RIVEN

MY MYTH TRILOGY, BOOK 1

JANE ALVEY HARRIS

7/17

RIVEN
Copyright © 2016 Jane Alvey Harris

Cover photography by Shalunx13
Cover design by Inkstain Designs
Book design by Inkstain Interior Book Designing
ISBN: 1944244166
ISBN-13: 9781944244163

For Jacob, Aidan, and Claire, my Purpose.
XoXoXo, Mom

P.S. I swear I'll whack you in the next book
if you don't keep your rooms clean.

AWARDS & PRAISE FOR
RIVEN

BEST YOUNG ADULT FICTION

EBOOK: YA FICTION

"The confusion of adolescence is captured in hi-fi...the seams of identity are exposed in all of their ragged beauty. A deftly constructed, hyper-real world reveals the effects of extreme pressure on a family torn by abuse."

—Forward, Clarion Reviews

"A fully engaging and unfailingly entertaining novel, "Riven" clearly demonstrates author Jane Alvey Harris as a genuinely gifted novelist who is able to deftly craft memorable characters and create a truly compelling story of unexpected twists and surprising turns."

—Midwest Book Review

"A whirlwind narrative about an imaginative heroine that uses fantasy to offer salvation from abuse."

—Kirkus Reviews.

"Harris's vividly realized novel, Riven, promotes a message of empowerment and obtaining emotional truth -- both for Emily and the young readers this impressive novel is aiming to educate and entertain."

—BookLife Prize in Fiction

"Riven is a beautiful, magical story about family, love, and overcoming the demons that haunt us, wrapped in an enchanting world where reality blends with the magic of the Fae."

—Amanda Hocking, author of the **Trylle Trilogy**

"Ms. Harris' characters are beautifully drawn and truly come alive on the page, as do the exquisitely imagined hues and textures of her nether world. The overriding narrative of the internal battle to overcome dependency and psychological deterioration in the aftermath of an abusive childhood sends a strong and uplifting message for young and old alike."

—Neil A. White, author of **Closure**

"A parable of imaginary stories and true tales that will change the way you think about fantasy, reality, and the power to hope our way through despair to a life of meaning and purpose."

—James A. Owen, author of **Drawing out the Dragons**

ONE

Nasty sweat slicks my skin like I'm human flypaper. Everything sticks to me except the stupid makeshift bandage around my bicep, the one thing that *can't* fall off. One glimpse at my arm and the grown-ups would ban me from the pool, call the World Health Organization, and lock me up in a nuthouse, because I have zero explanation for whatever the hell it was that happened to me during the night.

Just my rotten luck to wake up to this disaster and not find a single Band-Aid in the entire house. I've wrapped the wounds as best I can with gauze and the last bit of medical adhesive scrounged from an ancient first-aid kit I found in the glove box of the Civic. Teeth clenched against the pain I press down hard on the tape, willing the glue to hold.

The concrete scorches my bare feet but I'll stand here until they catch fire if I have to. I've told Claire the rules half a dozen times and she's still racing around the pool like a rabid squirrel on crack. As she streaks past in a blur of red hair and freckles I snag the back of her swimsuit, pulling her around and crouching so we're face to face.

"Hey! What the heck? Emma, let go!"

"Claire. Stop. Running. It's dangerous."

"All right, all right, I will. Let go!" she squirms.

"No. I'm serious." The punch-drunk screams of a dozen ten year-olds combined with my throbbing arm, sizzling feet, and legitimate fear that my little sister will slip and crack her head open sends my stress hormones rocketing to the relentless sun.

"I don't care if you're the only one walking. We'll leave next time you run. Got it?" The words come out harsher than I mean for them to.

Claire's shoulders sag. "I'm sorry Emma. Yes. I promise. Can I go now? Please?"

I loosen my grip, untwisting the strap of her tankini. She walks the rest of the way to her friends in line at the bottom of the yellow waterslide, glancing back twice like I might grow fangs and pounce.

Sometimes I hate my over-active imagination, but it's way too easy to envision an accident. If Claire got hurt it would kill me. Every time one of her friends flies around a corner of the pool my abs clench in panic. But what can I do? Their parents don't even seem to notice and there are three lifeguards on duty. As long as Claire is safe I'll just have to calm down until the birthday party's over.

Muddled white on the ground catches the corner of my eye.

Oh no no NO. The worthless bandage swells with dirty pool water in a puddle at my feet, dried blood rehydrating in loud crimson. Snatching it up, I ditch it in the trash. Arm clutched tight to my side I retreat to our lounge chairs under the awning.

Even though it's a zillion degrees in the shade, I pull my long-sleeved cover-up over my head. Rough fabric scrapes like steel wool across my raw pulpy bicep. I lie down and roll over, forehead pressed against the top vinyl slat of the chair.

For a minute I stare down through the opening at a line of ants crawling up from a seam in the concrete, marching off on some unknown adventure. But my nose and lips are squished up against the next slat down. I can't breathe.

You'd better pray no one saw your arm.

I turn my head to the side to prevent suffocation and scan for Claire. Good. She's walking.

Groan…. beads of perspiration meld the cover-up's thin material to my back and shoulders while my lacerated arm thumps along with my pulse's almost-audible heavy-deep gong. July's viscous inferno presses me down against the chair like a fist until I swear I'm slowly oozing through the vinyl slats.

Desperate, I summon an image of a chill pond in a secret glade surrounded by sheer mossy rock walls. Icy water laps against fern-covered banks, mist from a tumbling waterfall whispers against my cheek. A soft tapping breeze grazes my ankles, lulling the heartbeat away from my skin and back to my chest where it belongs. Mmmmm. More light tapping…

Wait. Breezes don't tap.

Whimper. A cicada! A disgusting, swollen, red-eyed monster bug landed on my ankle.

Frantic, I jerk back, my foot connecting with something big.

"Ow! What was that for?"

I flail onto my back and scramble to sit up. One of the lifeguards is backing away from me, cupping both hands over his nose.

"I'm so sorry!" Mortification. "I thought you were a bug! Are you okay?"

"Nice reflexes," comes his muffled voice.

"Is it bleeding?" I'm frozen to the chair. "You can use my towel!" This can't be happening.

He pulls his hands away. No blood, but his nose has already grown too big for his face. He pokes it gingerly. "I don't think it's broken. Sorry I tapped you, it's just you were so still I thought you might be asleep and your ankles are getting fried."

"Oh." I look down to discover my calves are fresh-slap red. "Thanks."

"No problem. I've still got a few minutes left on break. Mind if I sit?"

He wants to sit? By me?

I look around. I'm the only one under the awning, but every chair is littered with belongings: beach bags, towels, sunscreen, flip-flops. He goes off in search of an empty chair before I can answer.

Like I could say no after kicking him in the face.

Rising swells of embarrassment crash over me while I watch him pick up a chair and carry it back over his head. Who is this guy? He looks about my age, maybe a little older. Except, do teenage guys have muscles that…ripple? There's only one high school in town. True, there are more than 2,500 students, but there's no way I could've missed seeing him there—he's way too hot.

My head swims with questions I'll never have the guts to ask: is he new? Home from college for the summer? I'm already composing a text to my bff Sophie:

'Le Gasp! Hot guy alert. Need back up. ALL UNITS RESPOND!!'

But Soph stopped sending texts weeks ago. I can't really blame her. I haven't responded to a single message from any of my friends since school ended. Soph pleaded at first, and then threatened. She drove by the house and left notes on the front porch. Finally she sent:

'Fine I give up. I guess that's the way things end #abandoned.'

After that I blocked all their numbers so I wouldn't have to know they'd stopped texting.

"I'm Gabe." He sets the chair down inches from mine, pulling me back to the humiliating present. "I moved here from Colorado a few months ago."

Oh. He's a mind reader.

"That sucks," I blurt oh-so politely. "Summer in Dallas is misery."

He's SO handsome, Emma. Shake his hand!

I extend my hand. "I'm Emily."

"I know who you are." Gabe grins, taking my hand.

"You … what?"

"I pay attention."

My mouth goes dry. Did he see?

"That little redhead over there with all the freckles? She's your sister. And you have two younger brothers. You go to CHS, right?"

I nod and watch my composure rush out to sea on the tide between us. "I'll be a junior this year."

"Junior, huh? So you must be what, sixteen?"

I don't even hesitate. "Nice deductive reasoning."

It's not really a fib because you didn't say yes, right Emma? asks the little girl's voice in my head. She always calls me Emma, just like Claire. Just like Mom.

Technically it's a lie of omission, counters the stern woman's voice. **I know you're ashamed about repeating the eleventh grade but you shouldn't tell lies, Emily.**

I wish both the voices would leave me alone. I'm nervous enough without them butting in all the time.

"What about you?" I dare. "Will you be at CHS this fall?"

"Nah. I'm done with school."

"Oh, that's cool. Where are you going to college?"

He searches my face long enough for me to realize I've made a mistake.

This is why you don't talk to boys.

"I haven't decided what I'm going to do next. Besides, what makes you think I haven't already gotten my degree?"

"I guess I assumed if you had a degree you wouldn't be a pool boy." How I'm managing to pull witty banter out of my shy-nervous butt is quite the mystery. I want to sink into the crack with the ants under my lounge chair and implode.

"Ha! Good point. Nicely made. Except I'm a lifeguard, not a pool boy." He looks deep into my eyes for a few endless seconds like he wants to say something else.

Worms wriggle themselves to knots in my stomach

"Listen," he says. "It might be none of my business, but there's a first-aid kit at the guard station."

My hands go ice cold. He saw.

That's it. We're done here, Emily. It's time to leave.

My cell phone rings. "Hey, what's up, Jacob?" I step out from under the awning. Searching the pool area I spot Claire, then look back over my shoulder. Gabe follows my every move with knowing eyes. I shiver despite the heat.

"Bring me food," my brother says.

I focus all my attention on him. "How are you hungry? It's only five o'clock!" At fifteen, Jacob is a six-foot tall food-inhaling machine. "Can't you find a snack?"

"There isn't anything, I looked."

He's probably right. I hate grocery shopping. I've been putting it off for days. But now it's the perfect excuse to get away from Gabe. "If you come get Claire I'll go to the store."

"Can't you just pick up burgers?"

"We've had fast food the last three days in a row, Jacob. Come get Claire."

"I'm wearing pajamas."

"Of course you are. Get over here." *Please hurry.*

Half-cured cement stiffens my knees as I walk back to the awning. "Claire!" I call, waving my good arm. "You've got five minutes, okay?" Claire waves back, grabs a friend's hand, and fast-walks to the diving board. I avoid Gabe's eyes while gathering our stuff into the over-sized beach bag.

"Emily, wait. Where are you going? Is everything alright?"

"It was nice meeting you." I'm as casual as I can be with my voice shaking. "I'm really sorry about your nose."

"But what about your arm?"

"I've got to get dinner for my family."

"Will you be back tomorrow?"

"I dunno." *No.* "Maybe." *Never.* "See you around!"

7

Both my brothers are rounding the street corner when I get to the exit. The sight of them hushes my buzzing nerves. They're only eleven months apart, but so different. True to his word Jacob wears plaid pajama pants and a ratty t-shirt. Aidan's dressed in the same shorts he wore yesterday. And the day before that. At least he changed his fedora.

"You know people can see you guys, right?" I call when they're within earshot. "You look like sad hobos."

"I look chiseled and manly." Aidan puffs up his scrawny fourteen-year-old chest. "Besides, you're one to talk. You look like a mutant zebra. What happened to your face?"

I rub at the indents on my forehead. I'd forgotten about those. "They're from the lounge chair…"

"Forget your face," Jacob interrupts. "What's wrong with your arm? There's blood all over your sleeve."

Ugh. I didn't realize it had started bleeding again. I move it behind my back. "Nothing."

Before I can stop him Jacob grabs my arm and pushes the sleeve up to my shoulder.

"Ouch, Jacob, stop!" Oh, God that hurt. Tears spring to my eyes.

Aidan grimaces. "Sick. What happened?"

A mess of congealed blood cakes the pale skin of my entire upper arm. "Nothing. I woke up with a rash. It itches. I guess I've been scratching too much. It's probably just hives."

"Are you whack?" Jacob demands, eyeing me like I've lost my mind. "No way do hives bleed like that. It looks infected. You need to go to the doctor. Like, now."

I snatch my hand away. "I'm fine," I snap.

Gabe's stare bores into the back of my head. Everyone is looking at me.

"At least show Aunt Nancy." Concern constricts Aidan's voice. "She dropped off cookies. You're supposed to call her."

Aidan get's anxious about stuff, just like me. I have to fix this.

"Listen, Dork, I'm all right, I promise. It's not your job to worry about me. I'm in charge, remember?"

"Fat lot of good you'll do if you die from a flesh eating bacteria." Jacob pulls his second-hand flip phone out of his pajamas' pocket and snaps a picture of my bloody sleeve. "I'll just send this to Mom."

"Don't you dare!" I lunge for the phone. "Fine. FINE! I'll call Nancy when I get home from the store, I promise. Happy?"

"Yes. But still starving, so hurry." He steps around me and cups his hands to his mouth. "Claire! We're leaving. Now."

"Do you have to be so loud?" I steal a quick glance back. Gabe hasn't budged.

Aidan notices too. "Hey Emily, that lifeguard over there is staring at you. I bet he has a first-aid kit you could use."

"He's cute," Claire runs up, eager as usual to join the conversation. "Emma was talking to him before you got here," she informs the boys. "I think they're in lo-ove."

"You think everyone's in love." Jacob grabs Claire's flip-flops from me, tossing them at her feet. "Come on." To me he commands, "You should buy Band Aids. And snacks."

Ducking my head, I escape to the car before anyone stares me down or says anything else about first-aid or boys or love.

TWO

Hurrying across the parking lot I've got the paper grocery sack on my hip while digging for keys in the mesh tote, wincing every time it brushes up against my arm.

The encounter with Gabe at the pool looms at me making my breath come fast and my fingers even more slippery with sweat. I want to call Sophie so bad but I can't. She'll never forgive me now. It's for the best. Seniors don't hang out with repeat-junior losers.

I just want to get home to Claire and the boys. They're my only solace these days. We can chill and watch reruns of *South Park* during dinner. Parker and Stone make the whole world better. Well, maybe not better. Definitely funnier. Mom would probably freak out if she knew Claire watches *South Park*, but Aunt Nancy says we need to laugh more.

I'm almost to the car when I spot Gabe leaning against a crossover a couple of rows away from the Civic. Oh no—I gave him a black eye.

His head is bent over his phone. He hasn't seen me.

Let's keep it that way, young lady.

The woman's voice is consistently critical, but she's also usually right. I would give anything to avoid Gabe right now. Head down, I pick up my pace.

At the car I set the groceries on the hood to sift through the beach-bag with both hands. There's an SUV blocking me from Gabe's view now. At last my fingers close around the keys, thank God.

As I click open the trunk the groceries start to slide off the hood. Lurching forward I save the food. And roll my ankle.

"OwOwOW. SHIT."

Emily! LANGUAGE.

Groceries clutched in my bad arm I hop in tight circles, cursing through my teeth. This whole day is an epic fail.

A lone grapefruit topples from the sack to the ground.

Can't you do anything right?

Tears wet my eyes. I wipe them on my sleeve, about to kick the stupid grapefruit under the car when Gabe appears.

"I've got it," he says.

Humiliation shrivels my insides but I hold his gaze as he rescues the grapefruit. He brushes bits of asphalt from the pale yellow skin before handing it to me.

"Thanks."

"No worries. You have your hands full. And you twisted your ankle, didn't you?" Without waiting for a reply he scoops the groceries from my arms.

Oh, Emma, the little girl in my head swoons. *He's like a handsome knight coming to rescue you!*

"I just came down on it funny." Limping slightly, I follow him around to the trunk. "It's fine. Really. Thanks again for the help."

He deposits the groceries in the trunk and turns to face me, leaning against the civic with his arms folded across his chest.

"I'm sorry Gabe. I've got to go. My family's waiting for me."

"No, Emily." Lightning quick he grabs hold of my right arm. I twist to get away but his grip is too tight. Slowly, gently, he inches my sleeve up to my shoulder. "Not until you tell me about this."

The scaly infection encircling my upper arm has blistered in the short twenty minutes I shopped for groceries. While I watch, angry pustules burst open, seeping milky yellow pus.

Nausea curdles in my throat, flooding my mouth with pre-vomit spit.

A shrill metallic chirr—the screech of a thousand cicadas—pierces my eardrums as panic chokes my lungs.

What the hell is happening to me?

The tendons in my neck ache for oxygen but I can't get any air. Everything around me slows. The only sound I can hear above the cicada's grating song and the pounding rush of blood in my ears is the little girl's awe-struck voice in my mind.

Emma, your arm… it's glowing.

A pinprick of light sparks into existence, floating directly in front of my chest.

Your Spark, Emma. Breathe it in!

Frantic, I obey, sucking air as hard as I can. The speck yanks back into my mouth. I swallow without thinking.

Bad idea.

The speck expands inside my chest, bigger, bigger, BIGGER until I know I'll burst into a thousand fractured bits. I have to get it out. I have to push it out. Focusing on my diaphragm, I force every ounce of breath from my body in short broken pants...

"STOP." Gabe shouts the word that can't penetrate the mad rush in my head. His hand tightens on my shoulder and I stumble back. I've got to get away from him.

"Stop," he repeats, his mouth softening. He lets go of my shoulder.

Lack of oxygen stipples my fingertips and lips. Dread rages against my edges from the inside out. I wrap my arms around myself, whimpering.

"Emily. Listen to me," Gabe's voice tunnels into my brain. "You need to relax."

Listen to him, Emma.

Emily. Stop this nonsense. You are embarrassing yourself.

The shapeless mass hammers my ribcage. Black dots cloud my vision—a horde of swarming insects—I shove them away.

They shove back. The world tilts.

"Emily. Stop fighting. Breathe. It's going to be okay."

Stop fighting, please! Stop fighting stop pushing! This is Magic, Emma. It won't hurt you.

I stop pushing. The mass shrinks ever so slightly.

Now breathe, Emma.

Oxygen fills my lungs. The swarming insects retreat. My vision clears.

"Good, Emily. Everything's fine." Gabe's voice is steady.

"Everything is NOT fine!" I pant.

"Relax," he says, as if it's the simplest thing in the world.

"I can't!"

"Yes you can. Give me your hand."

My hand is cramped closed in a bloodless grip, nails digging half-moons deep into palms, but I don't pull away when he reaches for me.

"You can trust me, Emily. I want to help you."

Trust him, Emma. We need him.

His touch is firm. Slowly, he pries my fist open. The vice grip of fear around my chest unclenches little by little as his thumbs rub color back into my blanched fingers in slow-tender circles.

And then the dark mass implodes back into a golden spark in the middle of my chest before winking out of existence as if it had never been.

My knees buckle.

Gabe encircles my waist as I sag toward the asphalt. My neck won't hold my head up.

"Emily, NO." He lifts my chin from where it slumps onto his shoulder. He's so strong. This feels good. This feels safe. I need to lean against him just for a minute longer.

But he's impatient. "Please open your eyes." His breath tickles my ear. "Please, Emily. Look at me. Please."

His please is scared. That can't be good. I will myself to open my eyes.

Relief floods his face.

"Whoa." I double over with my head between knees until the dizziness fades. "It's okay. I'll be okay."

When I finally straighten, Gabe takes the keys and steers me back around to the front of the car. "Sit down," he instructs, opening the driver-side door.

I sit. Yow. It's sweltering.

He reaches across me, turning the key in the ignition and cranking up the AC. The promise of cold air hits my face. I let my head fall forward to rest on the steering wheel.

"I wish you'd stop doing that." He shuts the door and walks around to the passenger side.

I stare at him in disbelief as he climbs in. "You wish I'd stop doing what? Putting my head down? I nearly fell on my face in the parking lot!"

"You didn't nearly fall on your face. Trust me. You were never in any danger of falling on your face."

"Excuse me?" Indignation floods my cheeks with shiny red heat that makes July feel wintery. "Who do you think you are, anyway?" I demand. "Why are you even in my car? Why are you following me?"

"Yes," Gabe encourages. "Get angry. That's good!"

Something snaps inside. "You're laughing at me?"

"I'm sorry." His smile disappears. "It isn't funny. At all. But anger's better than fear. At least you're breathing again." He smooths back a lock of hair that's fallen into my face, tucking it gently behind my ear.

My anger evaporates, leaving me naked. Outside the window, carts bang against each other in the return. Hickory-laced barbecue smoke from the Hard Eight across the street sends a growl through my stomach. It's several long seconds before I can look at him again.

"What happened?" My voice is weak over the blast of now mercifully cold air.

"You had a panic attack."

Oh. A panic attack.

"That horrible screeching sound...my throat was closing up, I couldn't get any air. And then my arm...it started glowing! When I finally caught my breath I sucked the spark into my lungs. It grew so fast...it was huge. I was trying to push it out..."

"You were hyperventilating."

"But what was making that horrible screeching sound? Was there a crash? What was that spark thingy?"

"There wasn't any screeching, Emily. Your arm wasn't glowing. I didn't see any spark."

It was all in my head? I press the heels of my hands against my eyelids, holding back tears. "My chest hurts. Something's wrong with my heart."

"There nothing wrong with your heart, I promise. That's from the adrenaline. It'll stop hurting soon. It's scary as hell, I know, but it's over now."

"This has never happened to me before. I'm so embarrassed."

"Don't be."

"Thank you. For staying with me. For making it stop."

"Don't thank me. I'm obviously the one who triggered it. I should probably mind my own business, but I had to say something. I saw what you did." He nods at my arm.

My head falls forward again, my hair shielding my face.

You ridiculous little girl. DO NOT CRY.

I scrape the tears away before they can fall.

"Emily, you can trust me."

"I don't even know you."

"I'm not leaving until you talk to me."

Trust him, Emma.

No, Emily. Don't trust strangers. Make him go away.

"It's not a big deal. Just an itchy rash. I guess I've been scratching it too much…"

"Bullshit."

I cringe at his curse. My hands twist themselves together. What exactly did he see, just the blood? Or more?

His low whistle is more frustration than contempt. "Come on, Emily. A rash in the shape of letters?"

All the blood in my body rushes to my skin. I can't see them, but I know giant shame splotches blossom on my neck and chest. I hate him for having seen the strange letters. I hate him for asking. But worst of all I hate that even if I tell him the truth he'll never believe me. Because the truth is, I don't know how the weird angular script got carved on my arm or what it means. And that freaks me out most of all.

Make something up.

"It was a game." I mumble the lie at my lap. "I just wanted to see if I could. What it would feel like, you know?"

You're a stupid, helpless child. You need to fix this Emily, so he'll leave and you'll never have to see him again.

"What do they mean?" he asks softly. "The symbols you carved. What do they say?"

I close my eyes in resignation and hug my arm closer to my side. "Nothing. They don't mean anything."

"They look like they mean something. What about the one from last week? Was that just a game?"

Oh my God. He saw that, too.

You careless pathetic baby.

"I was just messing around."

"It must have taken a long time. Didn't it hurt?"

Exhaustion pours over me. I don't even have the strength for humiliation anymore. "Listen. I'm sorry if it freaked you out. It's nice of you to be concerned. I'm fine, and I promise I won't do it again."

Always making promises you can't keep.

"You can't do it again Emily. Whatever you use to brand with was obviously dirty. Your arm is infected. You need to take care of it or the infection will spread. And you need to talk to someone. To a professional."

"I have a therapist." Had. Six years ago, in Utah. Not that it's any of his business. Not that a therapist would believe I'd woken up covered in weird symbols with no clue how they'd gotten there any more than Gabe would. Any more than I do. I force a tight smile onto my face. "I have to go now, Gabe. My brothers and sister are waiting."

"All right. But let me give you my number. You know, for when you want to talk." He grabs a pen from the cup holder and scrounges an In-N-Out receipt off the floor, scrawls across the back and hands it to me.

"Whatever you're going through is going to get better." He opens the door and steps out into the stifling heat. "I promise."

Now *he's* making promises he knows nothing about.

I pull out of the parking lot while he stands there watching me with his hands shoved in his pockets. The need in his eyes makes me more uncomfortable than anything else that's happened today.

As soon as I turn left onto Denton Tap Road I roll down the window and let the wind carry the crumpled receipt away.

Littering is illegal.

SHUT. UP.

THREE

I stop to put a few gallons in the Civic and check my phone. Eight missed calls and five texts. All from Aidan.

'WHERE R U!!???'

'U've ben gone an HOUR'

'We're STARVING'

'Aunt Nancy is waiting for you.'

'When r u coming home???'

I've got to be better at keeping my stress to myself. Aidan soaks it up like a sponge.

'SORRY!' I reply. 'On my way!!!'

Jacob must have called Aunt Nancy and ratted about my arm. The good news is that means they probably haven't bothered Mom.

Fresh shame warms my neck as I pull into the driveway. Nancy's car is parked at the curb.

Nancy Quince isn't actually our aunt. She babysat Mom when she was little and has looked after our family ever since. She's remembered every birthday and special occasion even after we left California and moved to Utah. She moved from California to Texas just after we did. She's kind of our guardian angel.

I shut off the ignition and sit in the silent garage. Moist Dallas heat rushes in to fill the void left by escaping air conditioning. It holds me back against the seat, drawing beads of sweat out on my upper lip, plastering wisps of wilted hair to my neck. I hate it but I make myself sit still. I deserve to be uncomfortable. I've been so much more than careless. Now Nancy will know I can't handle things. She'll know I'm unraveling.

With antiseptic wipes from the new first-aid kit I scrub away the blood and pus. It hurts like fresh hell, but this time instead of tensing against the grating sting I detach, observing like it's someone else's mutilated limb I'm poking and prodding, someone I don't know. And I, a curious surgeon, am only clinically interested in the macabre.

Once the blood is gone I peer closer, examining the edges of the strange, angular symbols, pulling apart the lips of the largest gash. They're cleanly cut and deeper than I expected. Gabe was right…the precision of these engravings would have taken a steady, unhurried hand. The symbols are uniform in spacing, height, and depth, beginning just beneath the dip of the deltoid and wrapping around the soft-pale underside in the path of a wide cuff. (But how, Doctor? How could these wounds be self-inflicted? How could she have even reached that far around?).

I blink against a bead of sweat, too late. The salty sting blurs my vision, the detachment shatters and I'm defenseless. Vicious vipers of pain strike the wounds again and again with needle sharp fangs. ShitShitShit.

Enough, young lady!

I spread Neosporin on extra thick and apply three of the biggest Band-Aids—no messing with gauze and tape anymore. Hands full of bloody trash, I slam the car door shut with my hip, cram the used wipes and ruined cover-up to the bottom of our city waste bin, then grab the groceries from the trunk and head inside, bracing myself for Nancy's reaction.

"I'm home," I yell, hanging the keys on the hook and washing my hands before unloading the rotisserie chicken, microwave mashed potatoes, and grapefruit onto the counter. The kitchen is too cool after the heat of the garage and I shiver, uncomfortably exposed in my bathing suit and cut-off jeans without my cover-up.

"Finally!" Claire's shout comes from the family room. The boys' feet pound down the stairs. Jacob and Aidan arrive in the kitchen the same time as Claire and Nancy.

"Mmmm. Smells good," Claire says. "I get the drumsticks!"

"What took so long?" Aidan asks, getting right up in my space. "Why didn't you answer your phone?"

"Sorry. The ringer was off." I keep my voice light, resisting the urge to pull him even closer; afraid my anxiety will infect him via osmosis. I reach for plastic plates from the cupboard instead. "I stopped at the pharmacy to ask about my arm. I would have come straight home if I'd known you were here,"

I apologize to Nancy over my shoulder.

More lies.

"Not to worry, Dear," Aunt Nancy replies. "What did the pharmacist say?"

"He put some cream on it." Finally I turn to look at her, my eyes swimming with guilt. I know I can't hide the truth from her for long, but I'll do almost anything not to confess in front of the kids. "He said it was probably a heat rash, nothing to worry about. It's much better now." Nancy's nod is slow and assessing.

It's okay, Emma. Aunt Nancy knows about Magic. She'll understand.

"A heat rash? Are you serious?" Jacob is incredulous. "Aidan, back me up. You were slathered in blood..."

"Never mind, Jacob," Nancy interrupts. "You boys wash up for dinner."

"Yes, ma'am," Aidan and Jacob mumble, heading for the bathroom.

"Emily, Dear, I have a batch of raspberry-apricot jam in my car. Would you come out and carry it in for me, please?"

"Bug, I'm fine, I promise," I say to Claire's big-eyed, questioning stare. "Get napkins and silverware for everyone." I tug on her damp braid. "I'll be right back."

When the front door closes behind us I peel back the Band-Aids.

Nancy inhales sharply. "Oh, Emily."

I shove the tears and shame rising in my throat downdowndown.

"I recognize these, of course."

What? There's a sudden sucking beneath my feet, as if the ground is sliding out from under me.

Nancy looks steadily into my eyes for a long moment before gently smoothing the bandages back into place. "They're from that box, aren't they?

That beautiful Celtic box your father brought back from his trip to Germany years ago."

The box.

"I wish you'd called me before you did this, Emily. These scars will be permanent." Her voice is pained and I hate myself for being the cause of her hurt. "Is this about your father, Dear? Because he'll be coming home soon?"

I have no voice. It's like a wave has picked me up and slammed me down against an ocean floor of broken seashells. I can't get my bearings. I don't know which way is up.

"You must be a nervous wreck. I know I would be after not seeing my father for so long. I talked to your mother. She seems to be a little stronger today. I think she's hoping your family will have a second chance, Emily. You'll feel better when he gets here, you'll see."

I nod but say nothing. I still can't find my voice.

"I need you to promise me you won't do this again, Dear. It would upset your mother if she were to see, and you must be strong for your brothers and sister." She takes a pen from her purse and draws an ink circle around the bandages. "Wash it morning and night with soap and water and then cover it with antibiotic cream. Sleep without the Band-Aids to let it breathe. If the rash moves outside this circle it means the infection is spreading and you'll need to call me, alright?"

"Alright," I manage. "Thank you. I'm sorry you had to come all the way back here again."

"Nonsense. I love seeing you children. I know things haven't been easy for you, especially these last few months. You've been remarkably capable, taking care of your brothers and sister. You are strong and brave, Emily. All of you are. The four of you are stronger together. Don't hesitate to call me anytime night or day. Steve and I would be happy to come stay with you for a few nights if you need us to. Now, let's see that smile I've been missing."

A puppeteer pulling strings, I tug my lips up in a dutiful grin.

"That's what I like to see. Come carry this jam in from the car."

FOUR

The kids watch *South Park* without me. My plate of chicken and potatoes grows cold on the countertop while I drip sweat in the garage tearing open plastic bins and cardboard boxes like something obsessed, making a huge mess I'll have to clean up all too soon but right now all I care about is finding that damn wooden box.

It has to be in here somewhere.

My back cramps as I bend over a giant cardboard box marked with **Kids' Rooms/School** in bold Sharpie, up to my elbows in what were recently organized stacks of elementary school projects and class photos.

Long undisturbed must clogs my nose and paper cuts pepper my fingers. A stinky combination of rudely awakened dust and perspiration turn my hair to strings but finally it's here in my hands.

The smooth polished wood glows like it's just been buffed. A wide rectangular ribbon adorns the top, etched with the same angular symbols around my arm.

Trance-like, my fingers trace the Celtic figures.

I had completely erased the memory of this box.

Collapsing on the concrete and leaning against the Civic, a low moan escapes from deep inside. Is this early onset dementia?

It's Magic, Emma, the little girl insists. *Open the box. See what's inside.*

A twitch starts at the corner of my right eye but my hands remain clasped in my lap, unmoving. I don't want to unclasp the lid. Not now, not ever.

I set the box down. On autopilot, I gather all the file folders and papers and pictures I've flung around the garage and put them back in containers, not really paying attention what goes where, just gathering and placing and covering and closing while in my mind I stand and stare at a locked door. There's movement behind it. I can hear shuffling and whispering, a flutter of large wings. The scent of springtime steals from beneath the doorjamb, beckoning me with curling fingers.

Almost, in my peripheral vision, the little girl skips in a delighted circle, eager and excited, while the stern woman folds her arm, tapping her foot in disapproval.

That's it, then. All clean. Well, clean enough.

"Hey, guys. Take care of your dishes," I say to the kids as I walk past the family room with the box behind my back. "I have a headache. I need a shower."

"But Emma you didn't even…"

"I'll be down in a little while, Claire."

"But will you read to me before bed?"

"Sure." I take the stairs two at a time to my room and bolt the door behind me.

Both bathroom doors are locked and the lights are off. The shower is roomy, with a bench in the corner but I huddle on the floor directly beneath the fall of water, unfolding bit by bit as the warmth opens me.

It's funny. Minutes ago I boiled in the garage, but the second my butt hits the cold tile in the shower I morph into an ice princess, shivering like I'm moments away from frostbite, like I've never not been nearly-hypothermic.

Time to face facts.

Fact One: I've branded runes into my arm from a box I didn't remember.

Fact Two: I have no memory of branding myself.

Assumption: I've been losing time.

Conclusion: I've got to stop taking sleeping pills.

That's another funny thing, (not funny ha-ha). I hate meds, especially since Mom became so dependent on them the last couple years, finally checking out completely. I blame pills for everything…for Mom losing her job, for me flunking out, for losing my friends, too.

I couldn't even make up the credits I failed last year in summer school because I'm suddenly the under-aged-unwed-mother of my own siblings.

But meds have always been part of our family's life—there's always been a pill at the ready for any ache or pain. A couple weeks ago when my insomnia got worse and I was exhausted and snapping at the kids, I was desperate enough to take a sleeping pill.

And ohmygosh it was amazing. After swallowing, I laid in bed trying to beat my fastest Sudoku time like I do every night, and soon I couldn't help giggling at how hilariously stupid I was, getting slower and slower until suddenly I woke up an hour later clutching my phone with all the lights still on. I switched them off and slept straight through until morning and woke up a brand new person.

Our medicine cabinet is practically a micro pharmacy. Mom has tons of stuff in there. She prefers painkillers and muscle relaxants to Ambien these days so I figured why not? No one would miss a few pills. If they help me sleep and I'm more patient, it would be stupid not to take them. When Mom's better and life is back to normal I won't need them anymore and I'll stop. Easy Peasy.

One problem. Apparently they make me sleep a little *too* soundly.

It doesn't quite add up, though. Sleepwalking is one thing, but sleep branding? And it doesn't explain how I remembered the symbols so exactly when I haven't seen that box in at least five years; or how I reached all the way around my own arm.

But there isn't any other answer.

Honestly, it's kind of a relief. Maybe I'm not going crazy. Maybe I'm just extremely stressed like Nancy said … stressed about taking care of everyone, stressed about repeating junior year, stressed about alienating Sophie and our squad—and even though I try not to think about it—stressed about Dad coming home.

Is it so unusual the symbols made it into my dreams when I finally got good sleep?

Every part of me is warm and pliant now in the dark. I slide down onto my side in a loose fetal position, my bad arm sheltered from the spray by my body. I wish I could live in the shower forever.

Contentment spreads into all my nooks and crannies like butter melting on toast when I think about the contents of the box. How silly I was...being afraid to open it, afraid to remember. Huddled against the locked door of my room fifteen minutes ago, my fingers had actually trembled.

I hoped/feared the list and definitions of the runes that had come with the box were inside, but the minute I unclasped the latch and lifted the lid, every thought of the strange symbols vanished.

Tiny eager fingers tug at a briar-patch knot in my chest.

I told you it was Magic, Emma.

All sorts of forgotten things have ended up in the box: a rainbow-colored enamel dragon pin from China, rough-carved figures from a nativity set, a Polly Pocket, an engraved letter opener, a beaded cuff, and a souvenir-shield from Medieval Times.

But it was the smallest object that made the breath snag in my throat.

Two sections of the translucent cicada wings were still attached, top to bottom, resting dry and weightless in my palm, luminous like a rose window, as if they held trapped sunlight.

I used to collect them as a little girl. Mom said I had 'an unhealthy cicada obsession'. She couldn't understand why I was so fascinated by the dead body of something that freaked me out so much when it was alive.

It's because at six, I was convinced cicadas were faeries in disguise. It made no sense—such delicately perfect wings attached to such grotesque bodies. It had to be a trick. I would trace the wings on paper and replace their horrible eyes and bulging thoraxes with lithe figures clothed in gossamer.

That's how I learned about the Fae. They began to visit me in their insect and spider forms, peering over my shoulder, curious about the drawings I made.

It took us awhile to trust each other, but before long, we were whispering secrets.

They told me about their home in the First Realm, where there are seven kingdoms ruled by seven brother kings. The Good King Foster was the seventh son of the High King and ruled the Seventh Kingdom with his wife and their three sons...

A slight drop in the water temperature interrupts my daydream. I reach up to adjust the knob, then sink back down in darkness. The tiles radiate heat throughout my entire body. I bask in head-to-toe peace.

One day when I was seven an over-excited spider crawled down from the ceiling and onto my shoulder while I was in the shower...just like I am now.

"You've got to come with me, Emma! Right away, hurry, hurry!"

Stop this nonsense at once, young lady. You're not a child anymore, Emily. Spiders don't talk. You don't have time for daydreams now.

Defiant, I stick my tongue out at the cross woman's words and turn my attention fully to the spider in my memory.

"What is it? What's happened?"

"No time to explain!" Spider practically hyperventilates. "Hurry up!" "But where are we going?"

"The First Realm, of course. The Seventh Kingdom!"

"Spider. I'm bare-naked," seven year-old-me protests. "Besides, I don't know the way to the First Realm."

Clearly exasperated, he takes a calming breath. "It doesn't matter what you're wearing or not wearing here. You're wasting time! Don't you want to see her?"

I realize it will be easier to follow instructions than try to find out what

Spider is on about. Plus, I already have an idea who the "she" is, and my belly squeezes in anticipation. "Yes. Yes, I want to see her."

"Quickly then, follow me!" and he scuttles through a smallish crack in the grout where the shower floor and wall come together.

When I emerge on the other side of the crack I'm not naked or wet anymore…I'm clothed in diaphanous fabric that shifts and moves with my body, swirling in constant motion.

And Spider isn't a spider anymore. He's a young boy with pointed ears and a sheaf of arrows slung across his back.

By now, I've already learned the basics about the Fae. For instance, in the First Realm the Fae are normal human-size. They're all Faeries, but the boys and men are called elves and don't have wings, while the women and girls are called maidens and do have wings. When they visit me in my world—which they call the Second Realm—as bugs, I can tell the boys from the girls because everyone with wings is a maiden and everyone without wings is an elf.

For months all any of them have been talking about is the birth of Princess Nissa.

Spider tugs at my arm, leading me down a cobblestone street toward a staggeringly tall lacewing iron gate. Beyond the gates soar spires of a fairytale palace.

"Everything's so slow in your realm, Emma, especially you! This is the first time she's been outside the castle walls. Hurry up or we'll miss her!!"

I'm a bobble-head on a bumpy road. My chin swings every-which-way, feasting on the sparkling honeysuckle air, the serene entanglement of polished stone and creeping wild strawberry runners beneath my hurried footfall, the chiming laughter of celebrating Fae.

"Spider, let go of her at once, you'll pull her arm off!"

I recognize my dragonfly friend's voice and suddenly she's standing next to me...minus the exoskeleton and antennae. I wonder where her sister Twist is?

"Xander, it's you! Oh my goodness. You're so... Your wings...they're so...big."

Her grin is huge and playful as she turns ballerina-slow, showing off just a bit. "You like?"

My heart pinches with longing. "More than anything."

"They've only just unfurled all the way. You can touch them if you want."

Oh. I want.

They're stronger than I'd imagined, and slippery, like the skin of the dolphin I met at SeaWorld last year. My finger glides across the tiny panels between veins, trailing cerulean and lavender ripples in its wake.

"You're taller than me, Xander."

"Of course I am, you Goose," Xander laughs. "I'm nearly fourteen and you're only seven."

"Seven! She's seven, and the princess is ten!" Spider jumps up and down. "Come on Xander, come on Emma. We'll miss the entire party if we don't go *now*. I've never seen a real live princess before. She'll probably have grandchildren before we get there if you don't hurry up!"

"Ten?" I scowl. "But she was just born! You said she was a baby..."

"That was weeks and weeks ago in your world, you Goose! Today is her tenth birthday!" Xander laughs.

There's no time for bewilderment. Spider leads the way. Our feet fly across a shortcut of quilted grass to an enchanted garden crowded with elves and maidens.

Glittering fountains flavor the sunshine aquamarine. A harp's scale plays hide-

and-seek with the breeze, together tumbling from dizzying heights to twine and untangle in dark lush secret places beneath the bowers of blossoming trees.

The princess sits dutifully, dwarfed on an enormous gilded chair surrounded by elaborate gifts in honor of her birthday. Oohs and ahhhs rise and fall through the congregated Fae as each gift is brought forward and unveiled.

But Nissa's feet wiggle restlessly as she thanks the bearer of each present, and when no one's looking, her gaze slips again and again to the handsome boy standing just to her left side, holding something behind his back.

What could he be holding behind his back?

Whatever it is, the princess seems as curious as I am, until her attention is entirely fixed on the boy and the teasing smirk covering his whole face.

On Nissa's right, her mother the Queen leans to whisper in the King's ear. He nods and assesses the situation with a good-natured chuckle, then rises to his feet and announces: "My good people. We are honored by your attendance at this celebration of my Nissandra's tenth birthday."

The assemblage's applause is genteel and sincere. They clearly adore the darling princess, whose tiara has slipped in her raven-dark curls down over one brow, and whose fingers pick and pull at the elegant ribbons adorning her dress.

Spider, Xander, and I have sneaked around back of the grape trellis in front of which Nissa daintily squirms. Through the curling vines I watch the King kneel before his daughter and pull her onto his knee.

"I had no idea," he says, "a heart could hold so much love until you came and showed it how, my darling Nissa."

Sweet, slender Nissa reaches up as high as her arms will go to grab round her father's neck and place a petal shaped kiss on his dusky cheek.

"I love you, Papa."

"I've sworn an oath, my daughter, to protect you from any pain, from every sorrow. You need only depend on me, and you shall never want. Tell me daughter. What is it you want right now that I can give?"

Nissa whispers in his ear. He throws back his head and bellows a laugh. "So shall it be. Young Kaillen, your Princess desires to know what you have hidden behind your back."

Kaillen steps forward. He's younger than Nissa, but already straight and strong and tall. Nissa's face lights up as he bows one knee before her.

"Don't be a knave, Kaillen. Show me what you're hiding!"

"I'm not a knave, I'm your bodyguard," the boy replies petulantly. "And the thing I'm hiding is your birthday present, as you know full well."

"Don't make me wait any longer," she pleads. "It's the only present I've wanted all day!"

The King rises and sets Nissa in her chair before addressing the crowd. "Thank you for your generous gifts. Please, enjoy the party and the Royal Gardens. You are welcomed here. Our bounty is yours as well."

With that the crowd disperses. Spider pulls both Xander and me on tiptoe feet closer to the small princess and her smaller bodyguard.

"Give it here, oh please Kaillen! Why are you such a tease?"

"A kiss first, and then it's yours."

"Is he allowed to talk to her that way?" I'm shocked. "She's a princess!"

"Kaillen is the General's son. He's sworn to protect Nissa. Besides, they've been closest friends since he was out of the cradle," Spider answers.

Nissa removes her tiara and her fingerless gloves, then stoops to kiss

Kaillen's cheek.

"Now hold out your hands and close your eyes and I will give a great surprise." Kaillen instructs. Nissa obeys.

Kaillen brings an enormous warty toad from behind his back and plops it in Nissa's outstretched palms. Her eyes dart open, she squeals in delight.

"Kaillen, oh Kaillen! You're the best knight and the best friend and the best boy in all the land. Thank you, thank you. I already know his name," she announces, hugging the great slimy thing against the front of her gorgeous gown. "I'm going to call him Peter…" Her voice grows faint as she and Kaillen skip off merrily toward the vineyard. The last thing I hear her say is, "Royal toads eat only late summer golden grapes instead of flies… they grow gardens in their giant bellies…"

The sun is setting behind the towering trees of the primeval garden. I shiver in my bare feet.

"Emma, are you all right?" Xander asks. "Only, you've gone a bit blue around your lips."

I touch my lips with chilled fingers when pounding starts right behind my head, so loud it makes me jump.

"You've got to go now, Emma," Spider says. "Before you catch pneumonia. Where's the Path, Xander?"

"Goodbye, Emma." Xander places a funny kiss on the tip of my nose and playfully pushes me backwards. "We'll visit soon."

The sensation of falling and incessant knocking pulls me bolt upright from the shower floor. Oh God. It's freezing.

Banging continues on the hallway door.

"I'm in the shower! Who is it?"

"It's me, Claire. I need to pee. You've been in there forever."

"Claire. We have other bathrooms."

"Ugh. But when are you coming out? You said you'd read to me and I'm tired. It's way past my bedtime Emma."

I scramble to turn off the water and hunch into first one towel and then another. One more for good measure. I don't know how long I'd been sleeping when the hot water ran out, but I'm chilled to the bone. I may never be warm again.

"I'm sorry I took so long, Bug," I say through the door. "I'll hurry, okay? Brush your teeth and get in bed. I just need to comb my hair. I'll be right there, I promise."

"My toothbrush is in there, though."

"Well, brush them extra good in the morning. Go get in bed. I'm coming."

FIVE

It's been two weeks since the day I kicked Gabe in the nose. Two weeks since I found the box. Two weeks since I took my last sleeping pill. Four weeks until junior year starts. Again.

Ten days until Dad comes home.

The brands on my arm have healed to puckered pale-pink ridges surrounded by low purple valleys. There are no new symbols to hide, thank God.

I buried the box in the back of my closet. The woman's voice in my head is right: I don't have time for silly memories and make-believe now.

I focus on acting like everything's normal. We're a normal family; I'm a normal seventeen-year old completely friendless girl who may or may not be losing her mind. Everything is super normal. Fake it till you make it, right?

WRONG.

Before, the problem was sleep deprivation. Now it's the exact opposite. I can't stay awake. And for all my resolve to focus on reality, the Seventh Kingdom invades the theatre of my mind as soon as I fall asleep, even when I don't remember falling asleep. I'm re-living dreams I had as a little girl…the dreams I used to make into stories for the kids, until Mom made me stop.

At first the dreams were pleasant, like Nissa's tenth birthday, but they've changed. Now I wake drenched in sweat, my heart thumping to escape an unseen menace and half-remembered torture.

At night I guzzle energy drinks to stay awake, but it only seems to make the dreams more intense.

Xander and her twin sister, Twist, have come for me this time in their dragonfly-forms hovering above my bed in the air, inches from my nose. Their transparent wings buzz so fast they don't seem to move at all.

"Quickly, Emma. There isn't much time." Xander insists, speaking directly into my mind the way dragonflies do.

I want to go with them, I really do, but I'm tangled up in my sheets. I wriggle and squirm but can't break free.

"She's wasting time," Twist complains, impatient. "Our Path won't stay open forever. We're going to have to leave without her."

"No!" I shout, but my mouth is sewn shut and no sound comes out. "Please," I think as loud as I can, "please don't leave without me." I struggle harder but the bedding has hands. I'm trapped. A single silent tear slips from the corner of my eye.

"We need you, Emma. He'll be home soon and he'll be furious. She'll listen to you."

The dread Xander conveys kick-starts panic in my heart. My throat starts to close up when suddenly I remember Gabe's words from that day in the parking lot: "Emily. Stop fighting. Breathe. It's going to be okay."

I go limp. Make myself focus on the twins instead of what's happening to my body. "What is it, Xander? Who will listen to me?"

"There's no time to explain. We'll guide you. Our Path is just above the lamp."

Weightlessness envelops me. I'm wrapped in calm at the center of a rushing wind. I open my eyes in the Seventh Kingdom...

...and immediately shut them again. It's brighter than blue blazes, and puke...what's that disgusting reek?

Metal clangs on metal amidst impact grunts and the overpowering stench of B.O.

"No way. Is that Nissa?" Scandal and horror mingle on my tongue.

Covered in grime and dressed in her brothers' too-large clothes, the princess attacks one of the Queen's guards. Not with practice weapons, either, I notice. Her sword hand brandishes a long gleaming dagger. A studded dragon-hide gauntlet protects her sword arm from elbow to wrist, the leather extending between her knuckles. She's using the large circular shield on her left arm for defense, but also to smash with, and even though she's beaten back again and again, each time she stumbles she regains her feet and charges.

All I can think is that she's lost her mind.

"Xander! What is she doing? Where's the Queen? The King will murder them both!"

Xander and Twist, dressed in matching lavender gossamer which accents their wings, point to the edge of the practice field where the Queen stands next to her most trusted councilor, the Ovate Drake.

Shivers breed across my neck like they always do when I see him. "When did he get back?"

"You always ask when, Emma," scorns Twist. "Like you understand the flow of Time here."

Why is Twist such a Grade A bitch? She makes me feel like pond scum.

"Never mind about when, Emma," Xander says. "The point is he's returned, and King Foster is gone."

"Thank goodness the King is gone! Has everyone gone mad? It's absolutely forbidden for maidens to study the Art of Combat, let alone train. Even I know that, and I don't live here!"

"Things have changed since you visited last." Xander says quietly.

My open-mouthed stare swings from one sister to the other. "Are you telling me that the King, who's own mother—the High Queen—perished on a Great Hunt while fighting a Dragon of Legend has suddenly repealed his own decree and is on board with his daughter—the Princess—learning to fight?

"Not exactly."

I've started pacing in a distraught little circle, my bare feet churning up a haze of dust. "I don't understand why the Queen is allowing this to happen."

"It's complicated," Xander begins. "The Queen is not herself these days…"

"How complicated can it be?" I'm pissed. "Nissa could get hurt! She's not even thirteen years old! This is exactly why maidens aren't allowed to train as warriors. She realizes that, doesn't she?"

"That's why we need you, Emma."

The cacophony of battle ceases behind me. I turn to see the guard bend on one knee in the dirt, ceding victory to Nissa. That can't possibly be right, can it?

Everything's upside down.

I survey the handful of other spectators and notice something odd…

"Hey. There are only maidens here. Where are all the elves?"

"That's what we've been trying to tell you, if you'd ever shut up," Twist scowls.

"Drake brought disturbing news back from the High Palace," Xander explains, her face pale. "There have been crimbal attacks on three of the other kingdoms' borders."

"Crimbal?" I'm stunned. My Fae friends have always spoken of the wicked goblin-like creatures as things of nightmares…bedtime stories to frighten children. "I didn't think they were real."

"They're real," Twist says. For once, concern eclipses sarcasm in her voice.

"Foster and his army of elves left three month ago on a scouting party…" Xander begins.

"The minute the city gates closed, the Queen summoned Drake…"

"They holed up in her chambers for days…"

"As soon as they came out, they started Nissa's training."

My thoughts whirl while Xander and Twist talk over each other, eager to tell what they know.

"The Queen is afraid for Nissa," Xander continues. "No one's let her do anything for herself her whole life…"

"They tell her where to sit, what to eat, what to wear, even what to think…"

"What does that have to do with anything?" I interrupt. "She has a badass bodyguard and an entire army to protect her!"

"Do you even have a brain in that big head of yours?"

I'm sorry. What, now?

"Twist, be nice."

"But listen to her, Xander. She sounds just like one of those idiot elves!"

"Emma, no one knows where the crimbal have come from or who their Master is," Xander says. "The King went off like it's a lark, but Drake says there are hundreds and hundreds of them. Foster left an entire kingdom of women and children with only the Queen's Ovate guard to protect us. We are defenseless."

Twist turns on me. "Do you understand, yet? By order of the King, it's against the law for maidens to defend ourselves. Is that what you'd want for your sister Claire? To be a pretty, helpless little plaything, completely dependent on men who come and go as they please?"

"God NO." I take a step back. Except, I wouldn't want her fighting, either, she's ten...little girls shouldn't have to fight monsters.

"The elves are on their way back, Emma. If the King finds out what Nissa has been up to..." Xander shudders.

Dizziness pierces my inner ear. Each motivation makes sense to me. Each leads to almost certain disaster.

Silently I watch Drake and the Queen cross the training field to Nissa.

I'm not proud of it, but the sight of wings protruding through Drake's swirling black cloak has always weirded me out. They aren't nearly as large or elaborate as a maiden's, but they emanate dark opalescent light, casting surreal shadows around him on the ground. He glides instead of walking.

The Queen wipes grime from Nissa's face with a dainty white handkerchief.

"Perhaps we're pushing her a bit too hard, Drake. Nissa, darling, you look exhausted…and filthy…"

"Nonsense, she's magnificent." Drake's abrupt tone to the Queen raises my hackles, as does the way she defers to him with downcast eyes. When did he start treating her this way? When did she start allowing it?

I'm not a fan of the way he appraises Nissa from head to toe, either, like she's something he owns.

"You wonderful child," he purrs. "I've always known you were special, of course, but you have exceeded my expectations. In three months you have mastered what it takes most young elves three years to learn, and your wings haven't even begun to grow. Tell me, how do the weapons we fashioned together for you feel? Is the shield too heavy? The dagger too unwieldy? The gauntlet too tight?"

"They're perfect," Nissa gushes, practically glowing with pleasure at his praise. "I can't wait to show Father the progress I've made."

"Darling," the Queen objects. "I don't think it would be a very good idea to tell your father. At least not straight away…"

"You're being dramatic, Rhyannon," Drake rests his hand possessively on Nissa's shoulder. "Foster adores you above all else, my Pet. Tell me, has he ever denied you any request? How could he? You are so vastly different from the other simple maidens. You are mature, beautiful, intelligent, skilled. Why, if you weren't still a child I'd claim you for myself." He laughs lightly, but his eyes shine with greed and his red-red mouth is moist and hungry.

Queasiness encircles my legs, climbing up the backs of my thighs. They itch to run, to pull the princess away from Drake's grip. "Why isn't the Queen saying anything?" I whisper through clenched teeth to the twins. "The King will *not* be okay with this."

"You say something, Emma. You're the only one Nissa listens to besides Kaillen."

I want to. I need to.

But I can't. Not now. Not with Drake here. The truth is, he terrifies me.

"Emma!" Xander gasps. She's staring at a spot just above my lips.

Oozy wet creeps from my nose. I probe with my fingers, pulling them away dark with blood.

"She's stayed too long, Xander," says Twist. "The Path. It's closing."

Stricken, Xander leans in quickly, placing a funny kiss at the corner of my eye.

Weightlessness surrounds me again. Stillness shelters me within a maelstrom.

I wake upright on my mattress. The bedclothes lie in a twisted heap on the floor. For several dizzy moments I can't remember which Realm I'm in or how old I am…seven or seventeen?

My face is damp and sticky, but when I turn on the lamp I find my cheeks are only wet with tears, not blood.

SIX

O ne week left before Dad gets home and I am not all right.

My insomnia is back in full force. I started breaking up Ambien and taking them in bits. Maybe that's why bizarre scenes have been seeping from my subconscious into the world around me even when I'm fully awake. I startle at shrieks only I can hear, swat at sharp-toothed shadows only I can see.

Yesterday when I took the trash to the curb I caught myself zoning out, trying to send telepathic messages to a dragonfly.

My skin stings…like there's too much blood in my veins…like I'm trapped in my body.

Something terrifying is coming. I can smell it.

I push the door to Mom's room open with my shoulder, holding the silverware and cup in place on the tray so they won't rattle and wake her if she's asleep. It's dim and stuffy inside. White noise blocks all sound of the afternoon beyond the windows.

Setting the tray down on the ottoman I study the rhythm of her breathing as her chest rises and falls. She's so young, so beautiful. An ageless princess caught out of time in a magic spell.

I wonder what she's dreaming about.

There's fresh color in her cheeks tonight. She was happy this morning. When I came in to collect the laundry I found her humming to herself, towel-drying her hair after a shower.

My chest tightens with unexpected anger at her artless sleep. I want to shake her, to slap her awake. I can't do this anymore. I need her. The optimistic eagerness in her step the last few days hurts more than her strung-out binge-sleeping ever has. It means that she's forgotten everything. It means that it will all happen again.

I don't want it to happen again, Emma. Please don't let it happen again.

Quiet you pathetic little girl. You don't know what you're talking about.

The cup on the tray clatters slightly with my sudden realization.

The voices. The little girl who loves make-believe and the woman who is always upset with me. They started talking around the same time we got the release letter from Dad's Correctional Officer a month ago. They're almost never quiet anymore, always lobbying to be heard. But I feel removed from both of them right now, numb. It doesn't matter what anybody says anymore. It's too late. He's coming home and no one can stop it.

Maybe it will be different this time? Maybe he will be different. Maybe we can start over like Mom wants, like Nancy says.

A slow tear streaks a path to my chin as I turn to leave. "I hate you," I whisper without knowing who I'm talking to. Everyone, probably.

"Emily?" Mom's voice is soft but vivid.

I wipe the tear away before I face her. "I'm sorry. I was trying to be quiet."

"That's okay, Honey. I'm thirsty, what did you bring for me?"

"It's just lemonade and a peanut butter sandwich. Claire made it."

"My sweet girls. Maybe I'll come downstairs and eat with you tonight. How does that sound?"

I stare. She hasn't been downstairs since the school year ended and she lost her teaching job.

"Will you open the shades, Emily? It's so dark in here."

In a daze I open the blinds. Mom blinks in the sudden sunlight. "That's much better. Come sit down for a minute. I've been wanting to talk to you."

Obedient I sit on the edge of the coverlet at the bottom of her bed. She reaches for my hand, pulling me closer.

Her skin is smooth. She smells like spring. Ever since I can remember I've been her flower-garden assistant. I've always associated her with the tender late-May purple-evening scent of crushed lilac blossoms.

I look at our hands clasped together. When did my fingers grow longer than hers?

She hands me a prescription bottle from the nightstand. "I'd like you to throw these out for me. I'm feeling much better. I don't think I'll need pain pills anymore."

I don't trust my voice.

Mom sits up, adjusting the covers shyly before smiling and looking me in the eye. "You look so grown up, Emma. So pretty. You've been such a help since I got sick last semester. Before that, too. Since we moved here and I started teaching. I know... I've been struggling for a long time." She flattens miniscule wrinkles in the sheets again and again with restless fingers. "I'm sorry I've had to rely on you so much."

It's weird. While I'm listening to her I can see my thoughts and what the two voices in my head are saying instead of hearing them, like I'm reading from a script:

Emily: This doesn't mean anything. Just because she's saying the right words doesn't mean they're real. It doesn't mean she remembers how it was before he left.

Little Girl in Emily's Head: *It might be real. Ask her. Ask her if she remembers, Emma. Please.*

Woman in Emily's Head: *NO. Don't you DARE. Can't you see she's happy? Don't you dare upset her.*

"Honey? Did you hear what I said? Thank you. Thank you for taking care of everything while I've been sick. What if tomorrow we all go see a movie? Wouldn't that be nice?"

I nod and look down at the bed.

"It's going to be different now, Emma." Her voice is low, serious. "We all have some healing to do. I'm not asking you to forget what your father did, but I am asking you to forgive."

I raise my head, allowing tiny hopeful grubs to crawl across the moat I dug around my heart to protect me from her neglect long ago.

She remembers. She remembers what he did.

"Your father has served his sentence. He can't undo what he's done but the courts are willing to work with him in exchange for his cooperation. He didn't maliciously hurt anyone, Emma. He's a good man. He wants to pay back the money he took from those people. He wants to make it right."

She's talking about the securities fraud.

Frightened whimpers fill my head. Icy water pours into the moat, drowning the feeble pathetic worms wriggling across the dry cracked ground.

Make her remember, Emma. Make her remember. Please make her remember.

You HUSH.

Then it will happen again.

"Honey? Why are you crying? What's wrong?"

"Mom, please stop! Please don't pretend that everything's going to be fine. How can you not remember what he did? I saw! You were on the ground in the hall in your green robe…"

"Emily. Stop. That's enough."

"No. I can't! You were crying and crying because he hurt you and he wouldn't stop hurting you. I hate him! I'll never forgive him!"

"That's between me and your father, Emily."

"Mom, please!" I clutch at her abruptly rigid hands, desperate. Entombed demons scrape up from their packed dirt grave, clawing at my ankles. They're ghosts of something I can't quite remember. But she does…Mom knows, I can tell. "It won't be different if you don't remember *everything*. You can't let him come back! What about Claire..."

"Emily! I said that's enough. Leave my prescription and go to your room. Immediately. Go!"

Broken, I hurl the pills against the headboard and run from the room, slamming the door behind me.

Pressed against the wall outside her door, my body quakes with silent sobs.

You stupid STUPID Girl...

"Emma?"

Aidan and Claire stand at the top of the stairs. Aidan grips Claire's hand protectively. "What's wrong? Is Mom okay?"

The length and number of impossibly black lashes rimming Claire's wide innocent eyes crush me with their unblemished perfection. I would do anything for my little sister.

"Yes! She loved her sandwich, Bug. Sorry. I banged my stupid elbow on the door. Let's go eat."

SEVEN

*S*uffocating *gloom blankets the house,* each of us trail fog of unspoken tension. It gathers in the corners, piling up to the ceiling…a carbon monoxide cloud of toxic unwillingness to talk about anything that might be uncomfortable.

Or is it just me, projecting? Maybe the kids are fine. Maybe they don't feel the mounting pressure closing in around us, the crackle of static electricity causing my sanity's barometer to plummet.

After dinner and two episodes of Adventure Time, the boys left to play x-box and Claire banished me to the couch. "Stop petting me, Emma. I'm not a poodle!" Now she's weaving tiny colored rubber bands into bracelets at the kitchen table. Every time I glance over I swear the space around her grows heavier, darker.

Protect her, Emma. Don't let it happen again.

"Protect her how? From what?" I plead silently with the little girl who lives in my head, but her words are only wispy faded echoes.

I said those words to Mom earlier, but I don't know what I meant. Yes. He hit her. I remember that. She was on the floor in the hall, sobbing. But why? What happened? What made him so angry?

Remember. Remember. Remember. Remember or it will happen again.

It's driving me mad, watching thunderheads brew around my little sister.

"Aren't you tired, Bug," I ask when I can't bear it any longer. "I haven't read to you in a few nights."

"Are you serious? It's eight o'clock. You're being unchill, Emma. It's weirding me out a little."

"Come on," I plead, "I'm bored." It's a bald-faced lie, but I'm desperate. "It'll be fun. I could braid your hair. Let's have Claire and Emma time."

She studies me, considering, then a sudden light gleams in her eyes. She's thought of something she wants. She's always been good at negotiating.

"On one condition. We get to do whatever I want. Promise?"

"Yes, yes, absolutely. You're in charge, Bug. I promise."

"Yay! I have to go get something. You sit here and close your eyes. No peeking, okay?"

"No peeking." I agree.

She scurries away, her feet scampering up the front stairs. She's back before she was gone.

"Are your eyes still closed," she asks from the bottom step.

"Yep."

Her shadow falls across my eyelids as she deposits something heavy and wooden in my lap.

The box.

A peal of August thunder rumbles in the distance.

"I found this today while Aidan and I were playing hide and seek," she whispers. "It was in your closet behind your sneakers. Has it been in there this whole time?" She pauses, waiting for my answer but I am mute. "Emma? Open your eyes! It's the chest from the Seventh Kingdom," she squeals.

I'm being ridiculous. It's a harmless box of childhood memories. Besides, it's real whether I open my eyes or not.

"I want you to tell me the story of the Fae like you did when we were little, remember? About Nissa and Xander and Peter the Toad."

A chill traces my spine. The Seventh Kingdom isn't a safe place for children anymore. But no matter how hard I try, I can't keep the First Realm from trespassing on ours. It's one of the reasons Mom made me stop telling this story so long ago. Because they'd gotten out of control.

"BOYS!" Claire yells. "Come here, quick! Emma needs you!"

"Claire, the boys aren't going to want to hear a fairytale, trust me."

"NEVERMIND," she yells again.

"We're literally in the next room, Claire," Aidan grumps in. "You made me lose my turn. Why do you have to... oh Holy Balls, Batman! Is that the box from the Seventh Kingdom?"

"Aidan! Don't say balls!"

"Oh holy BALLS." Jacob almost trips over Aidan. "That's the Elder Futhark chest. You weren't seriously going to tell the story without us, were you?"

"No, I..."

"Uncool, Emily," Aidan frowns.

"Wait. You guys actually want me to tell you a story?"

Jacob takes the box from my lap and sets it on the coffee table. "I thought this thing got lost in the move or something."

They all reach inside, pulling objects out and lining them up on the table.

What if...what if I can fix the story? I mean, I created it, after all. I can tell it any way I want. I can make it safe, with a happy ending.

"Tell me what you remember about the Fae, Bug."

"They're fairies. Fae means faerie, right?"

"Right," Jacob says. "And they're Magic. The Fae get their powers from their parents during a Changing Ceremony at the beginning of puberty..."

"Ugh," Claire makes a face. "We had to learn about stinky puberty in school."

"Stop interrupting," Jacob says. "As I was saying, the dads give their kids a Spark and their moms give them a Flame at their Changing. For an elf the Spark and Flame combine to open his Mind's Eye so he can See the elements in Nature on a molecular level. The gift is called Keen, which means 'sharp sight'..."

"And is totally awesome," Aidan interjects. "It means they can learn to manipulate and arrange matter!"

"...and for the maidens the gift is called Blaze. A maiden's Spark and Flame make her wings start to grow and open her Inner Eye so she can See and weave the power stored in her wings into Intention."

"What's Intention?" Claire asks.

Jacob doesn't give me a chance to respond. "It means being determined to do something and not giving up."

I'm floored. Did I really tell them all this geeky science stuff? I was twelve the last time I told this story. I don't remember being such a nerd.

"Don't forget the weird ones," Aidan adds. "The Ovulaters."

Jacob cracks up. "Ovulaters? Aidan, do you even know what 'ovulate' means?"

Aidan grins. He knows.

"You guys are disgusting," I interject. "They're called Ovates, not Ovulaters."

"You know that means egg-shaped, right?" Jacob asks me.

"It's also a class of Druids. I did my research. It's a real thing."

"Whatever. Ovates aren't weird Aidan," Jacob continues. "They're beast. They're the maidens who can manipulate the elements and the elves who grow wings."

"So they're gay."

"Nice, Claire. Why would it matter if they're gay?" he asks. "The point is they're the strongest. That's why the Queen chose them as her bodyguards. A few of them have both male *and* female powers, like Drake. He's the Queen's High Counselor, and probably the most powerful Fae. Like, of all time."

"Jacob, how do you remember all this?"

"I might have written it down. I loved this story."

Their enthusiasm surrounds me, pushing back the oppressive gloom, soothing raw places left by my meltdown with Mom. This is exactly what I need.

"You guys. How about if we get in our pajamas and make snacks and I'll tell you a new adventure of the Fae?"

"Yes! I'll make the popcorn," Jacob says.

"Perfect. Let's have a race to see who can change the quickest. Bet I beat you back!"

I hang my clothes over the desk chair and pull on a loose tank top, matching pajama shorts, and a light cardigan to cover the brands on my arm. I feel like a completely different person than I did even half an hour ago. Optimism rises like fresh-blown bubbles up from my stomach and I decide right now: I'm going to unblock Sophie's number tomorrow and call her. I'll beg and plead if I have to until she forgives me for being such a wretched, miserable friend.

"OMFG." I enunciate each letter and start giggling like a loon because it's just occurred to me: in my dreams, Xander is Nice Sophie and Twist is Sophie In A Bad Mood. The twin faeries even look just like Soph: they're both petite blondes with lacquered lips and mischievous eyes. I miss my best friend.

How did I not recognize the infinite ways shutting myself away and hiding from the world for the past two months was going to make things even worse for me? Things have been getting pretty sketch. I shudder to think how close I came to losing it mentally: the voices, the nightmares, the paranoia and doom. Thank God for my brothers and sister. They are my lifelines to sanity.

I run a brush through my hair and reach for a lip-gloss on the vanity.

Lip-gloss and pajamas, Emma? The little girl giggles.

"Why not? My lips are dry."

EIGHT

"**P**opcorn *smells so gross.*" I skip downstairs into the family room and slam on the brakes. My stocking feet skid in a wild effort to back-peddle, nearly face-planting me on the slick hardwood floor. What. Fresh. HELL.

Gabe sits between Claire and Aidan on the couch. With a bowl of popcorn.

"Emma, look who it is!" A profound and wicked glee moves Claire's eyebrows to her hairline. Both boys wear wide grins.

They aren't stupid. They know it's all kinds of wrong they let him in. In fact, letting people in has never once been an issue because they hide whenever someone comes to the door in case it's a salesperson, or worse: missionaries. My awkward is funny to them, and subtlety is a communicable disease.

"Sorry." Gabe stands up. At least he has the decency to be embarrassed.

"They wouldn't let me leave."

"I'm in charge," Claire reminds me magnanimously.

I don't bother to hide my scowl. "Guys, it's time for bed."

Jacob snorts. "It's barely nine o'clock."

"Don't be mad, Emma. He brought flowers!" Claire points to a vase on the end table filled with white lilac, pale purple roses, and giant snowy gardenia. Oh wow. I can't stop from sticking my nose right in the middle of the blooms. The mellow-sultry mingling of fragrances tames me. Stupid Gabe, for disarming me so easily.

"You didn't call," he says. "I wanted to make sure you were alright. You look really good though, so I'll just go…"

"You should stay," Claire grabs his arm. "She's telling us a story."

He squirms.

The last thing I need is a swoon-worthy guy who probably already thinks I'm off my rocker in the audience, but his distress is endearing, and I feel too good to be cross.

"You might as well finish your popcorn."

"It's all right if I stay?" he stammers, shocked at the one-eighty I've done.

The truth is, he makes me feel safe. Tendrils of heat spread outward from my middle, climbing up my cheeks. "Why not? And thanks for the flowers. They're gorgeous."

Behind me Jacob snickers.

Gabe moves to sit on the edge of a cushion at the far end of the sectional like someone who wants to belong but knows he doesn't.

"You can trade spots with me if you want to sit by Emily," Aidan offers with zero attempt to keep a creepy leer from his voice.

As much as I want to smack my youngest brother, the irony of the situation isn't lost on me. My last meeting with Gabe was mortifying. Now the tables are turned and he is stuck.

"Aidan, give Gabe a brief background of the Seventh Kingdom."

"Well, basically there are these faeries. The boys are elves and the girls are maidens. The last time we heard this story, which was five years ago, the King and his elves had left to hunt a band of goblins called crimbal. All the maidens have to stay at home because they're fragile dainty treasures and the King won't let them do anything fun because his mom died when he was young so now he thinks girls are too dumb and weak to look after themselves."

"Aidan!"

"What? That's what happened. You just used different words."

"I like Emma's way better," Claire complains.

"Anyway," Jacob takes over, "the Queen is all worried because the whole kingdom is dysfunctional. As soon as the elves leave to hunt the crimbal she calls her Chief Counselor, who's a Shemale…"

"OhmygoshJacobSTOP." I cover Claire's ears and glare at him.

"It's okay, Emma. I know what a tamale is."

I can't help it. I hang my head to hide a grin. They're so stinking funny. Digging deep I compose myself. "Do you want me to finish the story or not?"

"Sorry," they say.

They're not.

I sneak a glance at Gabe. The dazed alarm on his face is one hundred percent justified. "You guys are only embarrassing yourselves, you know," I tell the boys.

"I'm pretty sure we're embarrassing both of you, too." Aidan quips.

"They're not really homophobes." I try explaining.

"We're not racists either, or even good at biology," says Jacob, tossing Jasmine-Polly Pocket to Gabe, who has no idea what to do with her. "This is Princess Nissa. Mary and Joseph are her parents."

"Hush," I grin. "Listen. Drake used his dual powers of Blaze and Keen to craft three extraordinary weapons for Princess Nissa's thirteenth birthday: a shield, a gauntlet, and a silver dagger."

Aidan hands me the toy shield, beaded cuff, and letter opener from the box. I fasten the cuff around Claire's skinny pink freckled forearm.

"Drake and the Queen began to train Nissa in the Art of Combat. They infused each of the weapons with a portion of their own power, making the weapons amplifiers that exponentially increase the power of the one who wields them. The Queen hoped that Foster would bless the weapons with his own infusion at Nissa's Changing ceremony, but she warned Nissa that the King would not approve of their lessons, that it would take patience to win him over, that they would need to stop training once he returned home."

"Nissa didn't listen, did she?" Claire looks up at me, eyes round with worry.

"No, Bug, she didn't listen. She couldn't wait to tell her father. She thought he would be so proud of her progress."

Claire mouths the words 'she should have listened' before pulling her cozy blanket over us and snuggling up against me.

A darting lavender flicker in the air above Gabe's head catches my eye. It's Xander. For one long disoriented second my vision spins like a cyclone before the Seventh Kingdom takes over. I squeeze my eyes shut and hold my breath, but it's no use. I'm not just telling the story anymore…the images Twist relays to Xander stream in real time directly into my head from the First Realm.

"The palace walls shake with Foster's fury. He orders the Queen to be thrown in the dungeons."

"Emily?" That's Gabe. I hear him calling my name like I'm underwater, but I can't answer. I can't do anything except stare in horror at Nissa and the Queen. Hot tears scorch their cheeks. Begging and pleading they scrabble for each other's fingertips as Kaillen holds Nissa back and the King's guards drag the Queen from her chambers.

"Are you okay, Emily?" Concerned unease fills Gabe's words. "Why does her voice sound hollow like that?" he asks the kids. "What is she staring at?"

Snap out of it, young lady, this instant!

"This used to happen sometimes," Jacob's reply is hushed. "When the story got too intense."

Pull it together, Emily! You CANNOT let that young man know you're crazy.

I let my gaze go soft and my eyes cross slightly so I can see both Realms simultaneously, superimposing the Seventh Kingdom over reality.

With monumental effort I manage a weak smile. "I'm fine. Sorry guys, I guess I zoned out for a second."

I reach for the nativity-Joseph. The slightest vibration starts where the crudely carved figurine touches my skin, spreading up through my arms to my throat. My tongue loosens; narrating the scene Xander and Twist show me. I do my best to keep my voice normal, but I can barely hear my own words over the pounding of Foster's boots eroding a heartless path down the palace's stone corridors as he stalks madness back and forth, night and day.

The Queen's handmaidens carry messages to the King pleading for an audience, but he burns them, unread, clawing patches of hair from his beard. With spittle flying from raw lips he dictates an edict to his privy council: "The Queen and her cohort, the Ovate Drake, are hereby charged with High Treason. They will be hanged side by side. The Queen's final act will be to bestow a Flame upon her youngest heir, the Princess Nissandra, at her Changing, to be held at sunrise."

At dawn, baffled Fae assemble to witness Nissa's Changing in a smothering press of bodies and discordant murmurs. General Raidho escorts Queen Rhyannon to the throne room, bound in chains.

I want to punch a hole through the cold-hateful mask on King Foster's face, to make the princes acknowledge their mother, but I'm powerless—trapped between Realms—and they refuse to meet her eyes. Nissa kicks like a wildcat in Kaillen's strong arms, reaching and sobbing for her mother.

I can't watch anymore. I need to retch.

"No, Emily. You must watch. We need you." Xander's voice rings like a bell in my ears.

Dazed, I lean forward, my fingers fumbling around on the coffee table for something real to hold onto. Aidan nudges the toy shield into my hands.

Lightning strikes in my chest. Someone—was it me?—has drawn a three-pronged Y on the front of the shield with thick black marker. I remember now: The rune Algiz. It was the first rune to appear on arm, the one Gabe saw at the pool the week before I gave him a black eye. How could I have forgotten its name? When I was a little girl I put Algiz on everything I loved.

PROTECTION

Foster forces Nissa into a straight-backed chair. He lays his hands beside the Queen's on his daughter's brow.

My brothers and sister's presence are the only things anchoring me to the couch. Without them I would fly away with Xander to the First Realm and shout and scream at the King until he listened to reason. But I'm dimly aware of Aidan slow-spinning his fedora on his finger next to me, of Jacob's forehead pressed against his knees on the floor, of Claire leaning against my shoulder with the big furry blanket pulled all the way up to her chin. I stay for them.

I rest my cheek against Claire's wavy hair, hollow inside at the crushing weight of mute agony on Rhyannon's face.

And then she begins to glow.

Streaming light seeps from her pores, a strangled groan escaping her lips. Shouts erupt from the crowd; they're pushing against the guards' swords, grappling forward.

Acrid smoke rises from Rhyannon's singed wingtips.

Oh my God. Her wings. They're shriveling, shrinking into her shoulder blades.

An explosion of brilliant light blinds me. When my vision clears, Foster and Kaillen are on their backs, knocked to the ground.

Shivering noiselessness ricochets repeatedly throughout the cavernous vaulted ceiling, piercing my eardrums. The Queen is incandescent. Light gathers from every cell in her body, pouring into her center. Swirling and twisting, a ribbon of flame travels through her arms, coursing out her hands and into her daughter.

With a violent shudder the Queen collapses. Wingless, dead.

No. This can't be happening. She can't be dead. She can't leave Nissa alone.

Suffocating silence ravages the crowd.

Nissa rises, power humming through and around her, pealing like a struck gong. Her wings have unfurled all at once, bathing her in dazzling radiance.

But that isn't all.

Strapped to her left arm, the black leather shield appears, bristling with spikes in the shape of her mother's mark: Algiz. On her right forearm the studded gauntlet materializes, emitting a subtle glow. Belted low around her slender hips the silver dagger gleams.

But her face. Her beautiful, innocent, thirteen year-old face haunts me. How can one face hold so much guilt, so much pain?

Black energy emanates from the crowd. I can almost hear their riotous intentions. Kaillen pulls Nissa from the throne room as the murderous Fae begin tearing each other to shreds.

The vision vanishes. Xander somersaults in the air before flying straight up through the chimney.

A ragged image of Nissa floats before my eyes. Grief sits on my shoulders like this fairytale is true. Like I knew the Queen. Like I've lost something real.

The family room slowly comes back into focus. The first thing I notice is how quiet it is. Shit. I have only the foggiest idea what I said.

Bet Gabe wasn't expecting THAT when Claire said he should stay for a story. What must he be thinking?

I make myself look around the room at my audience.

No one is holding a straight jacket. They're all just staring back at me, expectant. Waiting.

"The End?" I venture hesitantly.

"Wait. That's it?" Gabe searches my face.

"Um, I think so."

"But you said Nissa was to blame for the Queen's death."

"Did I?"

"It *was* kind of her fault," Aidan says. "She should have kept her mouth shut."

Gabe looks a question at each of us, one by one. "You're serious? That's how it ends?"

From across Realms, Xander speaks into my ear: "They've killed King Foster and the princes. Drake has escaped the dungeons. The High King Ælfwig is coming to banish us to the Second Realm permanently and seal the Doorway against our return. We need you Emily. Help us. We are coming."

"They're being banished to the Second Realm?" Claire squeals like I've just announced a trip to Disney World. "You mean here in Coppell?"

"Sheesh, Claire, she didn't say an exact place. Use your brain," Aidan rolls his eyes. "The Second Realm just means this world."

But I **do** know the exact place the Fae have been banished. Xander shows me the bridge that marks the boundary between Realms. I recognize it. We've been there.

"You're kidding, right?" Gabe is incredulous. "Everyone dies?"

"Not everyone. Just almost everyone," I amend. "That's why the High King stepped in, to stop the fighting before it could spread to any other kingdom."

"I can't believe that's from a kids' book," Gabe shakes his head. "That's really disturbing."

"It's not from a book," Claire corrects him. "Emma makes it up, don't you, Emma?"

Jacob whoops. "Hey, Emily, your boyfriend thinks your story sucks!"

The pillow I throw hits him squarely in the head. He falls backwards laughing.

"Go. To. BED."

"Alright, alright! Come on guys, let's give them some *privacy*." Jacob can make any word sound dirty. He and Aidan pick up their empty popcorn bowls, winking and nudging their way to the kitchen.

"Brush your teeth!" I yell after them.

"We will, Madame!" Aidan yells back.

Claire still snuggles up next to me. I unfasten the cuff from her wrist and put the shield and letter opener on the coffee table. "Come on, Bug. I'll tuck you in."

I glance back at Gabe while Claire and I climb the stairs to her room. He's picking up objects from the table one by one, as if he's searching for clues.

NINE

"I know you said *Princess Nissa* has black hair, but I kind of picture her with orange hair...like yours," Gabe says when I'm only halfway down the stairs. He's arranged Jasmine-Polly Pocket with Mary and Joseph in a group on the table.

I smile despite my raw nerves. "Wow. Nice. First of all, my hair isn't orange. And second, I'm not Nissa, if that's what you're thinking."

He looks at me. "I didn't mean orange-orange. I meant yellow-orange. Like honey, except..."

"Except orange?"

Ugh. Why is he here? And why does he have to be so...gorgeous? I guess it was too much to hope he'd politely let himself out in my absence.

"My mom says it's the color of marigolds." I'm trying to scrape up some of the confidence I felt before dragonflies took my brain hostage and made me look completely daft in front of the only non-family member I've had a conversation with in months, but all my courage has gone to bed with the kids. I stand by Gabe's shoulder, awkward, not knowing what to say or do.

"Is your mom here?" he asks. "I'd like to meet her."

"She's not feeling well. She went to bed early." Really early. Hibernating for the summer.

"What about your dad. I mean...are your parents married?"

Unfortunately. "He's been away for awhile. He gets back next week."

"Tell me about these symbols." He picks up the Celtic box and pats the spot on the couch next to him.

The house is quiet. Listening. I sit down. "What do you want to know?"

"Some of them are on your arm. I thought you said the brands didn't mean anything."

"I wasn't lying. I didn't even remember this box existed when I met you. I don't know what they mean."

I'm ready for him to tell me that I'm crazy, that of course I remember since I copied them so perfectly, but he doesn't and I'm grateful.

"Let's figure it out," he says.

I push the sleeve of my cardigan up to my shoulder and hold my right arm in front of me. He asks permission with his eyes before touching me. When I nod he takes my wrist, rotating my palm up, exposing the tender skin of my inner arm.

His long finger traces the puckered scars, leaving tingles in its wake.

He leans in, the back of his short tousled hair next to my face. I hold very still but can't stop the quick thump of my heart and I'm so glad he can't see me inhaling the clean, moving-water scent from the back of his sun-brown neck. God he smells good.

ᚠᛚᚢᛋ

"You don't remember anything?"

"Only a couple things. They're called the Elder Futhark runes. There was a glossary, but it's probably lost. This is the one I really remember." I twist at the elbow to show the first mark. "It's called Algiz."

"The one on Nissa's shield."

"Yep. It means Protection."

"May I?" he asks before cradling my wrist in his hand. The contrast of my pale arm against his tan skin makes me blush.

His chivalry is a little over-the-top, but I get it. He knows I'm a flight risk. Though where he thinks I'd go is a mystery. I'm already home.

He moves the box to my lap and pulls out his phone. I'm floored. I never once thought of doing that. After a few seconds he starts reading out loud:

ᚠ

Ansuz: (A: The As, ancestral god, i.e. Odin.) A revealing message or Insight, communication. Signals, inspiration, enthusiasm, speech, true vision, power of words and naming.

"Hmmmm. Trigger any memories?" he asks.

"Nope."

"Right. Okay, next up, Laguz.

ᛚ

Laguz: (L: Water, or a leek.) Flow, water, sea, a fertility source, the healing power of renewal. Life energy and organic growth.

I giggle while he's reading. That can't be what it says. "Did you say 'leak' as in 'take a leak'?"

"No, leek, like the soup," he squeezes my arm playfully. "Stop interrupting."

"I think you meant 'Lake.'"

"Ha! Probably, but it says 'leek'. Now try to behave and *focus*." He googles the next symbol and holds up his phone so we can read it together:

ᚢ

Uruz: (U or V: Auroch, a wild ox.) Physical strength and speed, untamed potential. A time of great energy and health.

As he scrolls through the symbols on the webpage for the last rune its name is suddenly on my tongue: Jera. Excitement bubbles up inside. It's an effort keeping quiet. I'm impatient to see if my memory is right.

Jera: (J or Y: A year, a good harvest.) The results of earlier efforts are realized. A time of peace and happiness, fruitful season. It can break through stagnancy. Hope...

I gasp, remembering all at once. I didn't choose the runes because of what they mean individually. I chose them as letters.

"What is it?" Gabe asks, "Did you remember something?"

"Yes! I remember what they spell! It's my last name: Alvey. Oh wow. This is so cool. Quick, google it Gabe. Google 'A L V E Y surname meaning'!"

He's quick with his phone and his 'hmm' is impressed. He reads:

This unusual and interesting name is of Anglo - Saxon origin, derives from a personal name, 'Ælfwig', recorded in 1095 ... The given name is composed of the elements 'ælf, meaning 'elf', and 'wig', meaning 'war, battle'.

"Isn't that amazing?" I gush, not waiting for him to answer because I already know he'll think it's amazing because it *is*. "My last name means 'elf warrior'!"

He regards me in silence. I deflate.

You're acting like a ridiculous child. I told you: you're too old for this NONSENSE.

Great. She's back again.

"It is a cool name, Emily. It's just... Do your parents know about this? I feel like branding yourself isn't healthy."

"Yeah, well, my parents aren't healthy either." The intense urge to run away grips me. I move into the corner of the couch.

"I have a question," Gabe's tone lightens. "If your name means 'elf warrior' how come only guys can be warriors in your story? Do you really believe girls aren't strong enough to take care of themselves?"

He's trying to distract me from my embarrassment by changing the subject. "Of course not. It's just a story I made up."

"I think it's cute you like elves and faeries so much."

I stare at my hands in my lap, flat inside. "I was just a little girl. I had to do a research project in school about my last name…"

"Hey," he says, "I'm sorry. I didn't mean 'cute'. Sometimes I don't say things very well."

I can relate but I still can't look at him. Shame glows on my face.

He lifts my chin with one finger. "Emily. You fascinate me. I want to know everything. Your story is incredible. Not at all what I was expecting. You really made it all up?"

"Yes." I only smile so he'll let go of my chin.

"My sister was really into faeries."

His words have an empty tone that catches me off guard. He's staring at me. A knowing comes over me like it sometimes does. His sister is dead.

The loss in his eyes skips like polished river rocks across my surface. I tense reflexively but either I'm not quick enough or it's already much too late. On the next descent the arc of his pain sinks below my skin, coming to rest in my lungs with the other stones of permanent crackle.

Whywhywhy?

My arms are big enough to hold countless jagged cuts, yet too small to hold Mom's hurt, my hurt, and Gabe's hurt too.

Tell him, Emma. Tell him about our faeries.

"*What are you talking about?*" I ask the little girl silently.

I'll show you, she says.

Suddenly the solid door I've leaned against for as long as I can remember—the one that keeps unsafe memories locked away—is vapor. I'm unable to stagger back from the great gaping rift at my center. I'm falling, falling…not graceful or weightless…heavy and hard. There's nothing to grab onto. I put my hands out in front of me to break my fall but I don't know which way is up or when I'll stop.

"I was seven when I first went to the Seventh Kingdom. The water in the shower was getting cold but steam was everywhere. Little icy drops fell on me from the ceiling and I shivered and wanted to get out but the man said NO, I wasn't all the way clean yet. I looked up and saw Spider hanging above my head in the corner…he was fat like a cantaloupe and had longlong legs. He took me to the First Realm through a crack in the wall. It was Princess Nissa's birthday. When I got back I was covered in a towel. I'd fallen asleep on the shower floor. Mom scolded me for using her bathroom when she found me there and for getting her towel soaking-wet but then she put her cool lips on my forehead and said 'you poor baby you're burning up'. She bundled me up in her cream colored robe and carried me to my bed and laid next to me for a long time petting my hair and singing songs about a swan and an oyster shell while she held ice on a bruise where I must have bumped my head. It was just before Thanksgiving right after I turned seven because I remember I stayed in bed for almost a week with an infection in my chest and couldn't go downstairs for dinner and even though I waited and watched Spider didn't come back."

Shut up, shut up, what are you doing? What are you saying? *Stop* talking. Shut your mouth. It isn't true you, little bitch. Shut *up*.

Tell him about Xander and Twist, Emma.

"The next time I went to the Seventh Kingdom two dragonflies came for me, Xander and Twist. When I woke up they were hovering at the side of my bed and I was scared. My body hurt. I tried to get away but he said Hold Still, Shut Up. I only cried inside my head a little because Xander and Twist took me to the First Realm until he was finished. When I woke up again I was back home alone in my bed and my face was wet with tears.

Gabe takes hold of my hand, anchoring me beside him. I've been gouging a piece of torn flesh by my fingernail. It's bleeding but it doesn't hurt and he doesn't say anything. I squeeze my eyes shut against more visions, but they play on the backs of my eyelids. The little girl sits front and center, mesmerized by the dragonflies. The muscles in my neck ache, trying hard to close my jaw and shut these dirty words deep inside where they belong but my tongue won't stop.

Tell him about the butterfly, Emma.

"The last time it was a butterfly. Silver. She was beautiful, fluttering up in the corner of Mom's shower. Have you ever seen a butterfly dance? I hit my head on the tile wall and almost slipped but then Mom kicked at the bathroom door so hard it broke her toe but she didn't stop kicking and beating even though she had bruises on her shoulder until the hinges came off and the steam pushed the butterfly out into the hall and there was yelling and screaming. By the time I got there she was already on the ground in her green terrycloth robe with her back against the wall crying and my little brother Aidan in just his diaper was covering up her swollen tummy with his arms and Jacob stood in front of her like a knight in his snap-up overalls until He left. I lay down against her with unborn Claire kicking against my naked-wet back and fell asleep to the rhythm of Mom's sobs. I promised myself that when the faeries came again I would be ready, that I wouldn't be afraid. But that was the last time. They didn't come back until..."

See, Emma? They didn't come back until NOW.

My traitorous throat closes at last, leaving me on this couch out in the open, completely exposed. I press in towards my knees and close my eyes, praying something will make them stop, the images and feelings and knowings.

Gabe's hand is on my back. "Emily, you're hyperventilating. You need to breathe. Slowly, in through your nose, out through your mouth."

I'm trying, I really am. I'm sucking air in through my nose. I can feel it going in. My chest expands but it's stuck, I can't exhale. My lungs are over-inflating. This isn't like the panic attack in the parking lot. I know this. This is asthma. I'm choking on my own breath.

"Emily, listen to me." Gabe gently touches my wrist, setting off an explosion that hurls me back off the couch and sends Gabe flailing over the coffee table.

"DON'T TOUCH ME!"

I huddle against the wall, crazed, tortured. I can't hear what Gabe's saying, the rasping from my strained lungs grates in my ears. "In…haler…" I wheeze, pointing to the kitchen.

He's on his feet, throwing open cupboards, knocking things aside. He's found the medicine cabinet and is back with my old blue inhaler, already shaking it, already placing it between my lips, already depressing the plunger, already opening my airways, already slowing my breath.

With my breath come tears, leaking down my face. Poor Gabe. He doesn't know what to do or where to put his hands. He's bleeding from a gash above his ear. But he doesn't leave. Thank God he doesn't leave.

I haven't used my inhaler in a year. It must have expired eons ago. I can't ignore these things that are happening to me anymore. Something is wrong with me.

"Emily, do you need more?"

"Gabe. I'm so sorry. You're bleeding. There's a new first aid kit in the…"

"In the medicine cabinet. I saw it."

He comes back with the clear plastic bin in one hand and a pill bottle in the other. Kneeling next to me he holds out the bottle.

"I can't believe I upset you like this again, Emily. Please, take one of these. It will help you calm down. I had no idea, Emily, I swear. I wasn't trying to pry. Just take it, please. I promise I'll go away and I won't come back if that's what you want. This will just help you calm down so you can rest."

"Calm down?" I grab his wrist. "You don't understand. Remember when I said my Dad's been away for a while? Well he has. For ten years. He's in prison, Gabe, and he's coming home next week. My mom's Aunt and Uncle own this house. They send us money every month. Mom lost her job two months ago. She's probably passed out on Oxycotin right now. How can I calm down?"

He's staring at me like I'm from a different planet and for the hundredth time I wonder why I can't keep my stupid mouth shut.

He opens the bottle and shakes out a pill. It's small and round and yellow with a heart cut out the middle.

Not a heart, you stupid girl. A 'V'. For Valium.

"I've never taken Valium."

Take it. You'll feel better in the morning. Forget this nonsense.

My whole body responds to that thought. That's all I want: to forget. To pull sleep up to my chin like Claire's soft blanket and wrap myself in forgetfulness. I take the pill from his hand and swallow it dry. "Thank you."

The anticipation of relief is potent. I reach for the wound on his head, brave with knowledge of escape. The cut is shallow, just a nick.

He's still like a statue, afraid to make a wrong move, I guess, which makes me smile. I twine my pale fingers through his tan ones and look at him, shy but steady. "I'm pretty sure that's as weird as I can possibly get."

"Bring it on."

There's something so gentle in his voice, so not judgmental. I tug him closer. He fills the space next to me against the wall like he belongs, shrinking the distance between us. I lean into him, resting my head on his shoulder. He's stronger and safer than any blanket I can imagine. I feel safe.

"I'm just going to stay until you get tired. Is that all right? Then you can lock the door and go to bed. But you have to call me in the morning, promise?"

I nod against him. "Promise."

"You're so brave." His voice is a whisper. "I know everything will be okay, Emily. I know we met for a reason. We'll get you help, for your mom, for you brothers and sister. I'm not going to let anything bad happen to you, understand?"

"I tried so hard to take care of everything. I'm just not strong enough." My voice is weak and I am small sitting here in the sleeping house pressed against Gabe.

"Are you serious? Is that what you think? That you aren't strong? Emily. This isn't your job. You're a kid. You're supposed to be hanging with friends and trolling Starbucks. Your parents are supposed to protect you, to take care of you, not neglect and abu…" My hands ball into fists again and he takes them, smoothing them out between his. "Yikes. I'm an idiot. Wow. Forget about that."

A loud thud jerks my head up to stare at the ceiling.

It came from Mom's room.

TEN

I stumble up the stairs. *My* knees are clumsy but they're MY knees and I'm determined. Gabe is right behind me. I'm glad, because I miss a step, and without his hands supporting me I'd be sprawled on the landing with my head split open.

I focus my energy out in front of me like a searchlight. The night splits open, soft wood under an axe. I shove Mom's door open and flip on the lights.

Strange auras surround the ceiling fan, spilling dark colors over the empty bed. Where is she? Heavy weights hold my feet to the floor as I search the room, willing her into my vision.

She doesn't appear.

Gabe crouches in the bathroom by the toilet. Is he sick?

No. No no no no. NO.

Mom is crumpled on the bathroom floor, smaller and thinner than the memory of her in my head. There are no sobs this time, no green terrycloth robe.

"Mom?"

"Emily. Call an ambulance." Gabe's voice is distant.

This isn't happening.

It is happening and it's YOUR fault for upsetting her.

"Emily!" Gabe says, urgent.

I wade through toxic shadows to the bathroom. There's blood. Blood everywhere.

"Emily, I think she's overdosed." Gabe's finger searches for a pulse at her throat, he holds an empty pill bottle in his other hand.

"Where is all the blood coming from? We have to stop the bleeding!"

"Emily, she's not bleeding. There is no blood. I need you to call an ambulance."

"Please, Gabe! Help me turn her over, we have to find where the blood is coming from!" I strain at her shoulder trying to tug her onto her side but it's like she's filled with uncured concrete. "Please, Gabe!"

He's ignoring me, on his cell phone. "508 Paris Street. I don't know how many there were. No. It says 'Roxicodone'. I don't know, maybe a hundred and twenty-five, a hundred and thirty pounds." To me he asks, "How old is your mom?"

"Thirty-five." Why won't she turn over? Where is the blood coming from? Did she hit the back of her head? I scrape the hair off her neck, delving for a wound.

Nothing.

There's too much blood. I take a deep breath and heave hard. Her lifeless body finally rolls forward onto her stomach. Her loose pajama top sticks wetly to her back, drenched in dark blood, but it isn't torn. I push her top up as far as I can. I still can't see where the blood is coming from. I pull off my cardigan, using it to soak up the blood, trying to find the wound.

My sweater hits a snag.

Something's stuck in her upper back by her shoulder blade on the right side of her spine.

Bewildered, I touch it with the tip of my finger and pull back instantly, lanced by needle-sharp pain. Is that glass?

I press down on her back with the sweater, careful not to touch the glass, hoping to staunch the flow of blood. I try to focus, but the Valium delays my response time. Gabe has disappeared.

The bleeding slows under the cardigan, but more blood oozes from somewhere else. It pools in the valley between her shoulder blades.

Continuing pressure with one hand, my other hand fumbles for a towel on the rack. It too is quickly saturated with blood.

Another protrusion exactly opposite the first juts out on the left side of her spine. Pressure. More pressure. "Gabe! Please, I need help!" Where has he gone?

I wait as long as I can stand it before lifting away the sweater and towel to look.

Two identical razor-sharp blades extend a fraction of an inch above Mom's ruined back. They're both several centimeters long, running parallel to the inside angles of her shoulder blades.

A loud scraping at the window above the bathtub steals my breath.

What was that?

Something's trying to get in the house.

Wrong.

Something is *in*.

Metallic liquid oozes from the corners of the window, spilling down the wall, flowing weirdly across the floor.

No. It isn't liquid. It's limbs…

Not limbs.

Antennae.

Hundreds of black and green cicadas skitter into the tub. Their thousand segmented legs scrabble sickeningly up over the porcelain and down the other side. The ground undulates as light glints off their too-slick bodies squirming over one another. They head straight for us.

Cocooned in a straight jacket of Valium I watch, terrified, as cicadas climb up Mom's bare arms and legs, tangling in her hair before finally converging on her back. They crowd around the two blades poking up from her torn skin and begin eating her flesh.

"Get AWAY!" I shriek.

They chirr in reply. Louder and louder their shrill song grows until it's vibrating in my chest.

The room brightens. Mom's entire body lights up from within. Runes like the ones on my arm crisscross her exposed skin, appearing, disappearing, re-appearing.

My mind somersaults. Movement in the corner of the ceiling pulls my attention away from the grotesque scene on the floor. Something small flutters up in the shadows. A gray moth descends from the dark.

It's not a moth and it isn't gray.

It's the silver butterfly.

The cicadas' mandibles shred Mom's back as the silver butterfly drops like a stone to the countertop.

My eyes won't stop blinking…

It's a faerie.

No! It ISN'T you ridiculous girl. It's the DRUGS. You're HALLUCINATING. Faeries aren't real. THIS isn't real. WHERE IS GABE?

But it is. The butterfly has transformed into a brilliant white faerie. I've never seen a real live insect-sized faerie in human form like this in my entire life. My mouth won't stay shut. She is very very small, no taller than the length of my hand. Her wings shine with the same iridescent light radiating from Mom.

The White Faerie stares at me. "They must work faster."

She's talking about the cicadas. What does she mean, work faster? Their exoskeletons are slick with Mom's blood. They're gorging themselves on her.

"GABE!" I scream. No answer. I ignore the White Faerie with all my might.

I can see the blades poking out of Mom's back more clearly now. They're longer than they were, extending several inches above her skin. They're growing.

The ground heaves.

Those aren't blades.

They're wings.

The cicadas aren't devouring her. They're chewing through layers of skin and muscle to free her wings.

But the White Faerie is right. Mom is fading. Her skin is gray, her body bent. The runes that crisscrossed her arms and legs have dimmed, barely visible anymore.

"Help her. She needs you." The White Faerie flits to my knee, looking up at me.

I can't ignore her anymore. "Please. Tell me what to do!"

"They're coming for her wings to give to their Master."

"Who? Who is coming? What Master? Tell me, please!"

"Their Master needs the Blaze in her wings to open the Doorway to the First Realm so he can return home."

Feet pound up the stairs.

"Emily, quickly!" the faerie says. "They're here, hide!"

The bedroom door bangs against the wall, but it's only Gabe.

"They're coming, Emily," he pants. "They'll be here any minute."

"I know! I don't know what to do! They want her wings, Gabe, for their Master!"

Gabe's shoulders droop. He shakes his head. His voice is quiet when he speaks. "I'm sorry, Emily. This is my fault. I shouldn't have given you Valium. You're hallucinating. You can't be in here when the paramedics arrive. I need you out of the way."

He tries to pull me to my feet.

"No. What are you doing? I'm not leaving! Let me go!" I struggle against his grip. "Gabe. You're not listening to me. Look at the cicadas, look at the wings! I'm not just going to let them take her wings!"

"You're high, Emily…"

"I. KNOW. I know I'm high! But this is REAL."

How do you make someone believe you when the things you're saying are insane? Hopelessness trickles into my gut because I know: no matter what I say, no matter who I tell, I know this more than I've ever known anything: No One Will Believe Me.

I believe you.

The voice is quiet. It sparkles. At first I think it's in my head but it's her—the White Faerie. She's vanished except for her voice in my ear.

Gabe stops pulling. I fall back to the floor.

He's beside me in an instant, kneeling. "Emily." He's talking like I'm five. "The ambulance is coming and you are in the way. They'll need to concentrate on your mom. Aidan is awake. Probably Jacob and Claire, too. They'll be worried, Emily. They need you."

He's right. I'm not even torn anymore because there's no contest. If push comes to shove—choosing between protecting them or Mom?—I'll choose them every time. They don't have anyone else.

ELEVEN

The hallway is dark. There are no sirens, but lights from an approaching ambulance turn the entry hall below into a silent fiesta. Aidan stands stock still against the wall, waiting for me to tell him how to feel, what to do.

Don't freak him out by saying anything crazy. Keep your hallucinations to yourself.

For once the stern woman says something useful.

"Emily. What's going on." Aidan's voice is flat.

The front door crashes open. I take my brother's hand and lead him further down the hall to Claire's room. "It's Mom. She passed out." I skip the part about her wings. "Gabe called an ambulance."

Claire peeks out from behind her door. Tears wet her cheeks. Jacob sits on her bed looking lost. I shut the door behind us and try to stop the world from spinning around me.

"What happened to Mom? Is she dead?" asks Claire.

For once the boys don't shush her. They just look at me, solemn.

"No."

"Is she dying?"

I don't have an answer. Part of me wants to scream 'No!' but is that right? Is false hope kind? The truth is, I don't know. Maybe she is dying.

What would it mean, if she did?

Something about her sprouting wings and the arrival of the White Faerie make me think it would be really stupid and selfish of her to die now. Then again, stupid and selfish sometimes win.

"Of course she isn't going to die, Claire. The paramedics are here. It's going to be alright."

Jacob's optimism grates. I want to tear my hair and stomp my feet and throw things. Is he really so naïve? Things haven't been 'alright' for a very long time. How will they ever be 'alright' again?

"Right Emily?"

He wants me to comfort Claire, to protect her from uncertainty and fear. But whip-thin threads of stubbornness stitch my lips together because in this moment I question what protection means. Is it reassuring my little sister that her absentee mom, who just tried to kill herself, didn't quite manage the job and is for now still somewhat alive? My tongue cleaves to the bottom of my mouth, refusing to say 'right'.

"It's okay, Claire." Jacob never once takes his eyes off me. "Dad will be home next week and Mom will get better."

Despair lodges at the base of my throat—a stuck pill that won't go down—radiating pain with every breath.

Be strong. For them, the White Faerie urges.

"Are you okay Emily? You seem…strange," Aidan says. They're all staring at me.

Lying and hiding are necessary for survival, but I don't like to lie to people I trust. In the whole world there are only three people I trust with my entire heart: my brothers and my sister. I trust them even more than I trust myself. I know they will never leave me.

Tell them the truth. Even if they don't believe you, tell them, the White Faerie insists.

"I'm not okay," I say. "I took one of Mom's sedatives. I keep…I keep seeing things that aren't really there."

"Like what things," Jacob says.

"Wings slicing through Mom's back. A butterfly turning into a faerie. She said something evil is coming to take Mom's wings. I think they want to kill her."

"Not on my watch." Jacob stands up. Behind him on the bed is the rune-covered box. He pulls out the souvenir shield, tossing it to Aidan. Claire snaps the beaded bracelet around her wrist, while Jacob slides the blade of the letter opener down the waistband of his slicky shorts. "I have a plan."

"What plan?"

"You are going to take her wings."

"WHAT?"

"You're going to take them. It's the only way to save her, Emily."

So now he's crazy too?

Claire takes my hand. Her bracelet morphs into Nissa's gauntlet. Black leather wraps around her fingers and palm, encircling her forearm from elbow to wrist. The studs flare bright before fading to a subtle glow.

Now I understand. This is another dream. I won't wake up and find out what really happened until after the Valium wears off.

Heavy footfalls pound the staircase.

Jacob takes charge. "Come on. They're taking her down the front stairs. We'll use the back. Claire, Emily is…impaired. Hold onto her so she doesn't fall. And be quiet. Remember, the third stair from the top creaks. Step where I do, got it?"

In a bunch we sneak down the back staircase. I'm hot and itchy in my skin; the cool kitchen tiles soothe my bare feet. As we pass the refrigerator, sparks of weird color light up the depths of the family room, punctuated by hissing and snarls. Jacob's shoulders go rigid. We freeze behind him.

The hiss isn't human. It's the screech of claws on sheet metal. I shrink against the freezer, moaning.

Claire squeezes my hand, hushing me with a finger to her lips.

My eyes lock on Jacob as he inches forward, easing his head past the corner of the wall that separates the kitchen from the family room. The glow from Claire's gauntlet casts deep shadows between his brows. His features tighten in anger.

Seconds pass but he doesn't move. I don't know whether to cover my ears and eyes and pretend I'm dead or plow into him with my shoulder. *"What is HAPPENING?"* I scream silently in my head, like I do with Xander.

Jacob's head whips around. Pointing to the laundry room he speaks into my thoughts. *"Outside. Be absolutely quiet."*

I hold my breath until we reach the door leading to the backyard. I turn the deadbolt and we slip into the warm night.

Huddled next to the fence separating our lawn from the neighbors, I stare at Jacob, Aidan, and Claire; shocked. They stand tall and strong like superheroes. Is bravery some weird recessive gene that skips the first-born?

A struggle shakes my insides as Reason and Logic battle Drugs and Dreams. Drugs and Dreams are stronger. My body begs me to seek the void hovering at the perimeter of my consciousness, to pull it down around me and sink into oblivion, but a desperate need in my brain insists I choose the one right version of Reality right now.

What is real? Who can say that the stories living inside you aren't real? Stay with us, Emily. We need you. FIGHT.

The White Faerie's voice sparkles from Aidan's lips.

I don't know why, but it makes me angry—no, furious—that my fourteen year-old brother is speaking with a fake sparkle-voice that I'm hallucinating, telling me to fight something that doesn't even exist.

"Fight with what?" I whisper-shout to the night. "Claire's bracelet-thingy? Your Medieval Times shield? Jacob's letter opener? We don't know how to fight! And even if we did, what are we fighting, exactly? Hissing paramedics? Jacob won't even tell us what he saw!"

"We'll fight with these." Jacob nods at Aidan, who places his thumbprint in the middle of the crude Algiz drawn on his wooden shield like he's been doing it his whole life. No one gasps but me as it expands into a real-life leather-bound shield with a golden Algiz sigil emblazoned in inch long spikes at the center.

The ground slams into my butt. My teeth pierce my lower lip and I'm glad to be sitting down because the very next second Jacob pulls Nissa's gleaming dagger from the sheath at his waist where the letter opener used to be tucked in his shorts. A quiet magnificent tone breaks the humid stillness of the night.

"FYI, it's not a bracelet-thingy," Claire says. "It's a gauntlet. The weapons make us stronger, remember, Emma?"

"Okay, listen up," Jacob commands. "We'll be fighting crimbal. Two of them."

Aidan shakes his head. "I smelled three. The other one must have gone upstairs. Looking for us, I'd bet."

"Well, the two I saw have Mom. She's unconscious."

Crimbal? Shit. How did crimbal get into the Second Realm?

"What are they doing with her?" I try to make my voice steady like theirs but fail. Miserably.

"Cutting the wings from her back, like you said. For their Master."

A trickle of blood slides across the tip of my tongue. I swallow hard. Monsters from a bedtime story all those years ago are here now trying to kill my mother.

"Don't worry, Emily," Jacob says. "We're going to help her. Are you ready, guys?"

Aidan and Claire both give solemn nods.

"Are you mental? Help her how?"

"Keep your voice down and trust us." Jacob says. "We know what we're doing."

"We don't have much time, Emma. You've got to stay calm and focus." In her American Girl pajamas barefoot in the dark, Claire flexes her wrist.

Metal claws extend from the leather between her knuckles. Aidan straps the enormous shield to his arm.

"All right," Jacob says. "Let's do this."

I follow my warrior-siblings in a crouch-crawl across the lawn to the picture window. Sprinkler-damp blades of grass stick to my bare feet. We kneel in the dirt of the flowerbed and peak inside. I can just make out the back of the sectional in the lightless room.

More sparks of color go off, casting an eerie pallor over the cushions.

I gape in horror.

Two short, gnarled creatures stoop over Mom's bent body. She's sprawled face down on the couch.

Crimbal. Exactly how I imagined them.

The sparks vanish, plunging the room back into darkness.

Red and yellow zags of afterimage swim in front of my eyes. Another flare shoots up, revealing details. One of the creatures' clawed feet digs into the leather armrest above Mom's head. The other kneels on the small of her back, lacerating her skin with a vicious scalpel. Every time the tool brushes up against one of her wings more sparks go off.

The light fizzles again.

I'm dizzy. I'd probably fall face-first into the flowerbed if not for Aidan's steadying hand on my shoulder.

Another flash forks the night. In the brief moment of brightness I spot Gabe hogtied on the floor in front of the fireplace. Aidan was right. A third crimbal bends over him.

"Emily." Jacob shakes my shoulder. He says my name twice more before

I'm able to tear my eyes away from the nightmare in front of me. "Emily. Time is running out. The cuts in Mom's back are barely bleeding. She's dying. Do you understand?"

My eyes won't blink, but I nod.

"Okay. Claire, Aidan, and I are going to take care of the crimbal. As soon as we get them off her you've got to take her wings."

This time I shake my head side to side. I don't know how to do that!

"Absorb them, Emily. You know this. Maidens store their Blaze in their wings. If you absorb the Blaze, her wings shrivel and Mom will be useless to the crimbal and their Master."

"Don't worry, Emma." Claire's voice is reassuring. "No one can take them from you if you keep them inside. Hold them there as long as you can."

"Emily. I need to hear you say you understand." Jacob insists.

I can't say anything at all. I can't find any words.

"She understands, don't you Emma?" Claire asks. "Just say 'yes.'"

I mouth the word yes.

"Good." Jacob puts his right hand in the middle of us. Aidan and Claire quickly cover it with theirs, then me. A jolt of energy races from the top of my head to my toenails. Immediately I'm stronger. I swear they just gave me a huge dose of Brave.

"On my mark," Jacob says. "Ready? One. Two. THREE."

They haul me up with them. Claire raises the gauntlet high above her head. A shrill vibration pierces the night, resonating in my chest.

The picture window shatters.

A thousands shards of glass hang suspended in the broken window frame, glittering crystalline teeth.

Claire rotates her arm toward the monsters. The glass pivots in the air, jagged tips aimed at the crimbal. She holds up three fingers. The hovering glass coalesces into three distinct spears. With a savage growl she jerks her arm down, fingers splayed wide.

Razor sharp shards fly straight at the crimbal, embedding in their skin. Thunk, thunk, THUNK.

The goblins thrash to the floor, writhing and wailing. But they're not down long. "The children!" the big one barks. "Get them!"

Aidan takes Claire's place at the window, shoving the big black shield around the frame, demolishing what's left of the broken glass. Claire leaps onto the sill, extending her glowing wrist towards the floor. Glass tinkles as it scrapes and shivers across the hardwood, blown back by a strong blast of wind. When the floor is clear she jumps inside, her eyes fixed on Mom's lifeless body.

"Aidan, hurry," she shouts.

Aidan leaps over the sill, landing in the room next to Claire. The spiked shield strapped to his arm is almost as big as he is. The crimbal charge. Aidan snarls and flings himself forward, swinging the shield in a wide sweeping arc. The outer rim connects with the big one's shoulder. A loud CRACK splits the night. The monster crashes back against the far wall, his arm ruined, his chest spattered with his own blood.

"Jacob, get in here now!" Aidan yells.

At the window, Claire holds her arm high above her head, bathing the room in glowing light.

Jacob steps inside. The gleaming dagger hums with energy, flaring white in the dim night.

The crimbal cower, shielding their eyes.

The air around Jacob ripples with menace. He speaks slowly and clearly, his words vibrating with power: "You will *not* touch my mother again."

Against the far wall, the big one rises. Panting raggedly, it clutches its ruined arm against its chest, muttering a menacing chant under its breath. The other two mimic their leader. Chanting and muttering, all three creatures hunch low, knuckles dragging on the hardwood planks.

Aidan adjusts his stance. Claire and Jacob stand on either side of him shoulder to shoulder.

"Now, Emily," Jacob says. "We need you now."

TWELVE

I can't remember the last time I was this close to Mom, the last time her arms were around me. She doesn't really like being touched.

I pick a cicada from her hair. Its legs twitch convulsively, abdomen swollen and glowing with fluorescent light.

Lying this way—foreheads pressed together—I'm struck how well we match...toe to toe we line-up: same height, same slender-limbed round-chested build. But my arms are golden-pink against hers, pale and gray. She is cold. Too much gravity holds her to the couch.

Shouts, snarls, crashes, thuds, and the clash of metal on bone rain down in the room behind me. Claire hurls insults and curses I've never heard at the crimbal, along with Mom's collection of books and paperweights. Jacob and Aidan beat them back from the couch with their enchanted weapons.

But me. I'm inside a barrier of stillness on this couch with Mom. She smells anemic, like dried leaves. The smoothness of her cheek mesmerizes me. Each pore is tiny and perfect. She's ageless, posed for a painting.

"Hurry Emily!" Aidan's leg smacks into me, jarring me back to my task. I move Mom's blood-stiff hair off her neck, lean forward and touch her lips with my own.

How to explain? She tastes buried. Unbreathing. The breath in her lungs is stagnant. When I inhale it comes at me in a rush, flooding my cells with her desperate need for circulation. I have to pay close attention so I won't lose myself in the simple task of exchanging oxygen for carbon dioxide, something asthma makes me not great at even when it's just for me.

Jacob said to absorb her Blaze, but it's not that simple. Have you ever tried to take the milk and leave the cream? It isn't impossible. The cream separates. But you can't just stick in a straw and suck.

I try to siphon only the Magic. I sip and pull. It races from her wings through her bloodstream before hitting me with a surge of cellular respiration. I choke, fighting back the urge to sever our connection.

Don't take anything except the Blaze.

The White Faerie's glittering voice helps me focus. She's right. Mom has already lost so much blood.

That's not what she means though. I'll take Mom's wings to save her life and I'll hide them inside as long as I can so the monsters can't get them. I don't want anything else. Not her addiction, not her suffering, not whatever rationalizations she has for leaving us.

Anguished tears prick my eyes. I can't do this.

Yes you can. The White Faerie's words effervesce in my ear. **You have everything you need inside you to do this hard thing. Trust yourself. Close your eyes and create a circle of calm in your middle.**

I don't know how to do that!

Listen to my voice. Imagine a single speck of light sparking within your chest. Concentrate only on that speck.

I do as she says. Where my ribs meet over my heart I see a single sphere hovering, emitting soft golden light, just like the Spark in the grocery store parking lot before it expanded and overwhelmed me.

My consciousness drifts down until I float weightless in my own chest. It is close and dark and full within. It is safe and quiet. The chaos around me recedes into the background.

The speck shimmers, daring me to come closer still, so I do and realize that it isn't just one sphere. There are countless points of light … so many, so uniform, so evenly spaced and equidistant from one another that they appear as a smooth, solid, single surface.

Gravity holds me just outside the curving planetary wall. Moving all around it in awe, I'm unable to comprehend the perfection of what I'm seeing. Tentatively, I reach out with the fingers of my mind, brushing against the closest light.

An unseen force yanks me down…

…down…

…I'm falling…

…I'm shrinking…

…I'm on the other side of the wall of lights.

Whoa. What I thought was a wall was just the first layer. There are endless layers and I am at their center. Infinite light radiates from me in a way I have never—could have never—seen before. It isn't seeing, really, it's BEING, in all directions at once. No front, no back, no up, no down.

Only everywhere.

Brilliant light streams from me. Light surrounds me. Light is me.

I am Light.

And suddenly, as if I just learned how to taste, I recognize the distinct flavor of my mother's Blaze.

Bathed in light I begin to pull her Blaze into my own body.

It hurts.

No part of me is in control as terrifying energy saturates my cells, filling me up to overflowing. I can't stop it. I don't know where else it can go or how much more I can expand. A swelling everywhere increases until I know my blood vessels, my lungs, my skin will split and spill onto the family room floor.

You're almost there, Emily, just a little more, the White Faerie encourages.

Needle-sharp blades strain against the skin of my back from inside me until it's paper-thin. The force threatens to knock me backwards while merciless hooks anchor my lips to Mom's. I am being riven.

The White Faerie starts to howl.

"She's taking the wings!" A crimbal shrieks. "STOP HER! SMASH HER! HE'LL KILL US!"

Something hits the back of my skull with a thunderous crash. Claire screams. Crazed, I gulp the last of Mom's Blaze and tear away from her. Propelling myself off the couch I trip and fall over what's left of the ruined coffee table. Splinters and glass crunch beneath me, blood oozes through my tank top.

Jacob pins a crimbal by the kitchen, one knee on its chest, the other subduing its flailing arms. He twists the glowing dagger hilt-deep in its eye socket.

At the end of the sectional Claire kicks and screams at the crimbal on top of her, its pointed fangs gnash inches from her neck.

And Aidan. Aidan is next to her on the floor folded under his shield, the third crimbal draped over him. Neither of them is moving.

A new energy electrifies me. I pick myself up and run at the monster on top of Claire. My kick lands squarely in its ribs, sending it crashing into the piano.

Instantly, my murderous hands clench its throat. I slam it back against the wall, pinning it just above my head. I want nothing more than to make its eyeballs burst.

The thing grins at me, pulling at my fingers, kicking at my waist. "You stupid little bitch," it hisses. "Don't you know what you've done? Your mother is useless now. A husk. But you … look how pretty you are. See how you shine. And the little freckled one, too. What nice pets you'll make for our Master. What lovely little playthings." Spittle foams at its lips.

I press harder with my thumbs on its windpipe. Its kicks grow feeble, its voice a broken clatter. "Yes, that's it. Kill me. No matter. There are plenty of others. This will not save you. Look at your arm. It will lead him to you like a vulture to rotting meat."

I stumble back, releasing my grip on its neck. The brands on my arm radiate phosphorescent light. I claw at the runes that spell my last name, desperate to scrape them off, knowing that if I don't he'll find us. He'll never stop searching until he finds us.

"Emily, behind you!"

At Jacob's warning I turn. The crimbal raises its arm above my head, a geode paperweight clutched in its fist. My hand snakes out. Grabbing its wrist I slam it down against the ivory keys on the piano. In a dissonant minor the paperweight falls. I catch it in my other hand and drive it into the crimbal's skull.

Bone crunches under rock. I'm pressing harder, grinding harder, smashing HARDER, pulverizing solid into sludge. Viscous blood dribbles between my fingers, heavy like mercury. Welts rise on my flesh where the blood touches me. It eats through my skin, spreading up my arm, exposing muscle and cartilage. I hear myself scream at the pain. I can't stop screaming at the pain.

"Emily. It's alright, your mom's going to be alright…"

Gabe. Jacob must have untied him. But someone is pulling him back away from me.

I'm lying down staring at the ceiling. There's a needling pinch in the crease of my arm at the elbow. Something presses around my mouth. It smells like lilac.

A beautiful black void settles across my shoulders. Jacob, Aidan, and Claire gaze down at me, their faces stunned and more than a little scared. But none of them is covered in crimbal guts, and after the night we just survived, that's a win in my book.

THIRTEEN

The clock on the wall loses seconds every time I look. A panel of buttons lines the railing on my hospital bed. Not that I want to push them. Or could if I wanted to. My hands are strapped down.

"Do they really think I'm a threat to anyone?" I ask the voices in my head.

No one answers. Not the little girl, not the woman. Not Xander or Twist or even the White Faerie, though I'm not surprised at all that she's gone.

Whatever they've put in the IV envelops me like a warm wet blanket. It doesn't stop me from thinking and remembering, just from caring. About anything. And even though I suspect I'll pay for it soon, I'm grateful soon isn't now.

I drift along on a makeshift raft lashed together with apathy. I don't **care** that there isn't a rudder or an anchor or even an oar. The river's current swirls around me, lulling me to the verge of deep sleep without letting me slip under.

Now and again gulls fly overhead. Sometimes they land on my raft and keep me company.

"How long does she have to stay here?" The Claire-gull asks.

"They said she's coming home tomorrow night." That squawk is Aidan.

"But we're leaving in two days. She doesn't even know!" The Claire-gull is upset. "She needs to wake up and tell them we aren't going with them."

"Calm down Claire. It's not like we have a choice. We can't stay here by ourselves. We're kids." This gull's voice is deeper, like Jacob's.

"Emma's seventeen. That's old enough. Mom's been sick for months and Emma has been in charge…"

"She's stressed out, okay? You saw her last night. The doctor said she had a drug induced psychotic break. That's why she's in this hospital, Claire. She can't be in charge of everything anymore."

"But Dad's coming home…"

"Yeah, Claire. From prison. Mom's family has never liked him. I heard Uncle Ian say we're staying with them until Mom's better."

"Can they even do that?" Claire asks. "Take us away without Dad's permission?"

"Yeah, I think they can. We'll be gone before he gets home."

"He's been gone ten years," the gull with Aidan's voice says. "It doesn't even feel like we're related anymore. I'm glad we're going with Aunt Meg and Uncle Ian."

"Aidan!" Claire-gull is shocked. "He's our dad. Mom always says blood is thicker than water. She says that no matter what, God commands us to forgive, even seven times seventy. She says the Atonement of Jesus will heal our hearts."

"You've never met him, Claire. You weren't even born when he went away."

The gulls' voices aren't good company anymore. I want to plug my ears but I can't move my arms. My feet twitch.

White-water rapids of claustrophobia threaten to overturn my raft. An alarm blares as I thrash against the smothering wet blanket of the sedative. Staccato beeps keep pace with my spiking pulse as the bed-straps constrict. I need to tell the Claire-gull. I need to tell her not to trust Dad.

Quick feet follow shouts in the hallway. Peace spreads thick and delicious through my nervous system. The ebb and flow of waves against the little raft hush all harshness, blocking out everything as I tip gently over the side. Bubbles of panic escape my mouth in a pleasant gurgle. Distant sunlight flickers through meters of silty water. I let go and sink...

How much time has passed? No more IV in my arm. The wall mounted TV glows blue in the dark room. A sports show is on. Gabe is here, slumped in a wooden chair, his head leaning awkwardly to one side. For a minute I just watch him sleep. His thick hair and smooth skin make my fingers tingle. And his lips, so full when relaxed...

I stifle the longing that shudders through me and focus on scanning my body: wiggle my toes... some pins and needles, but good. Wiggle my legs... fine. I clench and release my glutes and then my abs. Continuing up my torso I try to ignore the yellow straps across my arms and chest, wincing instead at the stabbing ache between my shoulder blades that must be from laying in one position too long. I hold my hands very still pretending I don't want to move them anyway, but sweat beads on my upper lip. The walls close in.

"You're awake."

Aunt Nancy's quiet voice pushes the shrinking walls back to their normal place.

"There, there, Dear. We don't need these ridiculous restraints. Let's sit you up a little. Are you thirsty?"

As she frees my arms the confusion the IV kept at bay floods over me—a tsunami of hopelessness. I can't hold back my tears. They sting where they touch my cheeks.

Nancy clucks in sympathy. Adjusting my pillow she raises the bed so I'm sitting up and presses a Styrofoam cup of apple juice to my lips. I drink, grateful.

"That's right. You just let those tears out. And no wonder. It's been too much, hasn't it, Dear?" She speaks in a whisper. Turning, she nods at Gabe. "That boy has been here all night. At first your Great Uncle Ian didn't want to let him in. He said family only. But I had some words with him and promised I'd stay, too. Your Gabe is quite extraordinary, Emily. He told me what happened, and I thank the stars he was with you when you found Sandra."

What did he tell her? Everything? You've never screwed up like this before! The woman's voice is back shouting louder than ever and I couldn't agree more. I've really messed up this time. I should have never confided in Gabe.

It wasn't his fault. The little girl's voice argues. *If he hadn't been there Mom would have died. Emma couldn't even call an ambulance!*

I cover my ears with my hands, but it doesn't stop them bickering. I rock forward, pulling my knees up to my chest.

"It hurts, Aunt Nancy."

"Where, Dear? Should I call the nurse?"

"Inside. Everywhere."

Nancy sighs. "I'm afraid the nurse can't help with that kind of hurt."

"When will it stop?"

She shakes her head. "That depends on you."

An aftertaste of despair distills on my tongue. Nothing good has ever come from depending on me.

"You're awake!" The happiness in Gabe's voice catches me off guard. He's by the bed holding my hand before I can blink. Stubble roughens his jaw and shadows smudge the skin under his blue eyes but my God he looks like an angel. Relief spreads through me where his fingers touch mine. I didn't even know how much I missed him until now.

Nancy hands me a tissue. I dry my eyes, very aware of my stale breath, tangled hair, and flimsy hospital gown. But Gabe looks at me like I'm a princess. The smile refuses to leave my face.

"Listen, you two." Nancy has never been good at faking stern. "We all need our sleep. You'll be released tomorrow, Emily, and I'm afraid things will be hectic when you get home. Ian and Margaret have flown in from California. They're determined to take you all back to the Vineyard with them as soon as possible. They've reserved Sandra a bed in a state-of-the-art detox and rehabilitation center. The plan is for Margaret to fly back with your mother. The rest of you will drive cross-country with Ian."

A string of silent exclamation marks marches across the stage in my mind. She can't be serious. My words stammer before they reach my tongue. "Wh-wh- what? I ... I don't ... I don't underst ... are you ... ? You're serious? I haven't seen them in years! I barely even know them! How long will we be gone?"

Nancy purses her lips. "I'm sorry Dear. I don't see any way around this. Steve and I have discussed it. I'll be going with you."

"I'm going too."

Nancy and I gawk at Gabe.

"I am. I'll drive there myself if I have to, and get a job. Your relatives can't stop me. They don't own California."

Nancy nods. "I just wanted to prepare you Emily. They're having a family council tomorrow evening to finalize plans."

"Why? It sounds like they've already decided everything."

"There are few things they want to discuss with you children. Logistics, I think."

I want—no, I need—the void. The last thing in the world I want to do is face Mom's rich Aunt and Uncle. I remember Claire saying that blood is thicker than water. Right now the only thought in my head is that I'd rather drown in water than blood any day of the week.

FOURTEEN

Claire sits cross-legged on the bathroom counter watching me get ready for the family council. She's a good source of information, recounting how she woke up to the sound of paramedics kicking in the front door the night before last. How she and the boys watched them carry Mom outside on a stretcher. I die a little inside when she tells me how I screamed; ranting like a lunatic about monsters, doing everything I could to keep them from taking Mom. How they finally had to sedate me.

The ER doctor did a toxicology report and found Valium and Ambien in my system. A hospital-appointed psychologist came and talked to me before I was released. She asked questions and made notes on her clipboard about prescription and non-prescription drugs and the scars on my arm, but she was just checking off boxes. There isn't anything she can do since I'll be leaving

Dallas indefinitely with my great aunt and uncle.

My stomach acids churn faster the closer it gets to the family meeting. I don't know why I have to be there, but Nancy insists it's important.

Maybe so I can act grateful.

Mom's aunt and uncle have been supporting us for a long time. They were named executors of my grandparent's estate after they both died in some tragic boating accident before I was born. Dear old Gram and Gramps didn't leave the money directly to Mom because they've never liked Dad and they didn't want him to be able to get his hands on it.

Whatever. I know Ian and Margaret are like Mom's second mom and dad but I haven't seen them in over seven years and I'm not fond of them. At all.

Claire chats away about them like she's stumbled across the world's greatest petting zoo. In her mind everything is better than good. Mom's alive, and except for the mental show I put on two nights ago, I'm home and relatively sane. Dad will be released from prison by the end of the week, and we're going on a road trip to California … where she was born.

"Have I ever seen redwoods, Emma? Aunt Meg says they live next to Great Basin Redwood State Park on a vineyard. They have acres of land and chickens that don't even live in cages. She says I can have my own baby chick! And she's going to teach me to bake and knit. She says she tried to teach you when you were my age but you sucked at it."

"Claire, her name is Margaret. Why do you keep calling her Meg?"

"She told me to."

That's interesting. Maybe she's rebranded herself with a fun nickname, trying to act nice so as not to frighten the youngsters. Meg certainly sounds less severe than the Margaret I remember.

"And oh my gosh Emma! Why didn't anyone ever tell me I have a cousin who's adopted? You named Kaillen in the story after him, didn't you?"

"Ugh. He's not your cousin and he isn't adopted. He's not related to us at all. Ian and 'Meg' are his godparents…"

"Uncle Ian has a riding lawn mower and he said I can help him mow the lawn…" I doubt she even heard me. Her words trip along like a swift-moving stream. Everything she says conjures up a memory. I felt the exact same excitement when I visited the Vineyard. We spent summers there when I was young. It was heaven. The lush landscape filled my waking hours with adventure and discovery, my nights with fairytale dreams. The summer Dad was sentenced there wasn't even a single empty space in my body left to worry about the way my family was falling apart, thanks to the Vineyard.

I hold my tongue, unwilling to take away Claire's enthusiasm. I'll do my best to shield her and Jacob and Aidan from any unpleasantness. I'll especially try to protect them from insufferable Kaillen. I have zero idea why I named Nissa's champion after him in the first place. I can't imagine why Ian and Meg brought him with them on this rescue mission. He's only a couple years older than I am, and everyone knows he resents Mom and hates Dad. I'm not looking forward to our reunion at all.

Thank God Nancy will be with me. I'm tensed like I'm going into battle. I'll take all the allies I can get.

Claire sets a tube of mascara down on the bathroom counter and tugs at my sundress. "Did you hear what I said, Emma? Don't you think it would be awesome? I've never been on a plane before!"

I stare at our reflections in the mirror. I must have zoned out again. "Yes you have Bug, you just don't remember. But we're driving to California, not flying."

"No! I knew you weren't listening. Dad called while you were still at the hospital. He said when he comes to get us next week we might all fly home!"

The earring I'm holding clatters into the sink, the silver back slips down the drain.

"What's wrong, Emma?"

"Nothing. I just feel stupid in this dumb sundress." It's true. Shorts and tank tops are my uniform. But it isn't why I'm shaking.

"You look pretty."

That just makes it worse. I don't want to look pretty. Ever. "Will you go tell them I'll be down in a minute, Bug?"

I lock the door after she leaves and sit down hard on the toilet. Sweat runs down my back. I long to ditch the cardigan but I can't leave my arms bare because even though I don't remember doing it, I'm a moron who carved my last name in runes on my arm for everyone to see. I can't imagine what they've all been saying about me behind my back.

Emma, you aren't a moron. The runes are Magic. They'll protect you... the weapons and the faeries too, just like in the story... just like when we were little before He left.

SHUT UP, that is NONSENSE. I'll tell you exactly what your family thinks. They think you're immature. They think you're selfish. They think those scars are a cry for attention. They pity you and you're lucky that's all they do, because they could have put you in an institution. Now they'll be watching. Waiting for you to screw up again. And you will. It's just a matter

of time because there's something WRONG with you. You're DELUSIONAL.
There are no faeries. If you have any sense at all in that ridiculous head you
will KEEP YOUR MOUTH SHUT AND FORGET ABOUT IT.

No Emma… Don't forget! Please… you can't forget.

I'm going to be sick.

I slide to my knees and push up the lid on the toilet. I wretch but nothing comes up.

The stuff I was wearing when they took me to the hospital is in a plastic drawstring bag on the floor in the corner. I crawl to it, digging inside, searching the pockets of the pajama shorts I had on that night.

The pill bottle weighs nothing in my hand. My breathing slows.

I stand up, run cold water over a washcloth and press it on my chest to cool the ugly red splotches, then twist off the cap.

You never learn, do you?

This is YOUR fault, not Emma's! If you didn't say such awful things to her she wouldn't need to run away.

Between my thumbnails I break the little yellow tablet in two, placing the smaller half on my tongue. "Just a little," I whisper. "This is the last time, I promise."

A quick drink from the faucet and swallow. When I straighten, two figures stand behind me staring back in the mirror: a tight-lipped woman with her arms crossed over her chest, and a little girl in braids with a jump rope trailing from her hand to the ground.

My voices.

Which one of them should I listen to? Maybe the woman's right and there's something seriously wrong with me. Maybe the little girl's right and something Magic is happening. The only thing I know for sure is they're tearing me apart.

"Go away. Both of you."

The little girl hangs her head in apology. As their reflections fade, the scowling woman sighs, unfolding her arms. *I'm not angry, Emily. Just very disappointed.*

I turn the corner at the head of the stairs. Ian and Meg stand in the entrance hall below. Jacob, Aidan, and Claire are by the tall round table at the back of the foyer. One by one, every head turns to stare up at me.

I concentrate on my feet. I don't want to trip and fall on my face.

Seven years makes my great aunt and uncle look smaller than I remember, maybe because I'm bigger. Ian's hair is more white than gray now, and thinning. He's still lean and tan like I remember, from working in the sun. His expression is serious but there are crinkles around his eyes. Echoes of his booming laugh fill my childhood memories. I have a longing to skip into his arms like I used to when I'd find him in the barn after a long day exploring the forest. But of course I can't… 'there's a time and a place for everything', and this is not the time nor the place for the kind of 'familiarity that breeds contempt'.

Most of the platitudes engrained in me come from Great Aunt Meg. She stands next to Ian, holding his hand. She's refined—almost formal—her skirt pressed with a crisp seam, her stylish hair frosted at the tips, her blue patent leather pumps polished to a shine. Zero crinkles flank her eyes.

Giddiness from the Valium turns me tipsy. Inappropriate questions zip around my brain: did I shave both legs? Which underwear do I have on? But I squash them. I'm determined the tiny piece of pill I took won't cause any problems. I've already decided I won't beg or cry or even say anything at all to these people. I'll just nod and accept my fate, whatever it is. I'm not going to shame Mom by acting like a silly child in front of her family.

I force false confidence onto my face and bend my left knee, bobbing a shallow curtsy. "Hello." Oh, brilliant.

Uncle Ian's eyes are clearest gray. He studies me.

Heat rises in my cheeks. Back straight, head erect, I can't seem to stop myself from offering him my hand.

"Come 'ere doll," Ian laughs, gathering me against his chest. He smells purpley-green, like sweet alfalfa. I'm caught off guard by how good it is to have his arms around me.

Aunt Meg makes a soft cluck of impatience. I step back from Ian. "Hello," I say self-consciously. I only know one word, apparently.

Meg nods, looking down her nose at a spot on my forehead just left of center. "It's been a long time. You look like Sandra." She sounds disapproving.

My feigned bravery wears thin. I'm exhausted and itchy in my stupid cardigan. How will I survive this family council? Why isn't Nancy here yet?

Awkward, I turn to join the kids by the table and see Gabe standing off to one side in front of a potted palm. He sparkles like an oasis in the Sahara.

"Gabe!" I bolt across the room, throwing my arms around his neck. "You're here!"

Before he can answer a commotion erupts in the entry—three loud crashes followed by a curse. A very good-looking youngish-man I've never seen before pushes past Aidan to my great aunt and uncle with a curt, "Get out of my way."

Crossing the foyer I kneel next to my brother, helping him gather up the fallen marbles from the stone solitaire game.

"Sorry." His voice is miserable. "He knocked into me and I bumped the table. He must not have seen me."

I tousle Aidan's soft blond hair. "Don't be sorry. I love you, you big dork."

"Your MOM's a dork."

I cram mad giggles back down my throat. Aidan is the most irreverent boy I know. Thank God for him. I stiffen my shoulders and walk over to the newcomer. He's talking to Ian. "Excuse me," I say to the back of his head. "We haven't met."

"Yes. We have." He doesn't turn around.

"Kaillen," Meg chides. "Say hello to Emily."

Kaillen? No. WAY.

He glances at me over his shoulder like I'm putrid cheese.

Sharp granite flecks harden my spine. I drop into a full-on Lizzy-Bennet-meets-Mr. Darcy curtsy, raising my Valium-brave hand sarcastically in front of me while never once breaking eye contact with stupid Kaillen whom I hate.

He stares at my extended hand, sniffs, and turns back to Ian. "As I was saying, the rain means an early harvest. We need to leave as soon as possible. I'm going to suggest—again—that we leave the younger siblings behind with that Nancy woman."

My nervousness evaporates. "What did you say?" I speak slowly because I know the anger seething inside me is dangerous. I can't lose my temper and embarrass my family.

This time he turns all the way around, appraising me from head to toe. I stare straight back.

"They'll be in the way. You can at least look after Sandra while she recovers from her latest attention-grabbing stunt. The detox facility recommends weekly family visits. I'm not going to let Meg babysit the younger ones. Our livelihood is more important than your ridiculous family drama."

"Oh? It's important?" I ask. "To whom?"

"To all of us."

"Why are you even here? What does any of this have to do with you?"

"Ian is training me as his viticulturist."

"I have no idea what that means and I couldn't care less."

"Really? Where do you think any of you would be right now if it weren't for your aunt and uncle's money?"

"Oh, so now you own us? You came here uninvited and think you can make decisions about our lives without asking any of us!"

"You didn't seem to be in any condition to make decisions yourself."

My teeth clench spasmodically. "I HATE YOU!"

Without warning a vivid hallucination hijacks my vision. Nissa's enchanted leather gauntlet encircles my right forearm, stretching over the back of my hand and between my fingers, spikes extending from the knuckles. I smash my fist viciously into Kaillen's jaw just below his left ear. His head snaps back and to the right. The spikes rip jagged gashes in his chin, spattering his blood hot on my face but it isn't enough. I want more. I need to feed him pain.

The delusion vanishes suddenly. My un-gauntleted right arm is caged in front of me ready to strike, my fist inches from Kaillen's chin.

Dizziness slams into me. My head swivels as the room tilts sideways.

Strong familiar arms encircle my waist as my knees buckle. "Gabe."

"I'm here."

Everything goes black.

FIFTEEN

I hate everyone.

I hate this stupid van, I hate this stupid drive, and I especially hate stupid Kaillen. His stupid head sits smugly on his stupid neck in the front passenger seat of the van; ignorant of the hatred-holes my eyes bore through it.

There's something extremely dignity-negating about being unceremoniously dumped in the back of a rented twelve-seat passenger van while you're unconscious. But at least I missed the family council.

This is entirely your own fault.

Shut-up shut-up shut-up, I write in the notebook on my lap. Shut-up you horrible woman in my head I hate you SHUT UP.

She doesn't shut up.

It's for your own good. Someone needs to tell you. Look what happens

when you don't listen to me. It isn't Kaillen's fault you took that pill and humiliated yourself and your entire family.

I've slept fitfully most of the drive so far in this stupid wrinkled up sundress, which is better than being awake, I suppose. I'm guessing they emptied the rest of the Valium down the toilet after I passed out again. I must be some kind of featherweight when it comes to meds.

I know they're all judging me. 'Like mother like daughter.'

FUCK. THEM. I scribble, pressing hard against the page.

Claire sits next to me. She notices I'm awake and leans over to see what I'm doing. Her eyes widen before I can cross out the word. OMG she mouths with what I know is legitimate concern for my eternal salvation.

I've never written or said the F word before but I'm too pissy to apologize. I'm amazed that bitch woman in my brain isn't yelling her head off at me.

But I am sorry Claire saw.

She takes the pencil and notebook from me, flips to a new page and writes in perfect round penmanship: Are you okay?

I write back: My back is really sore and I have a huge headache. Plus I'm grumpy. How are you?

BORED.

I write: I think we'll be there soon. Maybe two more hours?

Claire pauses then writes: Are you really okay?

Her lip quivers. I undo our seat belts and pull her next to me, buckling us into the same belt. With my lips against her silky hair I whisper, "I'm sorry Bug. I'm so sorry."

Instead of answering out loud she writes on the notepaper: What happened anyway?

I make myself write: I took one of Mom's pills again because I was freaking out about the family council. I thought it would calm me down. I shouldn't have done it. I didn't actually punch Kaillen, did I?

She writes: No. But I wish you had. He's a jerk. Even if he IS hot.

I write: FYI he was NOT hot the last time I saw him. I didn't recognize him at first!

She writes: Where did he even come from?

I don't write 'Hell' even though I want to.

Instead I write: His mom was a Hispanic migrant worker. Do you know what that means?

Claire makes a so-so gesture with her hand.

I write: Migrant workers are people who come to America from other countries to find work. They do really hard jobs for hardly any money, usually on farms planting or harvesting.

Claire gives me the thumbs-up to show she understands.

I keep writing: Well, Aunt Meg hired Kaillen's mom as a maid at the main house. Kaillen was just a baby. I don't know all the details, but they helped them both get citizenship. Kaillen's mom had a stroke when he was seven and he didn't have any place else to go."

"WHAT?" Claire gasps out loud. "He's an orphan?"

"Shhhhhh!" I glance up to the front. Thank God no one turns around.

Claire draws a frowny-face and a tear on the page and writes: He was only SEVEN!?

There's a photograph of Mom and Dad sitting on a couch at the Vineyard looking very young and kind of like hippies. Between them is the most beautiful, chubby-cheeked, black-haired, huge-eyed little boy I've ever seen in my entire life. Everyone was crazy about Kaillen. In the photo he holds a squirmy toddler on his plaid-panted lap. Me. But Kaillen isn't looking at me or at the camera. He's staring up at Mom, adoration on his face.

Claire nudges me and points to the paper with the eraser. She's drawn more frowny faces and tears and the words: That's sad.

Ugh. A kitten-soft paw of compassion prods at me. I smother it quick. Kaillen doesn't need or want my sympathy.

I write: Yeah. Super sad.

But I'm not sad. Ever since I can remember, Kaillen has been an enormous douche. He picked on me relentlessly when we were younger. Now he's like the prize-winning hog on Grandpa's farm.

I'm not bitter that Mom's family stopped visiting us. It must have been hard for them to admit they had a convicted felon in the family tree. I know they put pressure on Mom to divorce Dad, and kind of shunned her when she wouldn't. Kaillen's the only one who didn't stop calling her. But it wasn't to give support. I have zero idea why Mom kept answering his calls because whenever she hung up the phone after talking to him she would be in tears.

The memory of the photograph and the hollow ache that starts in my chest when I imagine what it would be like being an orphan at seven kicks my over-active empathy gene into high gear and now I'm weepy about him too even though I know better.

I write: I shouldn't have said 'I hate you' to Kaillen. And I'm sorry for writing the F word.

"It's okay," Claire whispers. "It's been a weird week. Besides, he really was being an ass."

I can't stop a giggle. "Claire!" I whisper back. "When did you start swearing?"

"About the same time you did."

Aidan turns back and looks at us from over his seat. "What are you guys laughing about?"

"Claire has a crush on Kaillen." I whisper.

She snorts and elbows me hard in the ribs. "I do not."

"You're the one who named Nissa's bodyguard after him." Thankfully Aidan lowers his voice. "I like the Kaillen in the story, but real-life Kaillen is kind of a dick."

"Aidan Michael Alvey!" I cover Claire's ears.

Claire moves my hands away. "Kids say that all the time at school, Emma. Speaking of the story, will you tell us more about the Fae when we get to Scott's Valley?"

Cracks form in the frozen pond that is my hastily patched façade of sanity.

"There isn't any more, Bug," I lie.

"There has to be. Where did Nissa go? What happened after the Fae got banished? Where are they now? Do they ever get back home?"

"She's right. It's a really lame cliff hanger," Aidan says.

Jacob turns around, taking out his earbuds. "I want to know what happens, too."

My brittle bravery begins to splinter and there is nothing I can do. Impending doom rushes to meet us every mile closer we drive to the Vineyard.

Through the van window I stare at a wake of vultures feasting on road kill. I'm afraid the First Realm won't let me go until I'm picked clean.

"Sure," I say. "I guess so."

The boys turn back around in their seats. Claire snuggles closer, pulling my arms around her tighter. She writes on the pad: Emma?

"What?" I whisper.

She writes: Will you maybe try to not pass out anymore?

I kiss her head. "I won't do that again," I whisper. "I promise."

SIXTEEN

The most delicious breeze from the open window sends a flurry of goosebumps up my arms. My eyes flutter open. Quietly, so I won't wake Claire, I swing my bare feet to the woven rug on the floor. The temperature balances between chill and warmth. I'm tempted to lie back down and bask in the perfection of the morning.

But I can't. The breeze pulls me up, a long lost best friend. It was late when we arrived last night and I went straight to bed, falling immediately into a dreamless sleep. Now, gazing out the guest room window, I'm shocked by how familiar everything is. How could I have forgotten this place? It was such a huge part of my life growing up.

It makes sense, though, that if I'd shut away memories of the Seventh Kingdom I'd have shut away memories of the Vineyard, too. This is where the

Seventh Kingdom was born. This is where it came to life.

I slide into the flip-flops at the foot of the bed, pull my cardigan over my yoga pants and tank top, and tiptoe into the hall. Opening the back door with an excited shiver, I slip outside.

The house nestles in a copse of birch at the edge of Big Basin State Park. Thick wet fog clings to the redwood canopy that marks the far-end of the property line. I wrap my arms around myself in the early light. Everywhere is cold compared to summer in Dallas.

My sensory input system shifts into overdrive. I'm more alive here in this place, in this moment, than I've ever been before. I don't need pills to help me discern the subtle kiss of each individual birch-leaf filtered sunlit shaft as it lands on my upturned face.

The creaky old rope swing still hangs from the biggest oak in the yard. I used to climb this tree, make circlets from her leaves, and when I'd kick up on the swing so my toes nearly touched the next branch up, I'd pretend it was my wings propelling me so high.

I sit down on the wide wooden plank and push off from the ground, arcing back and forth on a long slow pendulum. Eyes closed, I relive the hallucination of lying next to Mom on the couch the other night…of shrinking down inside myself…of the countless specks of light. What if two of those lights were my own Spark and Flame? What if they'd awakened my own wings, causing them to strain and stretch against my skin from the inside out, desperate to escape their cocoon?

My own wings.

It wasn't real.

Maybe it WAS real, Emma. Now you can let your wings out! The crimbal can't get you here. This Vineyard belongs to the Fae.

Stop it. Emily is too old for this nonsense.

My feet scrape in the dirt, halting me abruptly as a watery memory swims to the surface of my mind and I remember: I used to tell Mom about the Fae, about the First Realm and the Seventh Kingdom. She thought it was cute I believed in faeries. She liked it when I would entertain Jacob, Aidan, and Claire with my stories at bedtime. But around my eleventh birthday it stopped being cute.

In my memory dark smudges spread beneath Mom's eyes, blocking the light that used to shine from her face when she looked at me.

Not long after Dad went to prison, Mom took me to a psychiatrist. He had a beard and wore glasses at the end of his nose. He prescribed Ritalin and warned me that people who couldn't separate fantasy from reality were seriously unhealthy.

That's why she made me stop telling the stories. That's why she took away the Celtic box. That's why the woman and the little girl argue about the Seventh Kingdom.

Petulance gathers my lips into a bloodless crinkled bunch. How is it fair for a mother who self-medicates to the point of abandoning her children and attempting suicide because she can't handle reality gets to give her eleven year-old daughter meds so she'll stop daydreaming? I locked my imagination in a lightless cupboard so Mom would accept me. What utter bullshit. Well. Not anymore.

Kicking off from the dirt again I tip back on the swing and let my wings unfurl from their subdural prison, opening and closing them defiantly. Air moves in liquid streams along their surface the way hair flows weightless under water. The headache and pain between my shoulder blades that have been plaguing me for days disappear immediately.

I twist hard on the wooden seat, twining the two ropes together. A tight thrill of anticipation squeezes my stomach when the coil reaches its apex… pauses…then sends me twirling back the other way, a mad top.

Wings outstretched I taste the breeze. Woodsy hints of white pine and sweet clover flavor the air along with something wet and utterly refreshing. It must be the stream that runs downhill past the beehives to the vineyard.

"Emily?"

"Claire, you're awake!" Dizzy but happy I come to a stop and wobble to my sister. "We've got to get a drink from that stream, it tastes amazing!"

She eyes me skeptically.

A dragonfly zips close, flitting in front of me at eye level.

"Bug, look, it's Xander," I exclaim. Kneeling, I clasp Claire's hands. "Can you keep a secret?" She nods. "See those trees over there, behind the goat shed?"

"Are those redwoods?"

"Yes. And guess what. The Fae live in that forest."

Her eyes get big. "Our Fae? From the Seventh Kingdom?"

"YES."

She squeals. "Will you show me, Emma?"

"They like to keep hidden, but we can go exploring later with the boys. Wouldn't it be amazing if we found the Doorway and broke the Seal and traveled to the First Realm?"

"Oh. My. Gosh. YES." Her eyes light up. "Hey, Emma? Are there goats in the goat shed?"

"Yep. Aunt Meg and Uncle Ian have goats, horses, bees, and chickens. If you're really lucky you'll get to milk the goats, muck the stalls, and gather the eggs. Plus, Aunt Meg has a garden. Best pea-pods you've ever tasted."

"No thanks on horse-poo and pea-pods," she crinkles her nose. "You seem happy, Emma. I'm glad." She leans against my forehead with hers. "Do you know how to milk a goat?"

"I do. Funny, right? I forgot how much I love this place."

The back door opens. "Good morning you two!" Nancy steps outside. "I thought for sure you'd sleep in today after being cooped up in that van for so long. How are you both feeling?"

Claire rushes to give her a hug. "Isn't it amazing here, Aunt Nancy? Did you know there are goats?"

"I did know that, Dear. I used to live just down the mountain a little ways."

Claire goggles. "No one tells me anything."

"I'll tell you something right now. Your Aunt Meg's making pancakes and she's asking for your help."

Claire skips inside without another word.

"How are you, Emily?"

I know Nancy loves me, but I still can't help pulling my cardigan closer now that we're alone. I have a lot to be embarrassed about.

"I'm better. Sorry… about everything. Thank you for coming here with us. I haven't seen my mom's family in a long time. I don't think they like us very much."

"They're good people, Emily. They love you children and your mother. And I have to say, that Gabe of yours is rather fond of you too. For him to drive me all the way out here…. It worked out perfectly that Ian needs extra help with the harvest this year. You're awfully young to have a serious boyfriend, but there's something about him…"

"He's not my boyfriend," I stammer, turning the same shade of violet as the grapes in Uncle Ian's vineyard. "He just… I don't know… We haven't even…" Ugh. I can't explain. Because he isn't just some lifeguard from the pool, either. I can't deny we're connected somehow.

Nancy puts her arm around my shoulders and steers me to a bench next to Aunt Meg's garden. The sharp herbal tang from the tomato plants makes me long for chips and salsa. I'm never as hungry anywhere as I am when I'm here.

"Emily. Do you know what my profession was before I retired?"

I shake my head, squinting at the morning sun reflecting off her glasses. Strange. I'd never even wondered.

"I was a Child and Family Guidance Counselor."

Shame crams into my empty spaces. She knows something's wrong with me.

"I know you have a lot on your mind."

I study my hands.

"I've kept an eye on you in particular since you moved to Dallas, Dear. I'm impressed at your remarkable resilience. You've had to be strong for your brothers and sister for a long time, and that wears on a person. You've got a lot on your plate, and I want you to know that I'm here for you. You can tell me anything. You know that, don't you?"

Anything? asks the little girl.

Not anything, says the woman.

It's like I'm balancing on a tightrope meters above the ground. Below me on the left the little girl in two braids and a pinafore dress stands in a field of dried wheat gazing up at me. She holds a balloon in one hand and the handlebar of a bicycle in the other.

Below me on the right is the woman. She's dressed in a crisp pencil skirt and patent leather pumps with a single string of pearls around her neck. She stands in front of an immaculate house with fresh painted eaves, looking up at me with her hands on her hips.

Lean mangy lions stalk the perimeter of their landscape. The little girl and the woman don't seem to notice the lions, or the Gray Man.

The Gray Man stands in the distance where the two different landscapes meet. His face is obscured in shadow from the brim of his hat. His posture is casual, but menace underlies the easy way he holds the rifle at his side. The slick-oiled scope and eight-round clip of his Remington make me uneasy. I can't tell if the Gray Man is protecting the little girl and the woman in my brain, or keeping them prisoner. The only thing I know for sure is that he is lethal.

I waiver high above them on my rope while they stare up at me in silence. Are they waiting for me to fall?

"Talk to me Emily." Next to me on the bench Nancy covers my hands with hers.

"I think I'm going crazy." My voice is a whisper.

"Why do you think that?"

I squeeze my eyes shut, hoping the little girl, the woman, the Gray Man, and the lions will all disappear. What do they want me to do? Why aren't they saying anything?

"Sometimes there are voices. In my head."

"Can you tell me what they sound like?"

I look at Nancy, surprised. She doesn't sound like she thinks I'm nuts. Her voice is normal. Is this a trick?

"It's alright if you don't want to tell me, Dear. I was only curious if they sound at all like the voices in my head."

The little girl in the wheat nods at me. The woman studies her shoes, but I can tell she's paying attention. The Gray Man with the Remington isn't doing anything at all. It doesn't even look like he's breathing.

"There are two main ones." I choose my words carefully because they're listening. "One is a little girl. She believes in Magic and she always wants to pretend. The other is a woman. She … well … she isn't very nice."

"What kinds of things do they say?"

The Gray Man lifts his head. From under the brim of his hat he stares directly into my eyes, moving his chin from side to side: NO.

A shock runs through me. "I don't know," I answer abruptly.

Nancy nods. "Most people don't recognize the self-talk from their different egos, Emily. The voices get jumbled in with the rest of the mind's noise, but everyone has many ego states. If I'm correct, two of your egos are in conflict with each other, either because they feel threatened by something happening externally, or because they're holding onto traumas they haven't processed yet from the past. It will be important to learn to communicate and compromise with them so they feel valued."

"Wouldn't I know it if I had past traumas to process?"

"It isn't unusual to keep secrets from ourselves."

"It isn't?"

"Not at all."

"Everyone has these egos?"

"Everyone. Usually, egos navigate in our subconscious subtly without us ever noticing. I bet you didn't start to hear the little girl and the woman until they started arguing."

She's right.

"Those voices probably developed to protect you when you needed them, to help you cope at times in your past when you were struggling or afraid. They each have different ways of handling difficult situations. If you open yourself up to listening, you might hear other voices too—perhaps a nurturing parent or a natural child. You can refine these voices, Emily. You can integrate them into one True Voice all your own, based on your personal reality in the present."

"How will I recognize my True Voice?" The Gray Man still watches me.

"Well, your True Voice is the voice of the woman you're becoming. When you hear it, you'll feel more like you than ever."

I'm empty. Hopeless. The only time I've ever heard a voice like that was when the White Faerie spoke to me. I'm pretty sure talking to imaginary creatures isn't healthy. I just nod though. I don't want Nancy to know I'm a lost cause.

"Gabe told me about your panic attacks, Dear. I understand why you took your mother's medication, but there are other ways to deal with your anxiety and the situations that trigger those emotions."

I hunch forward on the bench. My feet are cold. It was stupid to come outside in flip-flops.

"He also told me about your story. About the First Realm and the Seventh Kingdom. About the Fae."

The little girl and the woman gasp. My feet slip on the tightrope above their heads, I barely keep from toppling. "It's just something I made up...I know it isn't real..."

"It's incredible. There's truth in the imagination, Emily. There's insight in dreams. Albert Einstein said, 'If you want your children to be intelligent, read them fairytales. If you want them to be more intelligent, read them more fairytales.' I hope you'll look for opportunities to be alone here, Emily, to dream and use your imagination. Will you try?"

It's like flying. The tightrope no longer digs into the bottom of my feet. My muscles aren't cramping to hold my balance. There isn't anything under my feet anymore, just sky. It's disorienting and exhilarating at the same time. Nancy thinks my imagination *is good*.

"Here's your homework: I want you to listen to the little girl and the woman, really listen. Ask them what they want, what they need. Experience your emotions and memories without judging them or reacting to them... just feel them instead of burying or ignoring them and soon enough they'll go away. I won't lie to you, Dear. What I'm asking you to do isn't easy and it won't be comfortable. But you're strong and brave, Emily. I know you can make peace with those voices. That is when you will find your True Voice. With practice you will learn to trust yourself the way I trust you."

Sitting on this bench next to Nancy I'm doubtful of my bravery and strength. Sometimes my emotions come out of nowhere. Sometimes they're so frightening and so powerful that I'll do anything I can think of to make them go away. The idea of just holding still and experiencing them terrifies me.

"Nancy, when is my dad getting here?"

"He arrives the day after tomorrow."

"And then he's taking us home with him." It isn't a question.

"What would you like to have happen?"

"I'm only seventeen. It's not like I have a choice."

"When you learn to hear and trust your True Voice, you'll discover you have more choice than you think." Nancy lowers her glasses to the tip of her nose. Her eyes are ringed by dark green, flecked with amber. They make me think of thick primeval ivy on ancient pitted stone. "By the way, how's the pain in your shoulder blades, Dear? And your headache?"

A tingle traces up either side of my spine. "Better, thanks."

"Good. Now, I was on my way to the hen house to collect the eggs. You don't mind going for me, do you? That's a Dear."

With that Nancy squeezes my hand, leaving me on the bench, speechless and unalone.

SEVENTEEN

*T*hings are getting pretty strange.

Scratch that. Things have been strange for a while now.

Nancy might be more concerned about my mental health if she knew I don't only make up fairytales for my brothers and sister—that just before she came outside I was pretending I have actual wings.

I braid my hair as I walk down the path to the hen house, ordering my thoughts while my fingers work, mulling over my conversation with Nancy.

Ugh. She's a child psychologist. She's probably been psychoanalyzing me for years. Waiting for me to mess up? No. That's not Nancy. She's never given me any reason to mistrust her. But I still couldn't tell her everything about the voices or what they say.

I'm disturbed by the appearance of the Gray Man. Where did he come from? What does he want? And what's with the lions?

I shudder in my flip-flops. The inside of my brain is a crowded, dangerous place these days. How am I supposed to find my True Voice in that mess?

I leave the path, cutting through a field of tall grass. Nancy said to trust myself. How can I when I'm not even honest with myself?

I take a big breath and clench my fists. Determined, I speak a truth I've been ignoring for a long, long time: "I don't want Dad to come home."

I've never said that out loud before. Never even admitted it to myself. Now I can't stop repeating it like a chant: "I don't want him to come home, I don't want him to come home, I don't want him to come home."

No lightning snakes up from the ground, no ominous thunder claps.

But no relief, either.

It's true, though. And not just a little true. One hundred percent true. There's not one fraction of a percent of a percent in my body that wants to see Dad. Does that make me a bad person? I feel guilty.

It's okay that you don't want to see him. It's okay to feel guilty. Trust yourself.

I stop in my tracks. The words are distinct, but far away. Like a thrown voice. A trick.

Did someone hear me talking to myself and answer back?

"Emily!" Aidan's voice calls to me from the tree line down the hill and across the stream. A second later he bounds out of the birches, scrambling along the rocky hillside and skipping across half-submerged stones spanning the running water. In seconds he flings himself into my arms.

I hold him close, awash with joy. It's feels like months since I saw my fourteen year-old brother last, not just overnight. Has he grown? "You look like an elf!" I exclaim. He's dressed in soft cords and a light woven shirt I've never seen before. His hair smells of trapped sunshine, warm and boyish. Someone must have made him bathe. "So, Mr. Dorky T. Dorklington, how have you been?"

"Ermahgerd," he answers in his groan-inspiring valley girl impression. "I been, like, totes fine, thanks for asking, Ms. Fartnose."

I gasp. He's carrying a small wooden bucket. It's a quarter of the way full with plump raspberries and I'm starving.

I shovel a fist-full into my mouth. "These are so good," I mumble.

"Nice manners."

Ignoring him, I continue snarfing ripe purple fruit. "So, Aidan," I say when I reach the bottom of the bucket, "how do you like this situation? Do you remember this place at all? Are you bored out of your mind yet?" I wipe the juice from my chin with my fingers and clean them off on the back of his shirt in exaggerated strokes. I'm not sure what, exactly, has triggered this ebullient high, but I want it to last. "Is Jacob awake too?"

"Generally speaking, I frown on nature," Aidan answers, "and the bunk house smells like a zoo, but otherwise it's alright. Uncle Ian says later Jacob and I can do target practice with him and some of the guys who work for him."

I picture tall canvas targets and bows and arrows like from Robin Hood. "That sounds cool I guess, as long as you're safe. I mean, with adult supervision, obviously. Huh. Do you think he'd let me play, too?" I link arms with him and pull him with me back to the path.

"I dunno. He just said Jacob and me. Maybe he thinks you're too delicate. Besides, you hate guns, remember?"

"I don't hate target practice with bb guns, Dork. I'm actually a pretty good shot." I bump him with my hip, twisting my leg to kick him in the butt while maintaining my place on the narrow dirt trail.

"Yeah, I don't think the guys who work here use BB guns. Uncle Ian said I could use his Glock. I told him you wouldn't like it but he said we've been raised by women for too long and we need to start acting like men."

"Nice, Aidan," I smirk. "I'm sure that's exactly what he said. Oooh, is there a merit badge for boys who shoot semi-automatic weapons?" I'm cracking myself up.

Aidan rolls his eyes.

I turn to face him, grabbing his bucket and blocking his path mid-stride. My mouth forms a straight somber line. "But for reals, Aidan. Have you been able to figure it out yet?"

"Figure what out yet?"

I lean closer, suppressing giggles. "Why I can't seem to stop myself from PUSHING YOU IN THE BUSHES!" Hooking my foot around his ankle, I shove him sideways off the path into the tall grass.

I laugh as he disappears. Adjusting the bucket handle in the crook of my arm I skip off toward the hen house...

...and freeze.

Jacob, Gabe, and Uncle Ian are coming up the path towards me.

"Oops."

"Did your sister just push Aidan into the weeds?" Gabe asks Jacob.

I back up, bend over, and haul Aidan to his feet. "How embarrassing, Aidan! You must have stumbled," I say loudly. "You should really watch where you're going…" my voice trails off. I pull a twig from his hair.

"Yeah, stumbled over your foot," Jacob hoots.

Aidan brushes dirt from his pants. "Why? Why must you always trip me and push me and pinch me and do whirling jump attacks on me? I'm the good brother!"

"Whirling jump attacks?" Uncle Ian asks.

"Yeah, she's got a black belt in the Art of Annoyance." Jacob smirks.

"What's a whirling jump attack?" Gabe wants to know.

"It's when you're sitting on the couch minding your own business watching TV or reading a book," Jacob answers, "and your big sister walks by and launches herself at you out of the blue like an uncoordinated giraffe while yelling, 'whirling jump attack!'"

Gabe raises his eyebrows.

"It looks really cool in my head," I shrug.

"It looks really lame in reality," Jacob quips.

"You boys need to treat your sister with more respect," Uncle Ian admonishes. "She's a young lady and needs to start acting like one."

"Oh, I totally agree." I'm unwilling—at least right now—to let Ian's judgment detract from this bond with my brothers. Jacob looks good, happy. "They're totes lamesauce on my tacos." I can't keep a grin from my face. Even after all the bizarre stuff they've endured the last week, my brothers and sister are all right.

"Come on, all of you. Meg will have breakfast ready." Jacob and Aidan obediently follow Uncle Ian toward the house.

"I'm just on my way to gather the eggs," I say. "I'll be there in a few minutes."

Gabe stands in his frayed jeans and T-shirt watching them go, his hands shoved in his front pockets just like they were the day I left him in the grocery store parking lot. He looks really, really...good.

"How are you?" he asks quietly.

A rush of gratitude for him envelops me. "Thank you," I say.

"For what?"

"For always catching me when I fall."

He steps closer. I look at the ground. "You must think I'm crazy ridiculous," I say.

"Hey." He lifts my chin with his finger. I'm too shy to look at him. "Hey." He takes my face in his hands, bending his head until we're eye to eye. "You listen to me. I think you're crazy *amazing*."

Before I can say or do anything he kisses me gently on the lips. Just one short touch but I feel it to my toes.

He leans back and glances over my shoulder. A boyish grin spreads across his face. "Cool," is all he says before turning and following the others.

"Cool what?" I glance over my shoulder as well. "Oh, lovely. That's just lovely," I grumble at the bright fuchsia blush emanating from my wings.

EIGHTEEN

Picking climbing beans is backbreaking work. Leaves and whirling vines stick like glue to everything they touch. I'm plastered in bean plant. My arms itch from the clingy little hairs on the undersides of the leaves. And I swear I put on deodorant this morning, but the stink from my armpits is grossing me out, even though Claire says she can't smell it.

Our strategy is simple: I start at one end of the row and Claire at the other, scooting along in the dirt toward each other in the middle, picking the underside of the bushes and ignoring the higher-up beans. I know it's not a great strategy. Aunt Meg *will* come out and check to make sure we've gotten every. Single. Bean. I can't avoid the higher-up beans forever, but I'm cherishing this time on my butt in the shade, willing to risk her wrath to survive the present.

Curling vines just above my head start to waggle as a cupped hand, holding a split peapod parts the leaves. "Behold…the magic BEANS."

Aidan. I grab his wrist, laughing. "You know these aren't beans, right? They're peas. You're such a dork!"

Aidan thrashes, hissing like a deranged snake. "It's got me! The evil faerie woman wants my precious BEANS!"

I tug on his arm like I'm going to pull him through the row. He pulls back, squawking louder, bringing Claire running to see what's going on. As she gets close I suddenly let go of Aidan's wrist. I can't see him fall, but the crash on the other side of the climbing vines is extremely satisfying. Oh, glorious day, I love my brother. "Stop messing around, Aidan," I fake-scold. "We have work to do."

"Yeah Aidan," Claire says.

"Here, Bug, try these peas."

"They aren't peas, they're BEANS!" Aidan's voice is muffled.

"Picking beans is boring." Claire complains. "Why can't the boys come work with us?"

"Yeah, Aidan. Go get Jacob and come help us pick BEANS and then Claire and I will come help you guys pick PEAS when we're done."

"Won't Aunt Meg get mad?" Aidan asks through the plants. "I'm afraid of her. She made me scrub all the counters in the kitchen because I left the back door open and a fly flew in."

"She is kind of grumpy," Claire agrees. "But she makes really good pancakes."

"Hurry up, Aidan," I say. "I don't think it matters as long as we finish the rows she gave us, right? I can tell more of the story while we pick," Nancy's encouragement has made me brave. The sun shines bright, chasing the shadows from my mind.

"JACOB," Aidan yells. "BRING YOUR BUCKET OVER TO THE BEANSTALKS!"

"Nice, Aidan. I could have done that."

"I know," he answers. "Why didn't you?"

We hear a distant, "WHERE?"

I cup my hands around my mouth. "JUST PAST THE SUMMER SQUASH!"

"Do you really think he knows what summer squash is?" Aidan scoffs. But before long Jacob's head appears at the end of the row. We divide and conquer: boys on one side, girls on the other. I don't even mind standing up. My fairytale beckons, eager to be told, and here in the Vineyard garden surrounded by my siblings, I'm brave enough to try again.

"When the High King Ælfwig banished the surviving Fae to the Second Realm he sent them back in time a hundred years…" I start.

"So now they're time traveling faeries?" Aidan arches an eyebrow.

"The High King wasn't so much concerned with which time or reality he sent them to… he just wanted them *gone*. When the Fae found themselves on the wrong side of the Doorway they were disoriented. But mostly they were pissed… at each other. The elves blamed the maidens for the banishment because of the Queen's disobedience and betrayal. The maidens blamed the elves for being controlling misogynists and for starting the riots after the Queen's death. They split into two factions directly divided by gender. Civil war would have decimated them if the Ovate Drake hadn't stepped in as their Mediator and organized a peace treaty."

The scene unfolds vividly in my mind, more like memory than imagination.

"Even though both sides were suspicious of Drake, they all agreed that being Ovate gave him insight into both elf and maiden perspectives. Also, he was a lot stronger than the rest of them. See, the Second Realm is different than the First…energy vibrates more slowly here. The Fae are still ageless, but their powers are way weaker. The maidens' wings shriveled up when they were banished. They only have access to the Blaze in their wings when they shrink down to insect-size, and even then it isn't much. Elves still have Keen here. They can See the elements, but aren't strong enough to manipulate them. Except for Drake. Nissa's grandpa, the High King used the Blaze in Drake's wings to seal the Doorway shut, so as long as Drake stays within twenty-five miles of the Door, he has access to his full powers."

"Then why didn't he just use Magic to break the Seal so they could all go home?" Claire asks.

"He couldn't. It would be like attacking himself."

"So they decided just to live here and be happy?" she asks. "Nope. They couldn't—wouldn't—forgive each other. The maidens and elves each picked a delegate. Every year for almost a hundred years, Lady Quince and General Raidho travel to the Doorway to meet with Drake. He's been looking for a way home for a century."

Jacob and Aidan wiggle through to our side of the aisle. They sit cross-legged on the dirt with Claire in a semi-circle in front of me between two rows of climbing beans while I continue to pick. I pray Meg won't notice the way they've butchered her beanstalks.

"What about Princess Nissa? What happened to her?" Claire asks.

"No one knows, Bug. Kaillen saw her for the last time on the afternoon the Queen died. He took Nissa to her rooms just as the riots began. Four guards stood watch outside her doors."

It's happening again. Without the assistance of drugs or dragonflies, the Seventh Kingdom takes over, and either my imagination is exponentially stronger here in Cali than it was in Texas or I have completely lost my mind because WHOA.

I'm pressed into a niche in the castle wall, watching Kaillen pace back and forth in the hallway outside Nissa's chamber.

Dark clouds blacken the afternoon. When the first lightning bolt strikes I nearly jump out of my skin. Kaillen shoves past the guards into Nissa's room and I'm right behind him. He knows as well as I do how much she hates thunder. But her chambers are empty. We race through the corridors shouting her name, desperate to find our princess.

She's not anywhere in the palace. My anxiety spikes. Where could she be? We race outside to the courtyard, searching everywhere.

Another lightning bolt strikes and I glimpse Nissa's slight figure in a narrow alley between two dwellings just beyond the palace gates. Kaillen sees her too. He runs toward her, screaming her name. Lightning strikes again and the ground lurches, knocking me off balance and tossing Kaillen to his knees. By the time we recover she's gone.

We scour the streets, but guards have arrived. They're dragging Kaillen back to his father, General Raidho. They're organizing a search party of men still loyal to the Crown, but with a sinking in my heart I already know: they won't find a trace of Nissa.

"She's not dead, though. I know she's not dead. Right, Emma?" Claire tugs on my arm, yanking me abruptly back to the reality of the garden.

My own breath is too loud in my ears. "I hope not, Bug."

"They haven't found any way of getting back to the First Realm in a hundred years?" Jacob asks. "Is Drake really even trying?"

"Drake is obsessed with returning home." I'm not sure where this knowing comes from, but I'm certain what I'm saying is true. It's almost like I have a tangible connection with Drake… I can't see him, even in my vision his face is obscured… but his obsession reverberates through me. I shudder. It feels *bad*. "Three weeks ago, Drake summoned Lady Quince and General Raidho to an unscheduled meeting. He showed them a vision he received."

"Are you talking about three weeks ago as in the year of our Lady Gaga two-thousand and sixteen?" Aidan asks.

"Yep."

"Whoa."

"Emma, you forgot to tell the boys about where the Fae live now!" Claire squeals.

"You tell them, Bug."

"In the redwoods," she points past the goat shed. "Over there!"

Jacob whistles. "Way to keep it real, Sis. By the way, it's freaky but cool when you go all zombie and tell it like you're watching it happen or something. You should be an actor."

"Will you guys shut up already?" Aidan asks. "I want to hear about the vision."

I wish I'd known before that they like it when I go all 'zombie'—not that I can really help it—but it's a monumental relief not having to be so worried about maintaining a semblance of normalcy. Now my biggest fear is that the story will suck me in somehow and I'll get stuck in some delusional part of my brain. But Nancy said my imagination is good, so I take a deep breath, sit down in the dirt in front of my brothers and sister, and prepare to let my freak-flag fly.

For this performance, I'll be the narrator and act out the final scene with the different voices, too.

Narrator: When Lady Quince saw the vision, all she could do was stare in wonder, the General, too.

Drake: Tell me what you see.

Lady Quince: Determination. And Power. Incredible Power.

General Raidho: I see unspeakable fear.

Drake: You are both correct. This situation is extremely complex. I need you to go deeper and tell me *exactly* what you See.

Narrator: Lady Quince connects with the vision again, breathing deep and diving beneath the surface. She speaks as if in a trance:

Lady Quince: Darkness descends early, spreading a frosted hush over the horizon.

Silence covers the pavement as brittle leaves blanket the frozen ground.

Slender naked branches stretch toward the moon.

The maiden is alone.

Damp fog shrouds her head,

Her pale uncovered shoulders tremble as Night whispers flattery

Along the bare curve of her Neck,

Slips sighing to curl in the hollow of her throat:

A cold, heavy, glittering gem clasped in wintry silver.

Desperate, she reaches in and up

Grasping the edges of the sky.

With frigid fingers she gathers silky corners, pulling them down around her.

She wears Night as a cloak,

A sapphire shawl trimmed in deepest indigo,

Shot through with brilliant diamond stars.

Narrator: Quince severs the connection with the vision and speaking to the General.

Lady Quince: We must find her. She is Ovate. With Nissa's weapons she is strong enough to open the Door.

General Raidho: We cannot afford to hate or blame each other any longer. We have work to do. The fate of our people depends on it.

I shiver, breaking a small clump of dirt between my thumb and fingers, grinding it to dust. Jacob, Aidan, and Claire are quiet, too. Could they see the scene as vividly as I could? Do they sense the escalating urgency of the Fae closing in around them like I can? Or have they finally started to question my sanity?

"You know," a voice too close behind me says, "It wasn't nice to tell more of the story without me."

Scrambling to my feet I grab the bean-bucket, my heart pounding a wild rhythm. "Gabe!" I turn to find him sitting in the dirt looking up at me, admiration in his eyes.

My face flames. He's not alone.

Kaillen sits on a planter box a few feet away. His deep brown eyes glitter with warmth that steals my breath.

Is that look for me?

Oh my God, oh my God, oh my God, oh my God. Oh. My. GOD.

"Wait for me next time, okay?" Gabe stands up, taking the bean bucket from my hand.

"You didn't miss anything," Jacob says. "You got here when Nissa disappeared, right?"

"They've been here this whole time and you said *nothing*?" I glare at Jacob, Aidan and Claire. "You are so dead to me."

"What?" Aidan's voice is innocent. "It's rude to interrupt."

"Emma, that face though!" Claire laughs hysterically. She'll probably start snort-farting any minute. She has very little control over her bodily functions. The boys grin obnoxiously.

"Thanks a lot, guys."

"Meg sent us to tell you it's time for lunch," Kaillen says. "You're supposed to take your shoes off before you go inside, and wash your hands in the back bathroom only. Food's on the porch."

My pulse sprints a three-minute mile as I make myself meet his bold appraising eyes.

"It's too bad Kaillen couldn't find the princess," Kaillen says. "He sounds like an amazing person."

Oh hells bells.

My shoulder bumps against Gabe as I walk stiffly down the narrow dirt path through the garden. I hate boys.

"Wait," Jacob says from a couple paces ahead. "Gabe, I should mention that the Fae's powers don't work in the Second Realm like they do in the First. The elves can still See the elements, but not manipulate them, and the maidens only have wings and power when they shrink to insect size. Drake lost his wings, but he can still use his powers if he stays within twenty-five miles of the Doorway, which is why he needs Lady Quince and the General to go find the girl in the vision. Any questions?"

"Just one," Gabe says. "Does the girl in the vision happen to have hair the color of marigolds?"

A bean smacks the back of my head. "Yeah, Emily," Aidan says behind me. "Does she?"

I stop short. Aidan collides into me but I hardly even notice him or Gabe or Kaillen or anything else. A thrill of dread flutters through me as the fog shrouding the girl in the vision disperses. I gasp as she looks up at me with my own eyes.

"Yes." I want to deny it but I can't.

"I knew it!" Claire's fist pumps the air.

My thoughts spin. Gabe bends his head down and whispers in my ear, "I can't wait to hear what happens next."

NINETEEN

At lunch Aunt Meg announces we'll be driving into town to meet Dad tomorrow. I can't wrap my head around it. He's out of prison. Less than 25 miles away from the Vineyard. I need to be alone or I swear I'll go mad. I escape the house as soon as I can and head for my secret place. The one I discovered when I was a little girl.

"Emily!" Aidan's shout draws me up short as I walk along the dirt path. "Wait up!"

He's jogging across the field of tall grass toward me, his blond hair flopping with every step.

"What's up, French-iest Fry?" Feigning normalcy is my new norm these days.

As Aidan gets closer my plan to sweep his leg with a stealthy roundhouse kick evaporates, replaced with concern. Dark shadows gather under his eyes and tight lines surround his mouth.

"I've been having this recurring dream," he says. "It's freaking me out."

"Why didn't you tell me before, dork? This morning you said you liked it here and you were doing good."

"I didn't want you to think I was a wuss." His eyes keep sliding away from mine and his shoulders twitch, bunching and unbunching. He's spooked, and I hate it.

I plop down on the ground, lying back so the vegetation towers above me. Sticks poke me from every direction and I imagine the excitement of the ants at the sudden appearance of a giantess to explore. Twisting a blade of sweet grass loose from its sheath I bite down, releasing honey on my tongue-tip, and wait for Aidan to join me.

He kneels next to me, hesitating. I tug him down so his head rests in the crook of my shoulder and close my eyes. "Spill it."

"I'm standing in this empty paved lot," he begins. "On my left is a redwood forest with birds chirping and moss growing and stuff. On the right is an abandoned parking garage and I walk toward it…I want to see if there're any junk cars in there. In front of the garage is a cracked sidewalk with a massive, ancient tree growing through it. Nissa's pet Toad from the Seventh Kingdom sits under the tree, only he's grown enormous…like as big as an elephant. He's wearing a wooden sign around his neck that says, 'Stay Away From Toad.'"

The scene comes alive behind my eyelids. I'm there on the pavement observing as Aidan approaches Toad. A pungent smack of decomposing moss and dark secrets drifts to my nostrils. It's so real I swear it's *my* dream, not his.

"That's when I notice the old wooden box on the sidewalk," Aidan continues. "It's the size of a piano bench, but without legs. The lid is about to open. I realize I've been waiting for it to open for a really long time, but I don't know what's inside."

I've chewed the sweet grass stem to a slimy pulp. Cold dread creeps up beside me. I almost tell Aidan to stop because suddenly I don't want to know what's in the bench. But that's silly. I've got to be strong and comfort him. I pluck another long grass stem and twirl it between my fingers. It's just a dream.

"The lid creaks open and someone tall climbs out," Aidan continues. "It's a man, but his face is vague. From inside the bench he pulls out three smaller boxes and sets them on the ground under the tree, then climbs back inside the bench and closes the lid."

I sit up, hugging my knees to my chest. The words coming out of Aidan's mouth aren't threatening in any way, but I am threatened. Aidan sits up, too, staring straight ahead. I hate that I know what he's going to say before he says it.

"You were there, Emily. You came striding out of the forest across the pavement straight toward the three boxes."

I thought I was used to the visions taking over by now, but I wasn't expecting it to happen when it's someone else's dream.

Mottled milky skin forms over the sun as I cross the paved lot, casting a sickly light on the dying cypress. I kneel in front of the tree.

The first box is simple and rustic but when I open the lid I find a gorgeous book bound in leather nestled inside. The weight and texture of the pages makes me sigh with pleasure. I almost forget about the dread that's scuttled up my back, peering over my shoulder at this book of the First Realm, written in curling calligraphy.

The second box is like the first. A heavy scrollwork lock and key wait inside for me when I open the lid. They're obviously a set, but to what? I slip them both in my pocket and turn my attention to the third box.

This one is different than the other two. Thick bubbly glass distorts my view of what's inside. Whatever it is, it's dazzling. But the intricate clasp is locked and the key from the second box is way too big to fit.

Aidan's words come from far away. "You stand up and walk over to Toad, knocking on the 'Stay Away From Toad' sign. He opens one filmy old eye and looks right at you, yawning wide. Inside is a beautiful woman. She looks so familiar...I think it must be Princess Nissa; only she's older than thirteen. She's frail and weak. She hands you the shield, the dagger, and the gauntlet from the story. As soon as you touch the gauntlet it wraps around your wrist like it's part of your body."

The woman inside Toad speaks directly to my mind without moving her lips. "These weapons will give you Purpose, but they are not your Defense. Your strength can only come from within you, Emily. No one else can provide it. Each box holds a portion of Hell, some less painful than others. But remember: pain is not Eternal. Sometimes regret cuts deeper. You must choose."

With that, Toad shuts his mouth, closing his black lily-pad eye.

"You kneel in front of the boxes again," Aidan's voice travels back to me. "You can't make up your mind which to choose. As you look at each of them, your clothes start changing. When you touch the first box, you're wearing a long sparkly dress. When you touch the box with the lock and key you have a plain skirt and sweater on, like something a Sunday School teacher would wear. When you touch the locked crystal box, you're in your regular clothes again: shorts and a tank top. It keeps changing like that, back and forth as you study each box. After a while you sit back against the tree, staring up at the three big rotting branches. I call to you, but you can't hear me."

A huge weight sits on my chest. Dread rests on my shoulders. The Toad-woman's words spin in circles around my heart while the worry in Aidan's voice squeezes at my middle.

"That's the dream. I've had it every night since the night you went to the hospital. Sometimes more than once." He's looking at me but now I can't meet his eyes. "Are you okay, Emily?"

I rouse myself. "Of course I am, dork." I ruffle his hair just like I'm not suffocating. "You have the best imagination, you know that?" He smiles. "I'm sorry you're having a hard time sleeping. Does Jacob snore?"

"Yeah, he does. Why can't we sleep at the main house with you instead of at the bunkhouse? I'd even sleep on the couch."

"I know. It sucks, but I don't think Aunt Meg likes couch-sleepers. It won't be for much longer, though. I can give you something that will help. You probably won't dream at all."

"Like what?"

"I found a few sleeping pills behind some stuff in the guest bathroom medicine cabinet. Mom used to give them to me when I had bad dreams. They made it so I didn't remember my dreams at all."

"Are you sure it's safe?"

"It must be if she gave it to me, right? I was a lot younger than you are. You can just take a tiny bit, like maybe even a quarter. You'll sleep so good, I promise. You're probably having a hard time being in a different time zone and sleeping in a strange bed and everything. Once we get home you'll be fine."

His face and body relax. "Thanks, Emily."

"Aidan. You know it's just a dream, right? You don't need to worry about me. Got it?"

He nods.

"Good. Now go do something fun. I want to explore by myself for a bit, find the places I used to go when I was little. I'll take you guys with me next time, okay?"

Aidan smiles. "Okay, Dork Princess. Don't get lost in the woods!"

He bolts out of reach as I smack at him. Once he's gone I lie back in the grass. Failure clogs my brain. I've got to do better at keeping my stress locked away where Aidan can't see.

TWENTY

I'm in paradise.

Holding back damp ferns, I peek around a birch tree. I'm in a small glade, hidden from view on three sides by rock walls that climb at least fifteen feet. On the far side a waterfall tumbles over a sheer cliff, landing in a pond surrounded by broad-leafed flowering plants.

I walk to the edge of the pool.

This is my secret place, exactly as I remember it from so long ago. I would sneak here, making sure no one followed. This is where I drank mist that collected in folded ribbon leaves, explored the recess behind the fall, washed my gossamer in the narrow tumbled river that rushes away from the glade.

My ankles ache at the water's first touch. Every instinct shouts: it's too cold! Jump out.

Wait, a quiet voice sparkles. **This isn't pain. It doesn't hurt. It's just unknown so it's scary.** I hesitate only a second more, then strip out of my dirt and bean leaf covered clothes and step into the pond. Chill invigorates me.

I wade in deeper, take a breath, and sink beneath the surface, my head heavy with thoughts.

Nancy said to listen to the voices, to experience my emotions without judging or reacting to them. Did she know what she was asking?

I climb from the pool. Naked and dripping wet, I sit on a lip of rock jutting out over the water. Large flat leaves of a vine cover the stony ground.

I don't think I can do it. I don't want my roller-coaster emotions. I don't want the voices. I don't want to meet Dad.

What if I refuse to meet him?

What if I stay here in the glade with my fantasies and never go back?

I lay down, adjusting my wings so they're open beneath me. Pulling my wet hair out from under my neck I drape it over one shoulder. Tiny droplets of spray shower like a blessing around me.

I'm connected to the earth here. A thousand hues and shades of green hold me captive. The scent of gardenia, jasmine, and something citrus intoxicates me.

The water gushes a hypnotic symphony. I focus on the distinct voices of the fall, distinguishing myriad tones and dynamics. The river hurtles deep and wide over mossy rocks above, echoing off the three wet stone walls encircling me, roaring a continuous splash into the pool, plunging low, gurgling to the surface, fanning out to the reed-lined edges.

And the spray. Spray is everywhere. Frenzied, it shoots skyward, ripped from the current as gravity pulls the river down, flinging twirling mist into the air. More spray clings to the clear water, desperate as it falls, twisting, arching, and finally escaping with a breathy sigh, clouding the air in a constant hush.

If I hold my breath I can even hear the bubbling movement of water beneath the surface of the pool swirling in every direction, absorbing and being absorbed by the calm depth of the blue-green pond.

Turning on my side I re-position my wings so they rest against each other, drooping drowsily ground-ward. Individual droplets of water caress my skin: heavily on my back and legs, lightly across my shoulders, whisper soft on my face.

One tiny drop lands at my hairline. It joins with dozens of still smaller drops, sliding down the contour of my cheekbone to the corner of my mouth. I lick my lips, savoring wet green life on my tongue.

Pulling my awareness back I experience the shower as a whole. It enfolds me in its constantly changing embrace.

Softly, slowly, I let go and drift off to sleep.

Something soft nudges my hand.

Hmmm. I've never been so relaxed. I don't want to move a muscle. Opening my eyes to see what nudged me is out of the question.

As I drift back to a place just below consciousness there's another nudge, this time more insistent. A bright trill of birdsong invades my ear.

I open one eye. A sparrow and a pink-nosed rabbit sit by my outstretched hand, both damp with mist. The bright-eyed bird hops up and down; the rabbit's nose twitches frantically.

"Mhuhmmm." I arch my back, swatting at the animals before curling up into a ball. "Go away."

The sparrow hops closer, touching my hand with its sharp beak.

"Owww!" I open both eyes. "What could possibly be important enough for you two to wake me?" I stroke the soft fur under the bunny's chin.

A purple dragonfly zigzags into view. Xander.

She sends a dizzying kaleidoscope of impossible images tumbling through my head. Several seconds pass before I understand what Xander is showing me: an elf is crouching behind a stand of redwoods. Watching me.

The bird trills again, hopping from one foot to another.

"Shhhhh," I whisper. "Haven't you seen an elf before? The forest is full of them. This is their home in the Second Realm."

Wait, an elf? Watching… me.

A shock in my middle yanks me fully awake. The voices go nuts.

Emma! This is so silly!

You're NAKED. What were you thinking? Skinny-dipping like a tramp!

Shame and guilt mingle in the droplets splashing over me, burning my skin.

Just listen, don't react, whispers the White Faerie.

I hold very, very still and reach out to Xander. She darts closer with a flick of her wings, feeding me more images from Twist. I see a pair of soft woven boots. If only Twist would fly a little higher… yes, just like that. The elf has thick black hair, brown skin and broad powerful shoulders.

Oh. My. God. Kaillen.

Kaillen is watching me.

Did someone send him to keep an eye on me? No. That's ridiculous. I know I wasn't followed. And no one knows this place except me.

He must have stumbled upon me by accident.

And then what? Stayed to watch me nap? Why?

Because you're NAKED.

Keep still and pretend you're asleep, Emma. He'll get bored and go away.

He doesn't budge.

What exactly can he see from his hiding place? My back, probably, and my wings. My bum, too?

Oh. NO.

How long has he been here? How could he?

My chest tingles with an unexpected surge of power.

Where did that come from? I'm more than just a modest person...I've perfected the art of privacy and keeping secrets. But I'm tackled by an intense thrill knowing he's watching me.

An image of his strong hands turning me onto my back springs unbidden to my mind.

Xander didn't send that.

This is all me.

His long fingers slowly trace the bare skin of my neck and shoulders, down my arm. His face hovers inches above mine, his deep brown eyes wanting.

I close my eyes. His breath grazes my lips. The weight of his body against my hips presses me into the rock beneath us. A barely audible moan escapes my throat. A powerful desire to pull him closer, to taste his mouth, grips me.

Stop this instant! This is completely inappropriate young lady!

But there are all kinds of new thoughts, new emotions, new sensations flooding me.

He's an arrogant young man with bad manners! You pity him because he was an orphan. The End.

That's true! I don't want him to outline my lips with his tongue... Do I?

I feel funny, Emma.

I steady my breathing. The rabbit hops closer, nudging me with his nose. The sparrow cocks her head to one side. They're waiting for me to do something.

What should I do?

What do you want to do? the White Faerie asks. Suddenly I know her name: Ava, the same as my middle name.

"The voices are supposed to tell me what to do." I whisper back. They'd never let me decide something like this on my own.

They already told you what to do: run away or pretend to be asleep. But you're still here, which means YOU want to do something different. Think, Emily Ava Alvey. What do YOU want?

I want it back... the image of Kaillen's golden-dark fingers on my pale skin. He's so... HOT.

STOP! You can't trust yourself, Emily. This is WRONG.

But I can't stop. No. That's not true. I don't want to stop.

There is truth in imagination. Trust yourself. If you could do anything, what would you do?

If I could do anything?

If I could do anything I would need butterflies. A *lot* of butterflies.

Xander zips in closer. "Okay," I think to her, "this is what we're going to do..."

From the input Twist sends Xander, Kaillen appears to be struggling—he's wearing a scowl like he's upset with himself for staying, like he wants to get up and sneak off—but the way his hand grips the bark of the tree next to him says he's not going anywhere. He settles into a crouch down on one knee, waiting. He doesn't know I'm awake.

Time to change that.

I stretch with both arms above my head. If his hearing's as sharp as Twist's, his ears would pick up my sensuous sigh. I turn over on my back, wings beneath me, and stare up into the overhanging vines confident in my modesty... Xander assures me the ferns and broad-leafed plants conceal most of my body.

Ablaze with a wild thrill I've never felt before, I prop myself up on my elbows.

With Xander zipping around my head, I turn and look directly into Kaillen's eyes.

"Dammit to hell," Twist relays. His voice is deep, breathy.

My heart pounds an intense rhythm as a fuchsia cloud of miniature butterflies descends from nowhere, encircling me as I rise to my feet in one fluid arc. They veil me in color and motion, swirling for a soft second before coalescing on my skin. Vivid pink wings open and close continuously, barely but chastely concealing my body, creating ripples of color and movement across my chest, hips, and the tops of my thighs.

My arms and legs are uncovered, as are my shoulders and back to the bottom of my spine.

He's holding his breath.

The butterflies move with me as I stretch on my tiptoes, wrists coiling high above my head. Pushing the girl and woman firmly from my mind I let this unexplored part of me take charge. Only one tiny question slips through: is this the real me?

I rock back onto my heels. My hands twist my wet hair up behind my neck. Both dragonflies appear, pinning my hair with their bodies, back and away from my face and shoulders.

Anchored in the moment I glance back playfully. Kaillen's deep eyes are fixed on me with an intensity that steals my breath. Turning, I step into the pool. It laps my calves, enclosing my knees.

As the water reaches the tops of my thighs the butterflies clinging there peel off in perfect synchronicity, skimming away across the surface of the pool, taking flight the second before my skin submerges.

I glide in further, the water rising to my navel, then my ribs. I spin so, so slowly, tipping my neck. Eyelashes heavy with mist, my wingtips part the pond behind me. I stop spinning with the water just above my breasts, several inches under the dip of my collarbone.

The butterflies have disappeared. Xander and Twist take flight. My hair tumbles down around my shoulders. Eyes closed, I bend back again, immersing my entire body.

Water rushes off me as I surface, my hair slick against my head. My wings drape down my back. I open my eyes and look right at Kaillen, unblinking with a boldness I didn't know I possessed.

He stares back.

Suddenly I realize: he must have voices in his head, too.

What if there are parts of him he has hidden away? What if there are places and desires in his body—right now—he didn't even know existed before this very moment? I want to discover those secret places. I want him to walk into the pond fully clothed and pull me against him.

The scowl is gone from his face. His body tenses. His primal covert heartbeat exposes him. He wants me like I want him.

He fascinates me.

He bewilders me.

I bewilder myself.

We look at each other. The falls, the glade, the hushed world, waiting. He takes a step toward me, eyes wide with naked hunger. Then he hesitates. Looking down he shakes his head and mutters something I can't make out.

When he looks up again he's pulled a mask over his face. He turns and walks back down the path that isn't nearly as secret as I imagined.

I squeeze my eyes shut. The daring façade I'd dressed myself in shreds like a tissue-paper moth's wing.

What were you thinking? What have you done?

I don't have an answer. I don't recognize myself.

You little slut. You should be ashamed of yourself!

Emma, you don't even like Kaillen! And you're NAKED. What about Gabe?

I hang my head. Slinking from the pond I pull on my crumpled clothes. I can't stop shivering.

Hush now, you two. Ava's voice is gentle. **I want to hear what Emily thinks. Close your eyes Sister, and experience your emotions. What if you didn't know the girl in the glade, the girl who dances with butterflies? The girl who bathes in Magic? Tell me, Emily, what do you feel when you think of that girl?**

I picture the girl as if she were someone else, as if she weren't me but the fairytale me Lady Quince and General Raidho saw in the vision pulling the night sky down her shoulders. Goosebumps raise on my arms...the good kind. An appreciative smile spreads across my lips. That girl is brave and smart. She's sexy, but innocent, too.

"I admire her." I whisper. "I want to BE her."

The woman and little girl gape.

Really? What if Kaillen tells someone? Would you want to be her then? What must he think of you, Emily? You hate him one minute and want to make-out with him the next? You need HELP. You can't be trusted.

What I need is an off switch. I know Nancy said it would be hard to find my True Voice, but this can't be what she meant. All I've accomplished is awakening insane hormones and sparking more confusion. Maybe I'm broken. Maybe there's no hope.

Whatever. Kaillen wouldn't dare tell anyone. HE was the one spying on ME from the bushes. And he'd definitely been staring.

I shake my head. How did I ever get the courage to do something like that? The woman is right: I do need help. But I'm way too embarrassed to tell Nancy about this. She likes Gabe. She'd think I was a two-timing skank.

I shove my feet in my flip-flops, desperate to be away from this place.

The roar of the falls is deafening now, the floral perfume coats my nose with cloying powdered-sugar sweetness. I'm wet, uncomfortable, and fed up with myself. I'm going to sneak into bed, pull the sheets over my head, and not come out. Ever.

TWENTY ONE

I'm one giant nerve ending. The half an Ambien I took from the medicine cabinet isn't helping at all. I'm trying to hold still so I don't wake Claire but what I really want to do is shed my skin and disappear. It's 12:38 a.m. About an hour ago I managed to convince myself that the episode in the glade this afternoon with Kaillen was a dream, that I'd dozed off and invented it all. After all, I saw him as an elf, and I had wings. No matter what the little girl says, Magic isn't real.

But I keep hearing what Nancy said about finding the truth in dreams. First Aidan's vision/dream about Toad and the boxes. Toad was Nissa's Secret Keeper. Nancy said the voices are protecting me from something in the past I haven't processed yet, from secrets I'm keeping from myself. And now I dream about making-out with someone I thought I hated. What the hell is happening to me? How many horrible things have I buried inside myself? Why are they all trying to surface at once?

There's enough nervous energy in my right calf and thigh alone to run three marathons. I'll never sleep again. The seconds until dawn stretch before me—evil plot-points on a line graph to infinity.

A host of wood-gray Daddy long-legs creep from the clustered ceiling-shadows in the corner of the room, inching closer with their tiny mouths and elegant all-seeing eyes. They know I'm going crazy. They're coming to feast on the decomposing remains of my sanity.

I can't stay in this bed another second.

I need carbs.

Normally I wouldn't scrounge around Aunt Meg's kitchen in the middle of the night. What would she say if she caught me? Probably nothing. But I hate the way she's been watching me…like she's waiting for my head to start spinning on my neck.

I've been avoiding all human contact other than Jacob, Aidan, and Claire since returning from the glade. There's no reason left in my head, only sensations of shame mixed with lust mixed with confusion mixed with dread, and I can't figure which emotion is attached to which situation in my life. How do I feel about Gabe? How do I feel about Kaillen? How do I feel about Mom? How do I feel about seeing Dad for the first time in seven years in less than twelve hours?

I pace back and forth in front of the refrigerator hugging my arms around my middle. Through the dining room a thin bar of light shines under the door of the den.

A cough. Uncle Ian.

My body pulls me in two different directions. Half of me scrambles off to hide in bed; the other half glides toward the light on silent feet.

I follow my feet when I hear Nancy's voice, too.

"She's still struggling, General. I think we should give her a few more days. Would you be willing to postpone this meeting?"

What's going on? Why did Nancy call Uncle Ian 'General'?

The door is open enough for me to easily hear Uncle Ian's reply: "We're running out of time, Lady Quince."

That's weird. Yeah, her name is Nancy Quince, but since when does Ian call her 'Lady'?

"We've waited this long, what harm to wait a few more days? Don't you care about her well being at all?"

"It troubles me you think so little of my humanity, Lady Quince. Like you, I've become rather fond of the girl. My concern for her wellbeing is not an act."

"I believe you. I've seen a change in all of you this trip. Then why push, General? The ordeal of absorbing her mother's Blaze, combined with her own Changing was nearly fatal. Why not let her recover a little longer? She'll need her full strength to break the Seal on the Doorway."

Am I being punked?

I peak around the edge of the door. Ian and Nancy sit opposite each other in matching wingback chairs. They look completely normal. Only their voices sound a little different… more formal.

"Which is exactly why we need to meet with Drake as soon as possible," Ian says. "He'll be able to assess her abilities, ascertain how much training she needs, and determine how long it will take. We're working blind here, Quince. Meanwhile, it grows more difficult to keep her hidden. Now that her wings have emerged, any predatory creature with the barest trace of Magic can see her power radiating from miles away. It won't be long before the crimbal or their Master discovers the Vineyard. The longer we wait, the greater the danger grows for Emily and her siblings."

Nancy leans forward in her chair. "I can't explain how, General, but I've come to love that girl. We can't just use and abandon her. She's had enough pain in her life."

They're talking about me. I back away from the door.

"She'll be welcome to accompany us to the First Realm if she chooses," Ian says. "Otherwise, Drake can scorch out her wings and she'll remain here. She would continue much as she has until now. She's always been looked after, Lady,"

"I'm aware of how she has been looked after better than anyone, General," Nancy replies. Her chair scrapes across the floor as she stands. "I'll agree to the meeting tomorrow, but we must tell her what we're planning..."

Her footsteps move toward the door. I trip over my own feet backing up through the kitchen and down the hallway to the small guest room I share with Claire at the back of the house. Once inside I pull the door shut, gripping the knob tight until my heartbeat slows. The clock on the bedside table reads 12:56 a.m. I've been gone fifteen minutes.

I lie down next to Claire's warm body, resisting the urge to wrap my arms around her and bury my head in her shoulder. I'm desperate to hold onto something real, but I don't want to wake her up.

My mind refuses to consider or even review what I just saw and heard.

Can I take more Ambien? No. I have to be careful since I'm giving them to Aidan too. I don't want anyone to notice they're missing.

I push images of Nancy/Lady Quince and Uncle Ian/General Raidho away and pick up the clock, placing it on my stomach so I can watch it's light-blue glow. I'll play a game. It's 12:58 now. As soon as it turns to 12:59 I'll close my eyes and start counting seconds. When I get to sixty I'll open my eyes and see how close I am to the actual time.

Start. One, two, three... At sixty I open and it's still 12:59. Too fast.

Again.

1:00 a.m., start. One, two, three... sixty. I've over compensated. Switching over to the second counter I find I'm only a little too slow: 1:01:07.

Again.

1:02, start. One, two, three...

I jerk awake, disoriented. The clock is back on the nightstand. It reads 12:35 a.m.

Claire stirs next to me as I bolt upright. What? 12:35? That means...

I dreamt the whole thing...

Relief pours over me. Nancy is Nancy Quince, not Lady Quince. Ian is my uncle, not General Ian Raidho. We are going to meet Dad tomorrow, not Drake

I am Emily Ava Alvey, a human girl—not an Ovate with special powers— just an over-active imagination and a bit of a prescription pill abuse problem.

I lie back down. I can't keep my eyes open. As I drift off to sleep I think I hear the bedroom door open. Bedsprings creak as someone sits on the mattress next to me. I smile at the calloused warmth of rough-tender fingers smoothing my hair off my forehead. I welcome this dream.

"Sleep well, Lady Emily Ava Alvey." Ian's gruff voice is low. "You are stronger than you know. I believe in you."

Peace settles into my chest as his lips press a feather soft kiss onto my brow.

TWENTY TWO

I want to bang my head against the van window.

On the one hand, I'm glad Ian didn't just give me the keys and punch the address of the diner into the GPS. I'm glad Meg is staying home with the kids, too. I'm happy Ian is driving and Nancy is in the front passenger seat...

But why oh why are Kaillen and Gabe coming with us?

Kaillen hates Dad, and Gabe has never even met him. It's like a sinister plot to make this meeting as awkward as possible.

Maybe this is another Ambien dream and my subconscious is punishing me for being an adulterer.

Gabe kissed me. Nothing really mushy or anything, more like a peck between friends. Oh, who am I kidding? I don't kiss my friends.

Just remembering the slight pressure of his lips on mine sends lightning straight through my core. And judging by the looks he's been giving me, and the way his knee rests against mine, he's feeling a lot more than friendly.

The warmth of his body next to me is…nice.

Meanwhile, Kaillen sits in the row in front of us. He's barely said two words to me today, but I know I didn't imagine the electricity between us as he helped me into the van this morning, or the way his glance lingered on my mouth. Even if I dreamt that whole thing and he didn't really see me naked, I can't deny the fact that I'm crazy attracted to him.

Does it mean I'm a bad person if I crush on two guys at the same time?

Yes.

YES.

I've got to stop taking the sleeping pills. Again. Right now it's a toss up between which is worse: not sleeping or the bizarre dreams I have when I do sleep.

Maybe it's a blessing in disguise both Kaillen and Gabe are here. It's so embarrassing, but at least it's distracting me from obsessing over lunch. With Dad.

I only remember driving to the Point of the Mountain three times to visit Dad at the Utah State Penitentiary since he was convicted, and that was years ago, before we moved to Dallas. The memories don't amount to much: my rubber-soled sketchers echoing down fluorescent-lit concrete hallways, muted conversations of inmates in the cafeteria where I sat by Jacob nodding politely to Dad's questions: was I practicing the piano? How were my grades in math? Was I helping around the house?

Ian parks the van and Gabe opens the side door, hopping out. I climb out to stand with my arms folded nervous and waiting next to him. No one else budges.

Why isn't anyone else budging?

"This must be really weird for you, Emily," Gabe says. "I wish I were going in with you."

I look at the van. Nancy and Ian sit face-forward. Only Kaillen returns my bewildered gaze with his serious black glance.

No no no no no.

I grab Gabe's arm. "Please don't leave me, Gabe. I can't go in by myself!"

"Don't worry. We'll be back in half an hour. You haven't seen your dad in a long time, Emily. He asked if he could meet you privately first and your great aunt and uncle agreed. I know things are kind of tense between your mom's family and your dad. It's best this way. Once you guys have a chance to catch up we'll all come back and have lunch together."

They're leaving me alone with him.

How is it okay that Gabe knew about this plan and I didn't? Did they think I wouldn't come if I knew?

They're right, I wouldn't have.

But how is that their decision?

They can decide they don't want him in their house, they can decide to keep the younger kids home, but why would they think they could make this decision for ME?

And why why why do they want me to meet with him alone?

Gabe kisses me quick on the top of my head. "It's going to be fine." He squeezes my arm and climbs back in the van, pulling the door shut behind him.

Ian switches on the left turn signal. They drive out of the parking lot without even waiting to watch me walk inside.

I'm completely alone.

Everyone's abandoned me, including the voices in my head: the woman, Ava…

No. The little girl stands beside me, hair in braids, pinafore dress faded but neatly pressed. She looks up at me. I take her hand.

I'm nervous, Emma.

"I'm nervous, too," I whisper. "But at least we're together."

We walk inside.

He's sitting beneath the window at the back of the restaurant staring straight at me. The fine hairs on the nape of my neck bristle.

His power vibrates around him, extending in every direction. How is it that the handful of people lingering over their lunches isn't disturbed?

He stands. I will my clumsy-stiff legs to cross the space between us, praying I navigate the waist-high tables without knocking anything over.

He takes my hand and everything is suddenly right. Real.

Exactly as it should be.

He cherishes me. He would never hurt or judge or blame me.

I hold Dad's outstretched hand in both of mine. I don't ever want to leave his side. I'm so eager to talk to him! I have to call Ian and tell him we need more time before they come back. I can't wait for Dad to see Jacob and Aidan and Claire. There's so much to tell him… where to begin?

"Emily. I'm so glad you're here." He hugs me and I don't want to let go. Finally I sit down, but reach across the table for his hand again.

His hand is just as I remember it: big and strong, with long tapered fingers, flat nails, and perfectly trimmed cuticles. He even smells the same: like warm leather and cedar.

I didn't know I remembered his hand or the way he smelled.

"Dad." I try it out on my tongue. "Dad." The stress and fear that have been building for the past several weeks seem silly now. Whatever he tells me to do will solve all of our family's problems. I don't care how long it's been or what happened in the past. I'm just glad I'm with him now.

It's like coming home.

No! I don't like it here!

Somewhere separate from the me sitting with Dad in the diner, the little girl and I stand together in the middle of a hedgerow maze. She stamps her feet and kicks at the bushes.

"HUSH," I tell her. *"You're FINE. I need you to be quiet, I'm BUSY."*

Across the table in the diner Dad is saying I'm beautiful, that seeing me is like the sun coming out from behind the clouds. His touch comforts me.

DON'T TOUCH US! The little girl screams. She's yelling at him so loud, how can he not hear her?

"You stop yelling and be quiet or you'll pay you spoiled little brat!" I push away from her, leaving the maze. I don't have the time or energy for her tantrums.

Dad is tracing the outline of the runes on my arm with his index fingers. "This is our last name, Emily!" His eyes gleam. "My dad would have loved this. Wow. Do you know what our surname means?"

"Elf Warrior."

"Exactly! Do you know anyone else who can beat that? Even though girls aren't actually warriors," he chuckles. "My family's name is old, Emily… ancient, like the blood in my veins… in your veins. Do you remember this?" He pulls the chain of a necklace out from under his shirt and over his head. A heavy gold ring hangs from the middle. "It's our family crest—the Golden

Boar Passant." He hands it to me.

A stylized boar stretches along the golden band; its front and hind legs rest on either side of an amber-colored crystal stone set in the center. Engraved on the inside are the same runes on my arm:

ᚠᛚᚢᛋ

"The boar is a symbol of bravery and tenacity," he says. "You used to wear this ring with a beaded cuff when you played elves and faeries as a little girl. Do you remember?"

A strange energy buzzes around the brand on my bicep. My scars begin to glow, white flames growing brighter, edges merging. The shrill metallic tone of a thousand cicadas reverberates in my ears as my arm goes super-nova.

I'm blinded. My skin is on fire. The pressure of Dad's fingertips at my wrist grounds me. A storm concusses in my skull but my body barely shakes.

The brands disappear as Nissa's gem-studded leather gauntlet encircles my forearm, extending over the back of my hand and through my fingers.

Approval emanates from Dad's eyes. "There's power in our name, Emily. You're an Alvey. Where are the other weapons?"

And for some reason, I'm not the least bit worried that I don't know where the dagger and shield are, or how to summon them. I simply reach out with my mind and they appear. The shield leans against my thigh on the floor, the dagger is belted around my waist.

"If you submit to me, I'll teach you how to use them."

I interlock my shorter fingers through Dad's long ones. Elemental energy pours in from all the weapons, super-heating my blood, liquefying cartilage into molten gold. His hand steadies me, guides me. Exultant power sears the marrow in my bones.

The little girl screams in the maze. But she's too far away. The howling energy pulsing in my body eclipses her voice. She bends down, scrawling something with a stick in the dirt. Stepping back, she points at the crude letters she's scratched:

T R A P.

"QUIET!" I command.

A piercing rush of wind swirls through the hedgerow, surrounding the little girl. Suddenly the Gray Man towers over her, his barrel stock raised above her head.

Everything becomes radiant and still.

The Gray man speaks.

ENOUGH. THIS ENDS NOW. YOU STAY IN YOUR WORLD AND SHE STAYS IN HERS.

Please Emma, comes the faintest whisper, soft like the fading echo of a child's voice. *Look.*

In the diner I raise my eyes and freeze. Dad's eyes are fixed on me, his tongue wet between his moist red lips. I can hear his charged breath.

I balk, losing control of the energy flowing through me. It waivers clumsily, dissolving altogether. The gauntlet on my arm goes dark, transforming back into pale pink scars on my upper arm. The shield and dagger vanish. I fight the compulsion to snatch my hand away from Dad's.

"Emily? What happened? Are you alright?"

Did I imagine hunger on his face?

I search his eyes and see nothing but compassion and concern.

Raw fatigue grips me. I want to sob but I can't. Not here, not now. Fear rises steady in my chest, becoming certainty: I am not okay.

I don't know what's true anymore. I don't trust myself. I can't distinguish between awake and asleep. I can't decipher between what is fantasy and what is real.

What just happened?

"Sorry…it …I don't know…I guess I'm a little nervous." I can't meet his eyes.

"I understand. I've been nervous too. But now that I'm here it's almost like I never left. You're amazing, Emily, to say the least. You've always been special, even when you were very young. You were more mature than any little girl I ever met. We were different together, weren't we? You were my little girlfriend. I could tell you anything and you always made me feel better."

He's right. He did make me feel special. I haven't felt special since he went away.

In the booth behind Dad a young girl knocks her cup to the floor. Her father grabs for napkins, her mother scolds. The girl shrinks into the corner of their booth…

Oh no. I left the little girl alone. With the Gray Man.

Panicked, I fly to the hedgerow.

She's gone.

Two shallow furrows gouge the ground in parallel lines leading away to the right. I sprint in that direction, following the tracks around twists and turns. Sounds of muffled struggle fuel my speed.

"*STOP!*" I yell. The struggle grows louder. Around the next bend I overtake them.

Hannah.

All at once I know the little girl has a name and it's Hannah.

The Gray Man's arm is around Hannah's slender neck in a chokehold. Her eyes bulge. A filthy piece of ripped linen binds her mouth. Tears streak the dust on her face as her heels pummel the ground. She claws at the arm choking off her breath.

A snarl rips from my throat. Lowering my head I charge at the Gray Man, my shoulder slamming into his ribs.

All three of us hit the ground, but his arm still chokes her neck. I roll over on top of him, grinding my knee into his groin, punching at his face until he lets go.

His backhand catches me in the throat, crushing my windpipe and knocking me flat.

I can't stay down. I'm back up on all fours, rushing him, ramming into his gut. My teeth clamp down on the skin just above his hip, tearing into his flesh. With every move he makes my teeth shred deeper, filling my mouth with rancid meat. He grunts, striking the crown of my head with his elbow.

My vision narrows. My jaws release. I grapple to bring myself closer, to cling to his body so at least she'll have time to get away but my muscles won't obey.

I'm on my back. His shadowy face hovers over me, his hands press down around my bruised larynx, squeezing... His face goes slack.

He topples over on my chest. Through dimming eyesight I see the woman —her name is Margaret—and Hannah peering down at me. Blood smears the butt of the rifle in Margaret's grip. She drops it to the ground, cleaning her palms on her crisply pressed pencil skirt as she walks away in her patent leather pumps. Seconds later she's back with a rope.

"Emily? Are you feeling all right?" In the diner Dad's voice is concerned.

"I'm... I'm okay..." I mumble. But I'm not. I'm in two different realities at once.

I scrabble out from under the Gray Man and pull Hannah onto my lap, holding her tight. *"I'm sorry,"* I whisper, rocking her back and forth. *"I'm so sorry."*

"I'm just tired," I make myself focus, and talk to Dad. "I didn't sleep much last night."

"I bet. You've had a lot on your plate, haven't you? Looking after everyone. I know your great aunt and uncle can be hard to deal with, but that will be over soon, Emily. When we get home, we'll hire someone to come in and take care of Mom. And you can teach me all about running a household. You're probably better at it than most actual mothers."

"Mom won't need help. She's going through detox and rehab. She'll be better when she gets home."

"I know all about what Ian and Meg have done, but Sandra's *my* wife, Emily. I'll make the decisions for my family. They took a lot of liberties, running off with you all in the night right before my release. And they'll be sure to remind me how much they shelled out to pay for this 'state of the art facility' they've sent her to, even though that money should rightfully be mine. I can't wait for them to hold that over my head for the rest of my life."

I shift in my chair. Am I supposed to agree with him? They aren't my favorite bunch of people either, but they've supported us for ten years.

"We shouldn't put too much pressure on Mom, Emily. Chronic pain is nothing to joke about. She needs her medications. You and I can handle things at home though, right? And of course Claire's is getting older. I bet she's gorgeous, like you. She'll be a huge help. My two girls will manage the house and I'll bring home the bacon. How does that sound?"

Hannah's lips tremble as she looks up at me. *I don't like the things he's saying, Emma.*

"*I know,*" I soothe. "*I don't either.*"

But it's my fault Emma. I'm wicked. I did bad things. The Gray Man didn't want me to tell you. I wasn't supposed to say anything, ever. I wasn't supposed to let you see me. But I'm scared. I'm scared of Dad. I don't want to be his girlfriend anymore.

"*Oh my sweet little girl,*" I whisper. "*It wasn't your fault. You aren't wicked. I will always love you, no matter what. You've been trying to protect me, haven't you? Now it's my turn to love you and keep you safe. I'm so sorry I got angry and yelled. I'm sorry I left you.*"

I look up to tell Dad he's wrong, to tell him that it's more than chronic pain, that Mom is sick with depression and tried to kill herself, but that she's getting better.

He's gazing at me.

The words sour on my tongue because suddenly I know: he's stronger than I am. Much MUCH stronger. And he knows everything. He knows that I won't argue, that I won't disobey, that I won't breathe a word about Hannah or the secrets she hides. He knows he's in control. I can't fight him.

"How does that sound, Emily?" He repeats his question with an almost-patient smile.

"It sounds nice," I lie.

"Good. Ah, your great uncle Ian is back. And look, he's brought that little wetback with him. Won't this be fun? Who do they think they are, telling me when I can and can't see my own children? Never mind. I'll play their little game for now. But I won't forget what they've done."

He stands. "Ian," his voice booms through the small restaurant, "thank you so much for taking care of my family while I was away…"

I'm numb. I have no idea what I order. When the food arrives every bite tastes exactly like the last: sand. In my mind I rock Hannah back and forth, humming a tuneless song. My arms fall asleep and my knees cramp but I keep rocking, rocking. Conversation at the table buzzes in my ears. I nod robotically in answer to questions I don't even hear. Every second I'm shrinking, retreating, falling-back deeper inside myself until finally I am all the way inside with Hannah and Margaret, wearing my tattered skin like a patchwork quilt. I'm not afraid anymore of getting lost in my mind. I don't want to go back to reality anymore.

TWENTY THREE

Hannah: I peek out at the world through Emma's eyes like I'm looking through binoculars. I may be too little to stand up to My Dad, but I know how to take care of Emma. Aunt Margaret does too, 'cuz we've been doing it for years and years. I know lots of games and stories to tell her now that she's here in the fairytale we created together. And since Aunt Margaret has tied up the Gray Man, he can't stop me from showing Emma anything I want, like where the Doorway is. The best news is that Emma is Ovate here. That means she's strong enough to use the weapons to break the Seal, and once she does we can go to the First Realm and stay there together forever. I like it here on Emma's lap. She's in our world now—Aunt Margaret's and mine—and she's whispering that she'll never leave me ever again. We don't have to be afraid anymore. I'll sing her a song to help her sleep on the drive home. When she wakes up, her dreams will be real.

TWENTY FOUR

Tires crunching on the gravel driveway bring me awake. Groggy, I raise my head from Kaillen's shoulder. Gabe's hand rests on my knee.

I sigh and close my eyes again so I can continue this bizarre but strangely pleasant dream in which both the hot lifeguard from Dallas and Nissa's equally hot best friend/bodyguard from the First Realm have crushes on me.

The van door squeals open. I wonder what will happen next in this dream. I hope it's something good. I need a distraction from thinking about the uber-weird meeting with the all-powerful Drake.

I sneak one eye open.

Lady Quince stands with her hand on the door looking in at us. A smile twitches her lips. "Are you three going to stay in there all day?"

Oh crap. This isn't a dream.

Kaillen and Gabe remain stubbornly still on either side of me in the back seat.

Without turning my head to look at them I crouch-stand out of the van, tugging my top down over my shorts so they can't see my butt. Crimson heat washes over me.

"You're exhausted, aren't you Dear?" Quince asks, plucking a leaf from one of my wings. "Drake is extremely impressed with your strength, Emily. There's no question that with his guidance and some training you'll be able to break the Seal on the Doorway. What he and General Ian seem to have forgotten is that even a normal Changing can be very taxing, and yours was far from normal. It's scarcely been a week since you took your mother's Blaze and your wings unfurled all at once. You haven't fully recovered. You'll need to rest this afternoon before you begin your training tomorrow…"

At that moment Claire, Jacob, and Aidan come careening out of the house. The screen door slams behind them.

"I can't believe you went to meet the Mediator without us," Aidan shouts.

"Yeah, that hardly seems fair," Jacob seconds. "When will we get to meet Drake? What did he say about your powers? Are you strong enough to break the Seal on the Doorway? How long will it take before you're ready to try?"

"Was he wearing his cape?" Claire interrupts. "The black one with red underneath that flows even when he's not moving?"

I grin. "No, Bug. He was business casual…slacks and a button-up shirt." It's kind of funny now that I think of it. "What did you guys do while I was gone?"

"Target practice," Claire squeals, "and guess what! I shot the target three times! I was the best one! Seriously, I was! Tell her, Aidan, tell her how I was the best!"

"She was the best," Aidan answers in a flat monotone through his barely-opened mouth. It's amazing how far back in his head he can roll his eyes.

"Awesome, Bug," I pull her close for a hug. "I was a pretty good shot with a bb gun when I was your age. We'd set up soda cans on one of the fallen redwoods and…"

"No," Claire squirms away from my hug and bounces up and down. "It wasn't with a bb gun, it was with a…a…what do you call it? A Glock!"

"Funny, Bug. How do you even know what a Glock is?"

"Uh oh," Aidan says. "I tried to tell you the other day, remember?"

I squint my eyes at him. "Why would you joke about Claire using a Glock, Aidan? It isn't funny."

"I believe she used a Glock 26 subcompact pistol, Lady Alvey," General Ian says. "Suitable for her frame and age."

"Did you say 'suitable for her age'?" My voice raises ten octaves.

"Don't freak out," Jacob says. "We need to be safe when we get to the Doorway. In case the crimbal and their Master come back."

I'm trying to steady my breathing. "We obviously have different ideas about what's suitable for a ten year-old girl, General. This isn't HALO, Jacob. It's real life. Using a Glock isn't about shooting inanimate objects for fun. It's about shooting live targets so you can kill them. With real bullets."

"I knew you were going to say something stupid about video games," Jacob mutters. "I'm not an idiot, I know this is real. But these aren't people we'd be shooting at either. They're monsters, remember? The ones who broke into our house and tried to kill us and take Mom's wings for their Master. The

General says they're still hunting us. Do you think we should just walk up to the Doorway unprotected?"

"This isn't our fight, Jacob. You don't need to go to the Doorway at all. You can stay here while I break the stupid Seal."

"You're going to leave us here alone? Nice. What if we're attacked?"

"You won't be alone. Some of the Fae can stay with you and then join the others after the Door is open and we know it's safe."

"I'm afraid that won't be possible, Lady Alvey," the General says. "The Doorway will only remain open as long as you hold it. All the Fae will need to be present. Jacob is right. It would be unwise to leave them here unprotected. The Vineyard offers no safety once we leave it, and I'm afraid the crimbal won't waste an opportunity to seize your siblings and use them against us."

My nails dig into my palms. "Fine. You'll have to come with us. But that doesn't mean I'm going to let you carry guns."

"Lady," the General says. "Your younger siblings handled Princess Nissa's weapons on the night the crimbal attacked. You've done an admirable job watching over them while your mother has been ill, but you can't keep them dependent on you forever. Their education has been neglected. Your brothers, especially, would benefit from the presence and example of strong men in their lives. Marksmanship and weapon safety should be part of every young man's training. I don't condone maidens training for combat, of course, but in this situation I concede it's necessary, and—as I'm reminded almost daily—I have no authority over the maidens in this Realm. Lady Quince insisted that young Claire be allowed to join the practice."

Quince insisted? I'm blown away. Isn't it obvious to everyone that guns are a necessary evil to be used by the military in times of war and by police to keep the peace and by my ten year-old sister never?

"She's not using a gun." I won't get sucked into a debate about the ethics of gun control with the General of the Fae army. I turn to Jacob and Aidan. "I can't believe you guys were okay with this. Listen. You were so brave the night the crimbal broke in, but I don't want any of us to go through anything like that ever again. Jacob, please tell me you understand the difference between an enchanted dagger and a semi-automatic pistol!"

"I do. Using a dagger means hand-to-hand combat, which is a lot more dangerous." The disgust in his voice hits me like an open-handed slap. "You're being stupid," he says.

"Jacob. You're fifteen years old. You can't even drive yet. Claire is ten. It isn't right," I plead. "What would Mom say? She'd ground me for life if she knew I let you carry guns!"

"Does that mean you won't be using one either?" Jacob challenges.

"Emily hardly needs a weapon as primitive as a gun," Kaillen says. "Drake says she IS a weapon."

Everyone stares at me.

"I...that isn't...I don't think...that's ridiculous!"

"We witnessed your immense capacity to wield power in the vision, Lady," the General says. "You are Ovate. It's why we were sent to retrieve you."

"Whatever." Ugh! Why aren't they listening? "That doesn't mean I have to fight. I'm going to break the Seal and when I'm done we're going home."

"So you just expect the Fae to risk their lives to protect us?" Jacob asks.

"No. I'll protect you."

"How?" Jacob asks. "You'll be busy breaking the Seal and not fighting, remember?"

Quince intercedes. "Perhaps instead of training with firearms you children would find it useful to learn about Blaze and Keen in preparation for your own Changings."

Shit.

I know she's trying to diffuse the situation, but Quince's words are like a punch in the gut. Of course I knew my brothers and sister have Magic, too. When I look at all three of them it's like being in a dim dusty room with sun-shafts shining through a window. Tiny specks of potential—millions of them—zip around each of their bodies. Jacob's follow him like a shadow of light.

I was just hoping *they* wouldn't ever have to know.

Jacob and Aidan watch me, expectant. They don't seem surprised.

Claire, on the other hand, looks like she won the lottery. "Oh my GOSH oh my GOSH oh my GOSH!" She jumps up and down flapping her arm. "Did you hear what Lady Quince said, Emma? Am I really going to be a maiden? OH MY GOSH!" her hands fly to cover the round O of her mouth. "What if I'm Ovate like you?" She squeezes her eyes shut, dancing a little jig in a circle.

"Oh good lord," Jacob mutters. "Claire you're embarrassing yourself. For the love of all that is Good and Holy, please calm down."

I kiss Claire's densely freckled forehead then look at Quince. "Thanks, but no. Drake says he can scorch the Blaze out of my wings when I break the Seal. Once you leave for the First Realm we'll take Mom and go back home."

"Great." Jacob's tone implies he thinks it's anything but great. "You've made this decision for me too. Maybe the biggest decisions of my life so far, and you've made it without even consulting me. Tell me why, exactly, you feel that my decision to Change is any of your business? You aren't my mother. I don't belong to you."

"Jacob, please. Let's talk about this later. I don't want to argue with you right now."

"I don't want to talk about it later. This is my life, not yours."

I don't like confrontation ever, but I will go an especially long way to avoid conflict with Jacob. He comes at me from all sides with his giant brain. It's like being flayed. His words and tone incise my flesh from bone with serrated sharpness while I hiss and spit—an animal backed into a corner. It's not something I recover from easily. We both tacitly agreed a long time ago to be on our best behavior when it comes to disagreeing.

Apparently he's changed his mind about that.

"Jacob, you're my brother," I plead. "Of course it's my business. You're only fifteen years-old and I'm in charge."

"Yeah, about that. You're barely two years older than me. And FYI, you're not in charge of this. You can't stop me from going through puberty."

His sarcasm cuts. "Jacob, please. No one wants to stop you from going through puberty."

"Oh really? You just want to control which kind of adult I am, though, right? You think that because you don't want to be Fae I shouldn't want to be either?"

His words make too much sense, like always. I'm frightened. "Jacob, even if I gave you a Flame, none of the elves are strong enough in this Realm to give you a Spark. You can't Change without both."

"Um, Emily?" Aidan says, "I don't think that's actually true."

"What isn't true?"

"Well, you're Ovate. You have male AND female powers. You could give each of us a Spark *and* a Flame. That way Jacob and I could have Keen and Claire could have Blaze."

I'm floundering, and the worst part is I'm not sure why I'm so upset. I only know I have to make Jacob understand how dangerous it would be for him to Change.

"Jacob, you don't even know if your powers would work here. Theirs don't!" I point at Ian and Quince and Kaillen.

"Yours do." His eyes bore holes through my logic.

"It's not like Claire and I can bop around with wings! Drake is going to scorch mine out to break the Seal. What would we do, go to the ER and have Claire's surgically removed when they start to grow? What's the point in Changing? As a mortal you can be anything you want. We'll go back to Texas and live normal lives together!"

"You really don't get it, do you?" Jacob speaks with something between scorn and pity. "I'm not staying here. I'm going with Drake and the Fae to the First Realm.

My knees dip ground-ward for a split-second before I lock them. A faint high-pitched ringing shatters what remains of my calm.

I'm crumbling. I want so badly to be back home in the sweltering heat of Dallas, back to how it was before the runes appeared on my arm and I took Mom's Blaze. Back when everything was predictable. It was hard, yes, doing the laundry and the shopping and the cooking. And sure, I was upset about losing my friends and nervous about repeating junior year and juggling homework with looking after Mom and everyone else, but in a way it was simple. There were no life-threatening decisions to make. There were no goblins or Glocks. No one was leaving.

Jacob is right—I can't control him or stop him from being who he wants to be. He glares at me, his expression stone. He knows he's won. But does he know what he's saying?

I look at my brothers and sister and realize everything has already changed. Moments ago I had a purpose, a plan. Now my family is falling apart. How could I be so naive to think things could stay the same? That just because I ignored it, this day would never come? That if I buried my head in the sand I could play house with Jacob and Aidan and Claire forever?

I've run out of time.

"It's been a long day," Gabe walks up behind me, placing his strong hands on my shoulders. His lips are close to my ear. "You should get some rest."

"Yes," General Ian agrees. "I propose we begin Lady Emily's training tomorrow. Lady Quince, would you be willing to meet with us in the morning at the grove to discuss our strategy?"

"Yes."

"Everything will feel better after a nap." Gabe whispers, moving even closer. His breath tickles the fine hairs on my neck. I shiver, giving just the teensiest nod. If I close my eyes I can almost imagine I'm alone with him. I want to lean back onto his chest and let him encase me in his arms.

But I can't. My wings are in the way.

I open my eyes. Kaillen is watching me. He doesn't look happy.

Shifting my weight, I take the smallest step away from Gabe. What the hell am I doing? Nothing makes sense anymore. Drawing my wings in tight around my shoulders I take Claire's hand. Tears threaten to spill as I turn to Jacob and Aidan. "I love you both. So much."

Aidan hugs me. "I love you, too, dork."

Jacob nods but doesn't say anything.

I clasp Claire's fingers tight. Together we walk into the house. I make sure the screen door doesn't slam behind us.

Ten year-old girls don't like to nap. Especially not when there's a vineyard full of maidens outside and a bunch of elves in a bunkhouse just beyond the stream. Claire runs off, leaving me alone and very lonely.

I'm glad when Hannah pushes open the door and lies down next to me on the bed so we're face to face.

"Hey," I whisper. "Don't you want to go play with Claire?"

"I like being with you."

She's playing with the wingtip peaking over my shoulder. I pick up one of her braids. "You must miss the First Realm."

She nods. "But it won't be long now before we go home. I'm excited, but I'm sad, too."

"Why sad?"

"Aunt Margaret says you're staying here. I don't want to leave you."

I love the way her eyes shift colors as I watch, like they can't decide whether to be green or blue.

I don't want to think about leaving Hannah. But I'm beginning to realize not thinking about things is my M.O. I shove everything unpleasant deep down inside myself so I don't have to deal with it. Only now I'm running out of space in there. Besides, it doesn't make the unpleasant things go away. Eventually they bubble out.

"Please come with us." Hannah says.

I lean closer so our foreheads touch. "Now you have one big eyeball, like a Cyclops!"

She giggles. "Come with us, Emma! The First Realm is amazing. We never grow old and we're Magic. We would never have to say good-bye to each other."

For a moment I allow myself to imagine what it would be like. Mom would come with us. All the people I love would be there...

"But what about Drake, Hannah? I don't know why, but I don't trust him. I don't want him around Jacob and Aidan and Claire. Or Mom."

"I know a secret." Hannah touches my face with rain-soft hands and whispers: "In the First Realm you're stronger than Drake. He can't hurt you there, or anyone you love."

"I need to think about it."

"I know," she says. "I brought you something. I found it in the medicine cabinet. It'll help you sleep." She cups a little white pill in her palm.

I almost moan in relief. "Thank you, Hannah. Thank you so much. This is just what I need. Will you tell the others I'm going to sleep for awhile?"

She nods, slipping off the bed. Tucking the blanket around me, she leans over and kisses my cheek, then draws the curtains closed before tiptoeing to the door. "I love you Emma."

"I love you, too, Hannah."

TWENTY FIVE

I wake to little girl laughter. Claire and Hannah sit at the foot of the bed. A purple dragonfly balances on Claire's knee.

"Good morning," Claire beams. "You slept for a really long time, all through the afternoon AND night! Did you know Xander can do tricks?"

Hannah holds her hands together, thumb and index fingers forming a heart. When Claire says 'now!' Xander darts through Hannah's fingers upside down.

I sit up, stretching. "Wow!" I'm glad Xander isn't sending images of her aerial acrobatics. The idea makes me dizzy. "Morning, you two. Hey, can you both see the things the dragonflies are seeing? Like, pictures and colors and stuff in your head?"

"I can't," Claire says. "But maybe I'll be able to after I go through puberty and my wings start to grow! Can you Hannah?"

Hannah shakes her head. "I've been seven for a really long time. My Blaze won't work until my Changing and I can't have that until we go back to the First Realm. But the grown-up maidens can talk to the dragonflies."

I tug on her braid, wishing I hadn't brought it up.

"Wouldn't it be cool if we had our Changings at the same time?" Claire says to Hannah, her eyes wide with excitement.

Hannah squeals and bounces up on her knees. "We can grow up together and marry elf brothers and have babies at the same time!"

"The grown-up maidens still have wings here, right?" Claire asks. "They're just hidden inside their bodies unless they shrink?"

"Yep."

"Why don't they just stay small then?"

Hannah shrugs. "Who wants to buzz around like an insect all the time?"

"Hannah! Why didn't I think of this before?"

"What is it, Emma?"

"Xander and Twist are maidens! Why are they always in their insect forms?"

"Oh Emma, I thought you knew," Hannah says. "Xander and Twist chose to stay this way when we were banished so they could serve as your guides. Most of the other maidens just use regular dragonflies. Insects have strong Magic."

I contemplate the sacrifice of the twins, and find myself missing Sophie.

Claire and Hannah lay at the foot of the bed chatting, Hannah's blond braided head resting in the crook of Claire's shoulder while Xander zips around them doing lazy somersaults. I think they've forgotten I'm even here.

"Girls!" Comes a call from the kitchen.

"Oh!" Hannah exclaims. "That's Aunt Margaret! I forgot, Emma. Xander came to get you for the meeting, but Aunt Margaret wants to talk to you first."

"Oopsies!" Claire giggles. "You're going to get in trouble, Emma. You'd better hurry." Grabbing Hannah's hand she whispers, "Let's sneak to the river and spy on the elves."

There aren't a lot of clothing options that work with wings. I pull on shorts and the same tank top I wore yesterday, wash my face, brush my teeth, and run a comb through my hair before heading to the kitchen.

Aunt Margaret is dressed the same as always—pencil skirt, simple elegant top, string of pearls around her neck.

In the kitchen she wears a starched apron tied around her waist. She's kicked off her patent leather pumps, going barefoot with her frosted hair pulled back. She's shaping dough with a rolling pin. A perfect smudge of flour decorates her cheek.

"I see those silly girls forgot to tell you to dress in something nice for the strategy council." She eyes my wrinkled clothes with disapproval.

"This is all I have."

"Never mind. I've sent some maidens to the stone cottage. Go there right now and they'll just have time to help you get ready. I need you to take this meeting seriously, Emily. It's extremely important."

"I know."

"I want you to pay close attention to what the General has to say and do what you're told. This isn't a time to be clever or get lost in one of your daydreams. Just listen and obey, do you understand?

"Yes, ma'am." I avoid her critical eyes.

"The General has centuries of experience and wisdom. You're just a girl. You may ask questions pertaining to your training, but that's all. Don't embarrass yourself. You will behave with respect to your elders and speak when spoken to. I don't know how on earth such an immature, fanciful girl could be the maiden from the vision. Frankly, I'm not convinced you have it in you. You may think being Ovate makes you special, but in reality it makes you a bit of a freak. Elves don't like girls who are too big for their britches. Do you think you can manage not to screw this up, or do I need to come with you and hold your hand?"

"I promise to behave, ma'am." I scour any emotion from my words and face.

"Good. You'll be fine as long as you remember your place. Now hurry along. Twist is at the cottage already. Xander will take you there."

"I wish we could talk face to face again," I confide in Xander as we walk to the cottage. "I miss you. And Twist too, even though she's kind of a brat." Xander bobs in the air. I don't know if she understands English, but it's making me feel less lonely all the same. "How old are you now, anyway? You were fourteen when I saw you in human form last...but that was weeks and weeks ago..." I smile. "Did I ever tell you that you remind me of my best friend Sophie? She's small and sparkly, just like you, Xander. I miss her so, so much."

It's true. Even with all these people wanting things from me, I'm more alone than ever. Quince and Ian are preoccupied with returning to the First

Realm. I'm crazy-shy around Gabe and nervous as hell around Kaillen, and I can't confide in the kids. I need to be strong for them.

I follow Xander around a bend in the path and spot the cottage ahead. It's more of a shed, really. Ivy invades its stone walls. Old growth trees tower behind. I imagine it was a shepherd's hut once, before the maidens and elves claimed this basin for themselves.

The wooden door of the cottage swings open as I approach. Two young maidens in airy sundresses skip into the clearing. The flowers in their hair dance as they bob curtsies.

Word must have gotten around that I curtsied like an idiot when I met the General and Kaillen. I'm such a moron.

Laughing, they pull me inside, closing the door behind them.

"Aunt Margaret said you'd help me find something more appropriate to wear."

"You're late," says a voice behind me. I turn to see a tall, slender maiden with long flowing brown hair drop an exaggerated curtsy.

The younger two walk around me, sizing me up. "You'll never attract a proper mate looking like this."

"No, I'm going to a strategy meeting for my training," I stammer. "So I can open the Doorway. Not attract a mate."

"Nonsense," the tall one says. "There will be eligible men there. You're nearly an adult. A maiden is nothing without a man, and this…" she waves her hand in front of my entire body…"is not doing you any favors."

Indignation pumps in my chest. Are they being rude on purpose?

The pretty one with upturned eyes laughs. "You look like a hillbilly."

"Who slept outdoors," the plump one with pin-straight hair chimes in.

I don't know whether to punch them or cry. I've never really had any experience with mean girls. But what if they aren't being mean? Maybe they really are concerned for me. Maybe they're right and I'm gross and pathetic. Look at them. They're flawless and immortal.

"Am I really that bad?"

The tall one surveys me with pity. "It won't be easy, but you do have a certain—natural—appeal. I'm up for the challenge. Are you with me girls?"

The younger ones nod and laugh.

"I'd kill for some mascara and a touch of lip-gloss," I venture, timid. I'm trying really hard not to remember all my previous encounters with Gabe and Kaillen and be retroactively self-conscious about my lack of make-up. It's not like Jacob packed a toiletry bag for me. They just dumped me in the van.

"We'll need a lot more than lip-gloss and mascara," the tall one clucks.

I appraise the room. How and when did they haul all this stuff out here? It's a legitimate set-up. A full-length mirror leans against one wall next to the only window. A dresser with a washbasin and water pitcher stands in the corner next to an open armoire, displaying dozens of stunning dresses in endless colors and fabrics.

They lead me to a swivel chair in front of a small elegant vanity. Bottles of perfume and jars of creams cover the top. An elaborate compact holds more eye shadows than I've ever seen in one place outside of Ulta.

I hold my breath before looking in the mirror. I don't look that bad. Not like the swamp creature I'd been expecting based on their comments. I just look like plain old me. Maybe a little more wild than usual, but the maidens can tame me.

The tall one spins the chair around. "You poor thing, I'm sorry you had to see that. Don't fret. We'll take care of everything. But no peeking. We want it to be a surprise." She begins applying creams and makeup to my face while the other two work on my hair.

I listen quietly while the maidens chat with each other, occasionally remarking on one another's work with an appreciative click of the tongue or admiring "oooh!" It isn't long before they're finished.

"No looking yet," the pretty one says. "We must dress you before you can see the finished product."

I sit with my back to the mirror wishing they'd hurry. I'm behaving like Margaret said to, reminding myself that in the big scheme of things I really have no clue what I'm doing and should always listen to people who do. But I'm fidgety. It's one thing to brush and moisturize. I'm going to a meeting in the woods, not a fashion show. I don't want to offend the maidens, but I don't want to get in trouble for being late, either.

"We'll start with some lingerie, of course," The plump one bosses. "I know how you mortals depend on your Victoria's Secret."

"Oh, she doesn't need lingerie," the pretty one protests. "Look at her! She's perfect au natural. Besides, it would defeat the purpose under this…" She pulls a shimmering silver floor-length gown from the armoire. It's sleeveless and backless and appears to be…sheer. She brings it over for me to admire. All three maidens gather around my chair as if waiting for me to stand up and put it on.

They're joking of course. There's no way in seven hells I'm wearing that.

I look at each of their faces. "You're joking, right? I don't think this is what Margaret had in mind."

"Aunt Meg may have power over you, Lady. She has no power over us," the tall one says.

"Lady Emily, I think it best you hurry," the pretty one admonishes. "I believe I hear some elves coming up the path. They'll be displeased if you keep them waiting."

"Thank you so much for your help," I'm determined not to show my abject fear. "I think I'll just wear what I have on. It's a gorgeous gown, though. Maybe another time?"

"I am afraid we cannot allow that," the tall one says as if she's speaking to a difficult child. "It wouldn't be proper." Her smile is sweet, but danger glints in her eye. "It will be best if you cooperate."

I don't know why, but these maidens want to humiliate me. If they get me in this dress they will succeed. I have to get away.

I drop my head in what I hope looks like sincere apology. As I stand and reach for the gown I hook my foot around the base of the chair, sending it crashing into the vanity.

Chaos ensues.

I bolt for the door.

Before I can reach it all three maidens shrink to insect size and dart around me. Their wings blaze bright with impudent power.

"I told you she would be difficult," one growls.

"Let's help her get dressed Sisters," laughs another. "We want her to look exquisite for her training."

Streaming sparks of power zip around me. I'm trapped, helpless against their attack.

TWENTY SIX

Xander dive-bombs the tiny maidens. They veer away from her, but aren't deterred for long. She's also feeding me images from Twist who is outside the cottage. While I thrash and try to defend myself I watch Gabe and Kaillen round the bend in the path. They're almost here. I can't let them see me like this!

Every time I gain some ground—a seam ripped here, a ridiculous spiked heel off there—they zap it right with Magic until everything sticks like it's sewn to my skin. Outside, Gabe and Kaillen stare open-mouthed at the sparks of light and color shooting from the small window. My angry shouts and the maidens' shrill laughter shatter the peace of the morning.

Xander shows me Kaillen and Gabe exchanging confused glances. They step off the path toward the cottage to investigate. I've got to get out of here. Is there a back door?

No. There's only one way out.

Whatever. I don't care anymore if they see me. I'll run straight past them like they aren't even there. The Fae can find someone else to open their Doorway.

Shit. The damn door won't open. Did the maidens Magic the lock?

"Tsk, tsk, you'll ruin your hair," one of them laughs as I bang my shoulder again and again against the wood.

All at once the lock magically springs open.

I tumble straight into Kaillen's arms.

His hands are everywhere. I disentangle myself and step back. Jungle drums beat a furious rhythm at my throat.

Kaillen and Gabe both stare at me, and my long, very snug gown with open mouths. It's way more scandalous on my body than it ever was on the hanger. The neckline plunges between my breasts. There's no back at all.

Gabe looks away embarrassed, but turns back to staring before long. If it weren't so humiliating it would be kind of cute how hard he's trying to figure out if the fabric is actually sheer or just really, really close.

I wobble in the heels. Kaillen's arms surround me again as I struggle to find my balance. He doesn't seem to be in any hurry to let go.

My hair falls all around my bare shoulders, getting in my eyes. I'm shedding blossoms from the countless miniature white flowers they've pinned in my curls. This is disastrous.

I kick off the heels and growl at Kaillen until he lets go. He chuckles as he steps back. Picking up the stilettos I hurl them with all my rage at the cottage.

"Give me back my clothes!" The tendons in my neck are close to snapping.

Giggles burst from inside the cottage. The three maidens fly through the open window carrying my stuff.

"Riley! Sybil!" Kaillen shouts, disapproval clear on his face. "Breena!" But it's too late. They're gone.

I stomp my feet. Tears well in my eyes.

"Are you hurt, Lady Emily?"

Kaillen called me Lady. He's never done that before. Is he mocking me?

I face both men. A crimson glow from behind me lights their features. Great. It's my wings. I'm blushing in my wings.

I need protection. Answering some voiceless inner command, the brand on my arm flares bright, transforming into the gauntlet and fitting around my wrist. Out of nowhere, the large black leather shield appears on my left forearm. I position it across my chest, blocking my body from their eyes as the dagger appears too. It hangs in gleaming silver filigree, loose and low around the curve of my hips.

I close my eyes and bow my head, silently begging the ground to open up and swallow me whole.

It doesn't.

I straighten my shoulders, moving the elaborately styled hair back from my face. There's only one thing to do: Pretend I'm not mortified. Holding my head high, I look both of them in the eye.

"Good morning, Gabe." I can't control the tremble in my voice and there's nothing to do about the color in my cheeks and wings—which shoot off little sparks like they're having a fiesta—but I won't squirm. "Good morning,

Kaillen. I'm sorry for knocking into you. And no, I'm not hurt."

"You're stunning," Kaillen says.

Gabe's mouth falls open.

I can't help smiling. Kaillen seems sincere. "I look like an idiot."

"Trust me Lady, that couldn't be further from the truth." Kaillen steps closer, wiping a traitorous tear from my cheek with his fingertip.

Gabe's hands ball into fists. "We should go." He retrieves the preposterous shoes from the dirt. "Here." Kneeling beside me he slips them on my feet.

"Thank you."

He clears his throat as he stands. "Do you want to change?"

Frustration makes me scowl. "I can't. There isn't anything better in there. Trust me."

"And to think I was dreading this meeting," Kaillen murmurs, exactly like a chivalrous knight.

Gabe glares.

"May I carry your shield, Lady?" Kaillen offers.

"Um, no thank you." I'm surprised roman candles aren't exploding from my wings.

"I may never forgive myself for this." Kaillen sighs dramatically, removing his linen jacket and holding it out for me to slip into.

I hesitate a moment before consciously letting go of the defensiveness I hold all around me. The gauntlet flares bright again. All three weapons wink out of existence.

Gabe doesn't know where to look. Kaillen makes no effort to hide his appreciative gaze as he helps me into his jacket with the opening in the back to accommodate my wings.

At the same time, both men extend their arms to me.

"Thank you." I hook my elbows through theirs. Together we walk down the path toward the clearing.

"Oh my God, oh my God, oh my God," repeats in my head over and over, "this cannot be happening."

Except that it is.

I'm going to strangle those mean-girl maidens and then light myself on fire.

I hold tightly to both men's arms as we go. The heels are break-neck tall ... one misstep on the dirt path and I'll crack my head open for sure.

I look mad-as-a-hatter traipsing through the forest in Kaillen's coat backwards over my almost see-through evening gown. The jacket smells amazing, though, and at least I don't feel naked anymore.

I glance up to find Kaillen staring at my lips. A small sound escapes the back of my throat, part cough, part gasp. On my other arm Gabe tightens his grip. I look up at his lean handsome face. He's pissed. His jaw contracts as he stares straight ahead. Is he mad at me? For taking Kaillen's arm? For being dressed like this? No. I know why he's pissed. He's pissed at Kaillen for flirting. He's pissed at me for enjoying it.

Those maidens had better watch their backs. I'm going to be the quickest study any Fae has ever seen. As soon as I learn how to use Blaze and Keen I'm going to teach them I'm not some easy target ...

I freeze in my tracks, pulling Gabe and Kaillen off balance. They turn to face me on the path, eyes questioning.

"That's it! I think I can do it!"

Kaillen and Gabe look at each other, confused, then back at me. "Do what?" Gabe asks.

I kick off the stupid heels. "I'm Magic."

Slipping out of Kaillen's coat, I hand it to him, crossing my arms over my chest. "Would you both mind turning around for a second? You're making me nervous."

They turn around.

I've remembered the part in Aidan's dream where my clothes kept changing. I was wearing a ridiculous dress just like this when I opened the first box.

What if I can change this dress?

This is the perfect chance to try using my powers for something other than summoning the weapons. Not that I even know how that happens or where the weapons go when they aren't with me.

I know nothing about seeing or manipulating the elements with Keen, but my wings pulse with the elemental energy of Blaze. What if I can use just a tiny bit of it to change my dress with Intention? I have loads of Intention.

I visualize my shoulder blades from the inside, feeling my way back with tiny hands to where my skin ends and my wings begin. Right away I smack into something solid, some kind of barricade where my human body stops and my Fae body starts.

You aren't different people stuck together with superglue. You're all the same YOU. Ava's voice glimmers in my ears. **Accept all your different parts. Sooner would be preferable to later.** Her tone is gentle, amused.

Mentally I feel along the barrier separating me from the Blaze locked in my wings, searching for any openings.

There, a seam! If I can only open it a tiny crack...

I hesitate. Massive power presses against the barrier, a swollen river behind a dam. If I open it—even just the teensiest bit—will it become unstable? What if the dam doesn't hold? What if letting out just a little isn't an option? Maybe I should wait until Quince can guide me?

No. I'm determined. I will change this dress. Now.

Eyes closed, I picture two needle-thin funnels at the base of each wing. They begin the slightest flutter and then a hum as the smallest amount of power trickles out, racing through my bloodstream like an electric car on a track. It isn't enough power to change the cut of the dress, but it's enough to make it less sheer.

That will have to do. I'm too scared to siphon any more.

I imagine the air above my head filled with opaque silver light. When the image is steady, I pull the energy down around myself.

Awash with tingles, I open my eyes. It worked!

The dress is solid silver now, with no transparent shimmer. It's still snug and low cut, but all in all it's a success.

I carefully remove the tiny funnels and patch up the hair-thin holes in the barrier.

"I did it!"

Both men turn around. I grab the dress by the hem and rip a knee-length slit so I can walk. "Much better."

Gabe's face registers shock and admiration. Kaillen seems impressed and maybe a little disappointed.

"Come on." I take their arms and tug them forward. "We're late!"

TWENTY SEVEN

S everal eyebrows arch at my bare feet and formal attire as we enter the grove, but nobody says anything. There are three elves and three maidens waiting for us. Two elves named Marcus and Jack flank the General. Two maidens, who introduce themselves as Lizzy and Kaye, stand next to Lady Quince. They've been appointed squadron leaders, tasked with getting us all to the Doorway safely.

I don't like being scrutinized by so many sets of eyes, especially when I'm bound to make a fool of myself, but in a weird way it almost helps being this insanely over-dressed. I'm so far out of my comfort zone in this gown escorted by two swoon-worthy guys who are both almost-definitely attracted to me that it's like it's happening to someone else. I manage to hold my fidgeting in check but fail miserably to keep from blushing like a fool.

General Ian takes my hand in his and kisses it fondly. Quince grazes my cheek with her heart shaped-lips. The maidens wish me a polite good morning while the elves each bow slightly at the waist with a murmured, "M'Lady," apiece. I allow myself to feel welcome, wanted.

The feeling lasts only seconds, though, before paranoia looms. They're probably just being extra nice after yesterday's cringe-worthy exchange between Jacob and me. Or maybe they realize how close they are to returning home and how skittish I am.

Gabe and Kaillen lead me to the moss-covered trunk of a fallen tree. A strong sense of déjà vu startles me. This reminds me of the place I saw in Aidan's dream. The dirt is strewn with the same pine needles and fallen leaves. The same wild clover sprouts in small patches here and there, and the same birdsong trills in the branches of the ancient towering trees.

No. I'm confused. Aidan's dream was of a paved lot with the Tree and Toad and the Three Boxes. He didn't mention a forest with a fallen tree. Did he? But somehow I know this is the place I rested before striding across the empty lot and kneeling in front of the boxes. I look over my shoulder to the right, half expecting to see the dilapidated parking garage.

Nothing but canopy stretches to the horizon.

Everyone sits on various stumps and boulders spaced closely together around the grove. Quince is on my right, sharing the fallen tree. My fingers run over lichen emerging from the springy bark of the decaying redwood.

"There's much to discuss." Ian calls the council to order. "Our meeting with Drake was very informative. We are finally ready to form our strategy for returning to the First Realm. Our purpose this morning is to reach a consensus on a clear plan of action and begin Lady Alvey's training. I ask that we put away our differences and work together in earnest. Our goal is close at hand." His pronouncement is met with brisk nods and murmurs of agreement.

"First, we have news of the crimbal and their Master. Several weeks ago, just after Drake received the vision of Lady Emily, he felt a weakness in the Wall. Closer examination revealed a hastily repaired breach. Drake believes the crimbal entered the Second Realm through this breach. From the tracks he found, he estimates there are forty crimbal here at most. He has found no remnants of any other crossing before or since, and unfortunately, the repaired breach is too strong for him to break."

"Even if the crimbal were creatures of High Magic, which they are not, how would they have the means to breach the Wall? Surely it's monitored from the First Realm?" Jack asks.

"The most plausible theory is that the High King Ælfwig sent the crimbal himself." The General answers.

Goosebumps flurry up my legs. Nissa's grandfather is the crimbal's Master?

Quince interlaces her fingers through mine, taking up the narrative in her clear voice. "The vision of Emily alerted High King Ælfwig, as it did us, that there was an extremely powerful Halfling on the cusp of her Changing with enough strength to wield Nissa's weapons. He knew what such an event could mean for us. He rightly guessed that we would act quickly to find and recruit her to our cause."

"So Ælfwig sent the crimbal to murder her." Kaillen's tone matches the anger in his eyes.

Ian nods. "We believe he sent them to neutralize the potential threat of our return by preventing Lady Alvey from opening the Doorway for us."

I try to ignore the words 'murder' and 'neutralize'. Something niggles at the back of my mind… "Wait!" I suddenly remember. "I thought the crimbal came to take my mom's wings."

"We must have been wrong. The crimbal were instructed to subdue a maiden and return with her wings. They would have been hunting an aura of High Magic. They obviously attacked the wrong maiden, as your wings had not yet emerged."

"They will be desperate to redeem themselves and recover Lady Alvey at any cost," Marcus interjects, "or risk harsh punishment."

"That is our fear." Ian is grim. "If they can capture and kill her, they would be able to return to Ælfwig with her wings as proof and receive whatever reward he promised them."

"They can't hope to attack us in the Vineyard," Lady Kaye says. "We're too well protected."

"It's unlikely they would risk such a suicidal mission," Ian agrees. "Which is why Drake believes they plan to ambush us as we approach the Doorway. Every day we wait is another day they have to formulate an attack. It's in our best interest to prepare Lady Emily to open the Doorway as quickly as possible."

"Then the only question left to ask regards Lady Emily. How long will her training take? When can we hope to attempt the opening?" Marcus doesn't believe in beating any bushes, apparently.

Quince speaks. "According to Drake, Lady Emily's natural abilities are nothing short of miraculous. She's able to wield the weapons using her raw power. It's only her lack of familiarity and control with Blaze and Keen that must be addressed before she can attempt to open the Doorway. At present, she becomes too easily overwhelmed."

The Fae turn to me.

Several seconds pass before I realize they're waiting for me to say something. "Don't look at me! I don't know how long it will take for me to learn 'familiarity and control'. And I haven't done any 'wielding' with the weapons. Sometimes they appear when I want them, but I don't know how or where from. Yesterday at the diner energy started rushing into me through all the weapons at once. It was awful." Even though I'm taking measured slow breaths so I won't hyperventilate, pins and needles prickle around my lips. "Just how big is this Doorway? Do I really need to use Blaze and Keen and all three weapons? That would be a ton of power."

"I understand your misgivings, Lady," the General says. "However, every ounce of energy you can access through all three weapons will be necessary to counteract the enchantment on the Doorway and hold it open long enough for us to pass through to the First Realm."

Why is he so calm? How can they all be so calm?

"The weapons only increase your ability to channel elemental energy. Once you learn how to recognize and access your masculine and feminine Sight you'll be able to wield them."

"My Sight?"

"Lady Emily," Ian says, "we won't force you to do something you're not willing or capable of doing."

"Remember, you won't be alone," Quince adds. "We'll be with you, and Drake will be there to help and guide you."

I know their words are meant to comfort, but they don't. "You won't force me? Really?" I challenge. "*None* of this has been my decision."

"Lady?"

"It hasn't. I took Mom's Blaze from her wings so those crimbal wouldn't hack her to bits. Then you people show up after we haven't seen or heard from you in years and the next thing I know my family and I are stuffed in the back of a van driving to the Pacific. So it isn't really true that you aren't going to force me to do something I'm not willing to do."

Ian looks at me from under gruff eyebrows. The Fae are silent.

An enormous headache gathers at the top of my skull. Is that what happened? Was it crimbal who came to get Mom? Why do I keep catching glimpses of a stretcher and three men in EMT uniforms? I try to pin the memory down but it's gone in a flash of pain behind my right eye.

It doesn't matter. Something doesn't add up. I don't know exactly how, but I'm definitely being manipulated. "Not for nothing, but there're some major holes in your story. I don't trust *any* of you. Especially not your Mediator Drake. He's creepy as hell. And especially not after finding out you plan to take my brothers and sister back to the First Realm without even asking me first."

"That isn't accurate, Lady," Ian says. "We merely welcomed them to join us, as we welcome you."

I have a moment where I know the things I'm about to say aren't rational, but they've formed themselves into legitimate sounding sentences held together with accusation rather than logic and they can't wait to leap from my mouth: "Why would you even say that to them? They're children. They belong at home with me. Of course they want to go to Faerieland, they don't know any better! We're going to go home and live normal lives."

"No one is forcing them to go anywhere, Lady," Ian replies. "The choice would, of course, be theirs."

"No. It's not theirs. They can't make choices like that. If you had any real concern for them you would never have suggested it."

"Emily, Dear. I understand you're upset, but I'm not sure exactly what you're upset about."

I flex my knuckles at Quince's reasonable, patient tone. She's patronizing me. "I'm upset because you're a bunch of selfish, irresponsible imposters. You don't care about us. You don't care about my mom. You don't care about anyone or anything except getting back to your stupid First Realm!"

My tantrum deafens the grove into breath-holding stillness.

"Emily." Ian kneels in front of me. I shrink back from his touch. "You've been hurt. You're hurting now. I understand you're frightened."

The next person who says they 'understand' anything is going to get throat punched. "I'm not frightened, General. I'm pissed. You can't just show up and ruin our lives."

"What is it about your life right now that you're so afraid of losing?" At least Marcus doesn't pretend to walk on eggshells. "Is it the fear that comes with having a mother ill and unreachable? Is it the pressure of running a household and parenting your siblings? The loss of your childhood?"

Oh. I hate him. Is that how they're going to spin this? They're rescuing me from my over-stressed life?

"If you cared so much about my 'hurt' or the 'loss of my childhood', why is it that you waited to show up until the exact moment you saw a vision and found out I could be useful to you?" My words drop as perfectly formed ice cubes and skate across the frozen tension in the grove.

"You're wrong, Emily. We have the utmost concern for your well being…"

"You don't act like it," I spit. "Jacob, Aidan, and Claire are everything to me. I'm not immortal. What if I fail? What if I die trying to break the Seal tomorrow? The Queen died when she scorched out her own Blaze. My brothers and sister would be alone. And what if I don't die? What then? Jacob wants to leave. No matter what I do my family will never be the same!"

A sonic boom whiplashes through the grove. Ian stumbles back like he's been struck. Astonished cries erupt in unison around me.

What happened?

"You saw that, Marcus, didn't you?" General Ian exclaims.

Marcus nods, eyes wide.

Saw what?

"We all saw it," Quince stands, backing away from me. "This is why she will not fail."

"She's insolent and ignorant. She has no idea what she's doing." Marcus insults with his words, but awe lights his expression.

"We're here to teach her, Marcus." Ian says.

I'm alone on my mossy log now. Whatever just happened cleared a wide swath around me.

"What's going on?" I'm spooked.

"You summoned a Dragon, Emily." Quince's voice is soft, wary. She keeps her distance. "An apparition, yes, but a very powerful one."

A Dragon?

"Even I could see it Emily, and I'm not Fae." Gabe speaks for the first time since the council began. He walks over, pulling me up from the log. "You don't need to worry about failing. You are beast."

"You don't need to worry about losing your bond with your family, either," Kaillen says. "Not even death could sever such powerful Connections."

Have they all gone mad?

"I'm amazed it took a vision for us to realize her capabilities," Jack says. "We sensed her potential awaken years ago. How did we not know the extent of her strength until now?"

"Because she's been hiding," Quince says as if she's piecing together a puzzle. "Very strategically hiding behind the most elaborate fortress for a very long time. Hiding even from herself. But her secrets grew too large for her body to contain and her fortress began to crumble. Her power began leaking out. That's what caused Sandra's wings to emerge. That's how the crimbal tracked her. When she absorbed Sandra's wings, the combined energy of their Blaze set Emily's own Changing in motion."

A chill snakes up my spine. The only warmth in my body rests in the small patch of skin where Gabe's fingers touch my arm. I made Mom's wings come out that night? Suddenly, all the secrets I don't remember burying overwhelm me with fear.

"I'm just a girl." My voice cracks.

"You can save us." Lady Kaye pleads.

I'm desperately alone. "I can't save anyone."

"You can restore our Connections." Quince says.

"What does that even mean? What Connections are you talking about?"

"It's a singularity of this Realm, Lady." I watch General Ian struggle to find words he thinks I'll understand. "In the First Realm, Connections are more than just emotions attaching people to things or other people. Our Connections are an organic physical link, binding us to each other. They don't form accidentally, nor are they something we're born with. They're a contract, an agreement we make with each other by choice, not by birth. When we were banished to this Realm, our Connections and our ability to Connect were severed. It is this loss that drives us more than anything to return to our home. It is your ability to Connect we envy. We're at your mercy."

I can't wrap my mind around what he's saying.

"She has Keen, General." Kaillen holds my gaze while he speaks. "Show her."

"Wait!" I'm suddenly nervous I'm going to let them all down, that I won't be able to see whatever it is Kaillen wants the General to show me. "Maybe we can start tomorrow. I have a really bad headache."

"Don't be nervous about your Sight, Dear," Quince soothes. "We already know you can use Keen or you wouldn't be able to activate the weapons."

"I don't even know how that happens!" I blurt.

"If you're quiet, M'Lady," Marcus forces politeness into his words, "we'll explain how it happens."

"Emily, you know both maidens and elves manipulate elemental energy in the First Realm," Quince begins. "The difference lies in how we access that power. Maidens are given the gift of Blaze at our Changings. Blaze activates the growth of our wings, where we store subatomic energy. It also opens our Inner Eye, which we use to See that energy and weave our Intentions into reality."

"Elves don't have wings, so we must reach outside ourselves for our power," Ian takes over. "We must grab hold of external elements in order to manipulate molecules and atoms and turn our Intention into reality."

"At his Changing, an elf's mother and father give him a Spark and Flame which combine to form Keen and open his Mind's Eye," Kaillen explains. "He also receives a medallion as a practice tool. It contains a small portion of elemental energy." He pulls a chain with a small medallion from under his shirt. "An elf Sees the elemental energy with his Mind's Eye. With years of practice using Keen, he's able to move beyond the medallion to grasp and manipulate elements in nature. The medallion becomes a focal point for his Sight."

"So Blaze and Keen are both ways of Seeing elemental energy, which maidens store in their wings and See with their Inner Eye, and elves get from nature and See with their Mind's Eye. Is that right?"

"Exactly right." Quince sounds proud.

Ian pulls a glittering necklace from his pocket. "Drake asked me to give this to you."

I've never seen anything like it. The links of the chain are flat and thick, made of a material that looks like polished sea-glass. They fit together seamlessly, reflecting the late-morning light as one sinuous piece. Each end is finished with a silver clasp. The chains join to a platinum circle engraved with the wild boar passant. A single chain dangles from the circle bearing a crystal orb. Inside the orb is a dandelion seed gone to puff, dizzy with innumerable delicate crystallites all perfectly arrayed around the faintest spark at their center.

"May I, Lady?" Ian asks.

I lift the hair off my neck so he can fasten the clasps. The chain is shorter than I expected, the crystal orb rests in the hollow of my throat just above the dip in my collarbone. I run a fingertip along the smooth chain. The clasp at the top of my spine is arctic.

"Are you ready to See, Lady?" Ian asks.

I can't find my voice. I squeeze his hand to let him know I'm ready.

"Close your eyes, Emily. Picture a Spark at the medallion's center. Pull it inside your body. Let it warm you, let it make you glow."

TWENTY EIGHT

Oh. *THIS. I smile inside. I* know this. The medallion warms at my throat. With the smallest movement I breathe in, watching with a twinge of excitement as the Spark sucks back into my body. I follow eagerly, slipping into my place at the center of the infinite pinpoints of light radiating outward from the center of my chest.

This time I don't panic or resist the unseen force when it yanks me...

...down...

...I'm falling...

...I'm shrinking...

...I'm with the Spark inside myself...

...brilliant light streams from me.

...Light surrounds me.

...Light *is* me.

I am Light.

THIS is my Mind's Eye.

I float, bathed in streaming color, full of Space, encompassing and transcending Time, aware in every direction. I stretch outward with my senses, leaving the confines of my body, gliding past edges, tasting my surroundings on the tip of my consciousness. First experimentally, then probing, now expanding in all directions. My giggles fizz around me, ebullient bubbles disseminating through me until I'm vapor thin, stretched out across the grove.

Ian's hand grips mine from a vast distance, anchoring my physical body to the ground. His words aren't sound; they're a rhythmic vibration traveling on waves through me.

The vibrations coalesce into a shimmering lens. Making the smallest adjustment in my Focus I can match the rhythm of his words, and…

Ohhhh. I can See…

…myriad ribbons of light flow from the center of my physical body to each person in the grove. More ribbons flow from my center outside the grove, stretching strong and thick away. At the other end of the ribbons the people I love resonate: Jacob, Aidan, Claire, and Mom. These are my Connections. I want to explore.

Drifting outside my skin I let this new world distract me from my fear and confusion. It's a sensory experience on steroids—I See with my ears, my tongue, even my sense of smell.

I examine the undulating ribbons of light, moving along each Connection's length, matching the distinct voices with my own pulsing music. I pass through several, savoring the vibrancy and strength swirling around me. It's easy to identify the unique flavors that belong to Aidan, Jacob, and Claire.

The ribbon flowing to and from Gabe is thick like blood pumping through healthy arteries. The spot where our ribbons meet emits a faint spark.

The ribbons connecting me to the Fae are thin and feeble compared to those that link me to my family and Gabe. A braid bridges the space between Quince and me, while my attachments to Ian and the others are thready, washed-out in the sunlight.

Except Kaillen. My Connection with Kaillen thrums, a just-plucked guitar string. It too sparks faintly, but not in the middle like Gabe's. This spark is so close to Kaillen's chest I'm surprised it doesn't singe his clothes.

That's when I notice.

There are no pathways of light linking any of the Fae to each other. None at all. In fact, they each have only one complete Connection. To me. Many short beams of light extend from their bodies, but go nowhere. They just hang impotently in the air a few feet out.

I stare at the Fae with my fully opened Mind's Eye, trying to apply the situation to myself, trying to imagine having no Connection—no instinctive caring, no innate concern, no natural affection—with my family and friends. I can't do it.

Dazed, I stray further from my body. A tremor slithers across my Awareness. I rotate in the direction of the disturbance to See a dark heavy Connection coiled on the ground below the other links, contracting slow and steady like the belly of a python around its dinner…

Chilled, I gather my particles closer together; all at once worried a sudden wind might separate me permanently.

There's a tug on my hand below. Ian is trying to get my attention. I ignore him.

This new knowledge changes everything. The Fae aren't arrogant and selfish, they've been lost and alone for a century...

I run the fingers of my Mind's Eye through the air. The elements ripple like liquid gold as the sun hanging overhead scatters miniature droplets of dazzling fire across every fragmented molecule it touches.

Another tug.

I'm not ready to go back yet. I need to examine the ribbons up close. I want to See how the Fae's Connections have been severed, how my links with them were formed. Quince said I could restore their Connections to each other, but how? Can they be re-made? Stitched back together? I have so many questions. I need more time to search for answers.

Ouch! Something pinched me.

Kaillen has positioned himself directly behind my body in the grove—alarmingly close. I can only see one of his hands...

He wouldn't dare actually pinch my butt in front of the council, would he?

Yep. He would. He does it again.

My surprised laugh diffuses around me. Hastily, I visualize my center, imagining the opposite of expanding. The dissipated edges of my Awareness shrink until I find myself inside the boundaries of my skin...my chest... smaller and smaller, more solid, less vague...separate from my Mind's Eye... back to my body.

I elbow Kaillen in the ribs. Composing myself, I open my eyes.

Ian places a kiss on my forehead. "I would dearly love to See this Realm through your Eyes, Lady."

The warmth of his kiss tickles my skin. My suspicions were wrong. The Fae don't pity me and they aren't just using me, either. I've Seen the Connections they share with me, even Marcus, who obviously isn't happy about it.

"I could See," I speak to the entire group. "I could See where your Connections to each other have been Unmade. But I could also See new Connections growing—they're like ribbons made of light—from each of you to me. They weren't strong like the bonds I have with my family, but they were there. I'm a little confused, though. I thought you said the Mind's Eye is for Seeing atoms and molecules. I'm not great at science but I know relationships aren't on the Periodic Table."

"This is what I meant when I told you that in the First Realm the Connections we form with one another are both physical and emotional," Ian says. "With your Mind's Eye you are able to See the physical component of this bond. When your Inner Eye is open you'll be able to See the emotional aspect as well."

"The rate of vibration in this Realm is so slow that our emotional and physical bonds dissolved almost entirely when we were banished," Quince explains. "You appear to be finely attuned to the vibration of power of both Realms, Emily."

"My Sight is too dim to See where my Connections with my people once were," Ian admits, "but I can See your incredible attachments to your siblings, and I can feel my attachment to you, Lady. It grows stronger as you grow stronger."

"I saw something else, too." I shudder. "It was different than my other Connections—heavy and dark on the ground."

"Not all Connections are positive. Or even healthy, Lady," says Kaye.

"But it was so big. Bigger and stronger than any of the others."

"Where did it lead?" Kaillen asks.

"I don't know. I was afraid to touch it."

"Sometimes an elf or maiden develops an unhealthy attachment to a person or behavior, or even a memory," Quince explains. "If an attachment between two Fae sours, the parties must petition to Unmake their bond. It can be a painful process, even when both individuals agree how to proceed. Connections feed on energy, Emily. They can be positive or negative, which is why we don't form them lightly. In the case of an attachment with a thought or object, the Connection would need to be Unpicked, thread by thread."

Instinctively I know I could spend every waking moment for the rest of my life unpicking the threads of that dark heavy coil and never be finished.

"I'm sorry to interrupt Lady Quince, but unpicking Connections won't help Emily break the Seal."

"Marcus, if you can't remember what empathy feels like, fake it." Ian's words hold reproach.

"No, Marcus is right. I need to focus. How will Seeing with my Mind's Eye help me break the Seal?"

"You have to Look in order to See," Gabe says.

"What did you say, Gabe?" Jack asks.

"Nothing. Just something I heard a long time ago."

"No, it's not nothing, Gabe." The medallion tingles at my throat. "Those Connections between us didn't just appear, right? But I couldn't See them until I learned how to open my Mind's Eye and knew what to look for." I turn to Ian, excited. "I know there isn't time for you to teach me how to grasp and manipulate the elements, but maybe if you tell me specifically what I'm supposed to look for when we get to the Doorway, I'll be able to See it and then I can use the Blaze in my wings to form Intention! I've done it once already… I bet with practice I could get good enough to break the Seal, maybe even in a few months!"

"Of course you will, Lady." The pride in Ian's voice makes me giddy.

"You won't be alone," Quince assures. "We'll be there to help you."

"We'll protect you and your family," Jack promises.

"Emily, your Mind's Eye is already sharp and true," Ian says. "Lady Quince and the other maidens will instruct you in opening your Inner Eye and using Blaze."

Hope reflects back at me from the Fae in the grove. Hope, conviction, and faith … faith in me. It leaves me speechless, but gives me courage, too.

General Ian claps his hands together once. "I propose we strike camp tomorrow at first light and make our way to the Doorway. Are we agreed?"

"Wait, what?" My throat closes up. "Tomorrow? NoNoNONONO! I thought I would have weeks to train…!" My words are trampled as each council member agrees in unison, raising a war cry in the grove.

When the noise dies down, Ian turns to me. "Emily, we wouldn't risk this attempt if we weren't convinced you're ready."

Vertigo hacks at my legs. This can't be happening.

Ian issues orders: "Marcus, you and your elves are to leave at once. Alert Drake that we will be ready by noon tomorrow. Secure the area and position a guard around the Doorway. Elizabeth, I ask that you and your squadron of maidens accompany them."

"We will," Lizzie answers.

"Jack, you will lead the short range marksmen. Lady Kaye, you will lead the long-range snipers. I'll coordinate defensive maneuvers if necessary. I want two warriors—one male and one female—assigned to protect each of the younger Alvey children. Lady Quince, I ask that you oversee this assignment."

"Of course."

"Son, will you act as Lady Emily's bodyguard?" Ian asks.

"With honor Father," Kaillen replies.

"Gabe, do you still wish to continue with us?"

"I do."

"I need someone to prepare the vehicles. Are you willing?"

Gabe nods, restless anticipation on his face. The council disperses.

TWENTY NINE

Gabe and Kaillen both hang back. I fidget with the tiny blossoms in my hair, wondering how long they plan to wait each other out.

Their stalemate breaks when Ian calls for his son to join him. Kaillen grimaces as he turns on his heel and follows the General out of the grove.

"Hey," Gabe says when everyone else has disappeared around the bend in the path.

"Hey." I'm glad he's here. The Fae were so excited they just up and left. They didn't even say when they were going to teach me how to open my Inner Eye.

"That was pretty intense. How are you?"

"Kind of freaking out."

"It's been a crazy few weeks." He rubs at the back of his neck with one hand. For the first time I notice how frayed he seems.

"Oh my gosh, Gabe, I've been so busy worrying about myself I haven't thought to ask about you! You've been with me this whole time…" It dawns on me how indebted I am to him. "You could have forgotten all about me after I kicked you out of my car in the parking lot. If you hadn't come to check on me that night, my mom wouldn't be alive right now…you drove to California…"

The enormity of the abyss he's filled hits me full force and for a split second I make myself suffer the way I would have suffered if I'd been alone. How can I ever repay him? I need him. I'm suddenly terrified of losing him.

"I couldn't have forgotten about you even if I'd wanted to, Emily. I've been searching for you my whole life. It just took me until now to find you." He takes my hand in his. "The first time I saw you I knew you would be important to me. Being around you feels good. It feels *right*."

"Are you really going with us to the Doorway, Gabe? I know you told the General you would help, but this isn't your fight. You could be killed if there's an ambush."

"Emily, I belong with you. I want you to come with me."

"Come with you where? Back to Dallas?"

"No. To the First Realm."

"I don't understand."

"We could make a place for ourselves there, for your mom and the kids."

"Make a place for ourselves? I'm seventeen. My place is at home with my family." I glance down at my bare feet in the dirt. "I'm not going to the First Realm, Gabe." The thought gives me waking nightmares. "I don't understand why you would want to go either."

"Because I want more, Emily. I want to know what it's like to See and manipulate the elements."

"How? You aren't an elf, Gabe. You don't have Keen."

"I met a man, Emily, a few years ago after my sister died. He's the one who told me I had to 'Look in order to See'. He sent me to keep an eye on you, he said you might be important." His gaze probes me. "Emily, I met that man again yesterday at the diner. He told me I could become very powerful in the First Realm."

A shock wave rattles through me. "You're talking about Drake."

"Yes, I'm talking about Drake. My mother knew him. He says I have ancient blood, that he can gift me power. That he'll craft weapons for me like he did for Nissa. He asked me to join him and help him usher in a new era in the First Realm. I'm going with him, Emily. I want you to come too."

"Why is everyone so anxious to leave everything here and go with the Fae? What do you mean Drake sent you to keep on eye on me? I don't trust Drake, Gabe. At all. There's something off about him."

"He's more than just the Fae's Mediator Emily. He's their Patriarch, too. We all need a strong leader, someone with vision who's powerful enough to control his people. Drake is the most powerful Ovate the Fae have ever seen. He has a plan to rebuild the Seventh Kingdom. Once you open the Doorway we'll march against the High King and take back what was stolen. We'll be unstoppable once the Master controls the weapons."

"Master? When the Master controls the weapons?"

Feverish light burns Gabe's eyes. He moves closer until our faces are only inches apart and grips both my arms. "Ælfwig will have no choice but to relinquish the Seventh Kingdom to us, Emily, and Drake has promised me a place of honor among his counselors. Say that you'll come with us."

"Drake is your Master."

Drake.

Drake is the Master.

I can only stare, my brain repeating it over and over.

"He would welcome you, Emily. He speaks very highly of your strength and potential, and the Fae admire you. Think of the possibilities! You could help us establish a new society where the traditional ways are enforced. And we wouldn't stop with the Seventh Kingdom. Drake plans to reform the entire Realm."

"What about our Fae, Gabe? What will happen to Ian and Quince when they return? What will happen to Kaillen?"

"Why do you care so much what happens to Kaillen? He's an arrogant ass who thinks he's better than everyone. Please tell me you haven't fallen for all his chivalrous bullshit. He's playing you."

I step back, yanking away from his grip. "Maybe *you're* the one being played!"

He takes a deep breath. His manic energy dissipates. "Don't worry, Emily," he placates, closing the distance between us. "Drake wants to make things right. I'm sure there will be a place for all your precious Fae in some part of the Realm. Come with us, Emily, and find out for yourself. You don't need to give up your power. You don't have to lose your family, and you can keep your wings."

"I need to think about it." I need to think about everything but his hands are on me and he kisses me, softly at first but his lips soon grow aggressive, then rough. His hands clutch me against him as he pulls back and smiles, "You don't know how happy this makes me. I won't lose you, Lady Alvey. I want to protect you and provide for you. Let me take care of you Emily. You won't ever need to be afraid again."

His lips take mine again and I don't stop him. I don't want him to stop. Excitement shoots through me at the wanting I taste in his kiss. It feels so good, being desired this way. The heady rush of euphoria drowns out everything else.

Responding to a hunger deep inside my gut, I trace the lean muscles of his back with my fingers. My hands travel up over the thin material of his T-shirt, across his broad shoulders and neck to tangle in the softness of his hair.

The insistent pressure of his hands leaves heat in their wake as they move over my hips and waist. My wings quiver when his fingertips brush against them.

I'm melting...

"Emily Ava Alvey! Stop this instant!"

"Aunt Margaret!" I pull my lips away and freeze, a mortified statue of embarrassment.

Gabe plucks a loose blossom from my shoulder, tucking it behind my ear, tossing a casual wry grin at Margaret. "I'll take care of you." He laces his hands behind the small of my back, pulling me back in against him.

I put my hands on his chest, pushing him away. "Let go, Gabe! I can take care of myself." Is he trying to get me in trouble?

He lets go, chuckling. "You're mine." His lips brush the tip of my nose. "I knew you would belong to me from the moment we met. Go on. I have some things to do. We'll have plenty of time for this in the First Realm."

He winks back at me as he passes Margaret, then disappears into the woods.

THIRTY

Margaret stares at me, zero emotion on her face. The hollow blanks of her unblinking eyes pierce me as she walks straight at me. I study the ground. Not even a speck of dust mars the blue shine on her patent-leather kitten-heel pumps.

I have vague ideas about how I'm supposed to act around boys from when we attended church as a family when I was young. I remember lessons on modesty and purity, about how a young lady should dress and talk, primary songs about how our bodies are temples. But that was a long time ago and I'm confused about the specifics. I'm seventeen. When will it be okay to kiss someone?

It doesn't matter. Obviously I shouldn't have been kissing him. I raise my head to apologize to Margaret.

Her open-handed slap cracks my head back.

Unstoppable tears sting my eyes. Stumbling, I raise my arms in defense. Not fast enough. Another slap catches me on my ear.

"I'm sorry! I'm sorry! Please, please, I'm sorry!" I hunch over where I've fallen in the dirt, expecting more blows. After several moments of silence I peek out from under my arms.

"Get up. You look ridiculous. You've ruined your dress."

I stand.

"Do you know why I slapped you?"

"Because I kissed Gabe."

"That's right. But do you understand why it was wrong of you to kiss him?"

I can't stop humiliating snivels. I know if I don't answer the right way I'll anger her more. My thoughts scurry, horrified. Nothing I come up with sounds good enough.

Old spores of despair expand in my lungs, choking off my breath. "I...it's because I shouldn't...because kissing is bad..."

Margaret clucks. I jerk up, surprised.

"Kissing isn't bad."

I flounder. Is she making a joke?

"There, there, Sweetheart. Dry your eyes. You've always been overly dramatic, haven't you?"

She dabs at my cheeks with a white embroidered handkerchief.

"You're a lovely young woman, Emily, and boys will be boys. Don't get me wrong. I like Gabe, and heaven knows you need a strong man in your life. But you're much too young to be kissing like that. What do you think will happen next? Do you think he'll be happy for long just kissing? It's always the same story. One thing leads to another and before you know it you're alone with a broken heart and that's all...if you're lucky." She lifts my chin. "I just don't want my little girl getting hurt."

I peer into her perfect blue unblinking eyes, dazed. Seconds ago they glowed with rage.

Her pupils. They're too big. How did I never notice before that she doesn't blink?

She gazes back for a moment before wavering and glancing away. She straightens the string of pearls at her neck and wipes her hands on her skirt.

"None of what you said makes any sense," I breathe.

Her eyes flicker back to mine. "Watch your tone, young lady."

"Why?" I take a step closer. "You said you hit me because you didn't want me to get hurt. News Flash: getting hit hurts."

Margaret turns her back to me. "That was nothing. Trust me, they'll hurt you a lot worse."

"Boys? How? I liked kissing Gabe. I wouldn't have done it if I hadn't liked it. It felt good."

"I'm sure it did," she smirks. "Just wait until he starts asking for more. Until he pushes a little harder. You want to please him, so you say yes. You don't want to lose him because he makes you feel good, so you do what he asks. What about then?"

"I'm in charge of my own body. I do what I want when I want. No one can make me do anything I don't want to do, period."

"I seem to remember things a little differently." She laughs. It isn't a pretty sound. "Fine. Do it your way, if you're so smart. But mark my words. If you don't listen to what I say you'll get hurt again. And the only thing we'll be able to do when that happens is what we've done for years and years. I guess some things never change."

She sits on the fallen trunk now. Wisps of hair escape the bun at her neck; a twig sticks to her skirt. I wait for her to continue, but her mouth has compressed into a small rigid line.

"What? What have we done for years and years?"

She puts her thumb and index finger to her lips and twists, then motions throwing something over her shoulder.

I'm dizzy.

I know what that was... with her fingers and her lips. She was locking up secrets and throwing away the key.

This is another freaky part from Aidan's creepy dream. There was a lock and key in the second box. I slipped them into the pocket of my skirt... a skirt that was just like Margaret's...

Homework. I suddenly remember I have homework. I'm supposed to talk to Hannah and Margaret and find out what they want. I already know what Hannah wants. She wants me to pretend that every hurt and problem in my life can be solved with Magic. She wants me to escape to the First Realm and live with her forever and forget whatever happened in the past. That's why the first box in Aidan's dream had a book of the First Realm inside.

And now I know what critical Margaret wants, too. She wants to stop me from getting hurt. Stop me from making mistakes. She wants me to keep all the bad things I've done locked away. That's why there was a lock and key in the second box.

I'm supposed to make peace with Hannah and Margaret. I'm supposed to find my True Voice. What if…? Could my True Voice be in the third box?

Except I don't know where the third box is, and how am I supposed to open the lid? It's sealed shut?

First things first.

I sit down next to Margaret and wrap my arms around her neck. "I'm sorry I was so rude. I didn't understand. But now I know you're trying to protect me the only way you know how."

She leans against me for a long moment before pulling back and wiping at her cheeks. This close, I notice how bent and tired she is.

"I love you Margaret. You're important to me. I promise I'll always listen and consider the things you say. I won't push you away. But I'm not seven anymore."

"I know you aren't Emily. It's easy to forget. You're growing up so fast. Thank you," she stands. "I love you too."

Alone now in the grove the events of the morning press in. Pent up energy and emotions threaten to overwhelm me. Maybe I shouldn't have kissed Gabe. Maybe I shouldn't have flirted with Kaillen. I'll definitely need to sort this out, but right now hormones and boys are the least of my problems.

The Fae are packing right now to go to the Doorway tomorrow where I'm supposed to submit to Drake so he can guide me in breaking the Seal and then scorch out the power in my freak-wings so the kids and I can go home. No biggie.

Sitting on the fallen tree I slump hard onto my white-knuckled fists with my stomach, forcing a harsh groan from my tight throat. I might explode.

I rake my fingers through my hair, pulling out the ridiculous flowers. My skin itches. This stupid gown is driving me mad. I want to tear it to shreds, but that's not an option since I'm absolutely done traipsing around naked in the forest.

Did those maidens bewitch the gown while they were forcing me into it? The glimmering material constricts, like it's trying to suffocate me.

Is this a psychotic break? Am I having another psychotic break?

"Hey, Ava!" I shout out loud to the White Faerie. "I'm throwing an 'experiencing my emotions party' and you're invited!"

Her reply sparkles immediately in my ear. **No offense, but your party sucks.**

Caught off guard, I laugh. "I'll lose my mind if I don't get out of this dress. Like, now."

Then change it, If you don't like what you're wearing, use Blaze to change it, like you did before. You're Magic, remember?

"I only made it less sheer before! How's that going to help?"

Shhhhh. It will be easier if you relax. Look.

An image appears in my mind of that yoga pose…I don't know what it's called…the one where you do crisscross-applesauce with one ankle over the other leg and sit up tall.

I'll try anything. I hike the hem of my dress up almost to my bum. Sitting down cross-legged in the dirt I place my right ankle over my left thigh and rest my palms face up on my knees.

Sporadic chatter from a squirrel and the soft chirp of a Meadow Lark are the only sounds interrupting the stillness of the grove. Not even Xander or

Twist is nearby.

I remember from a section in phys. ed. last spring that yoga is about being 'present'. It's about 'gentle strength'. I can't force the pent-up anxiety away from me, but if I concentrate on my breath I might be able to free it.

The pain from the murderous dress recedes as I follow my breath in and out. My shoulders ease down from where they'd bunched up by my ears. My calf and feet muscles go soft. I deepen each breath like this is the only moment I have to live in this body.

Little by little I unclench. My blood slows.

With tiny hands I probe at the barrier separating my wings from my body, pushing, searching for a weak point. It pushes back.

I need to open my Inner Eye so I can See what I'm dealing with in there. But how? No one's taught me how to do that yet.

Use your Mind's Eye.

"I thought the Mind's Eye was a guy thing for Seeing molecules in nature! How will that help me See my what's blocking up my wings inside my body?"

Are you really going to argue with me? I'm the White Faerie! Her silver laughter ricochets through my ear.

I grin in spite of myself.

Open your Mind's Eye. I want to show you something.

THIRTY ONE

What have I got to lose? I focus on Drake's medallion, visualizing a speck floating at its center. An ember ignites, warming the sphere from within.

I inhale the golden light from the crystal. My Mind's Eye awakens easily now, bathing me in light. I relish this dance of distinct particles spinning along the outer reaches of my awareness.

Fixing my attention on my shoulder blades, I seek the barrier that binds the power in my wings.

There is none. These wings extend from my shoulder blades the same way my arms extend from my torso and my fingers from my hand. Blood flows back and forth between torso and wings, fascia seams and binds wings to torso, sinew gives them motion.

"I told you, Ava! My Mind's Eye can't See any barrier. My yoga pose sags, the dress cuts off circulation in my arms. "My Eyes must be broken."

They aren't broken. Think about what you've learned for a minute. If you can't See the barrier with your Mind's Eye, what does that mean?

"That it doesn't exist…?" DUH.

You know better than anyone that just because you can't See something doesn't mean it doesn't exist or that it doesn't have power.

"Does it mean it isn't physical?" An utterly profound idea takes shape in my brain… "It means it's intangible…?"

Now you're getting it. If it isn't physical or tangible, what else could it be?

I think I know. "Quince said their Connections are physical and emotional…" Fresh excitement lengthens my spine. "That's it, isn't it? I can't See it with my Mind's Eye because the barrier is emotional not physical!"

My Inner Eye spills opens.

If Seeing with my Mind's Eye is like peering through an über-strong microscope, Seeing with my Inner Eye is like looking at the sun through a prism. Light refracts into a million rainbow bits, each uniquely holographic and crystal clear.

I can see it now…the barrier blocking the power in my wings. Layers and layers of dense interlocking mesh create a wall of thick blackness I can't penetrate. A wave of dread hits me when I poke along the edges.

It's made of fear.

"Ava, there's no way I can get past that. How did I ever get any energy out of my wings before?"

You were angry and humiliated. And no wonder.

"Now what am I going to do?"

There's no pressure. It's just an itchy dress.

"It's trying to kill me!"

Shhhh. You are smart, you are strong, you are brave. Be kind to yourself.

As the words of her mantra encircle me, the fibers of doubt and fear in the barrier relax. Small chinks appear in the knit of the mesh.

Just go slow. Open your heart. Of course you're nervous! But Emily, this is who you are. Trust yourself. I do.

The mesh loosens even more.

Beams of energy seep through the gaps from my wings into my body. I hold my breath—resisting the power—trying to control it. The fibers constrict.

You can do this.

I focus on inhaling and exhaling.

Remember the 'experiencing your emotions party'? Just sit and experience. Emotions aren't bad and they can't hurt you, though some can be very uncomfortable. Always remember that you are more than your emotions. I'm here for you.

The flow of power scalds white-hot. The pain becomes worse…hotter as I start to panic. "What if I burn up?"

You won't. Trust yourself. Think of something cool and refreshing. Think of this…

A memory of the glade surfaces. I relive the first touch of wintery water as I step into the waterfall pond. My ankles ache. Every instinct shouts: it's too cold! Jump out!

"Wait," I speak to the Emily in the glade. "Wait! This isn't pain. It doesn't hurt. It's just unknown so it's scary."

I smile. I remember hearing those words in my head when I first stepped into the pool. At the time I thought it was the White Faerie speaking, but it was really me all along!

I concentrate on the Emily in the glade wading deeper into the pond; I'm so glad we didn't jump out.

Mist from the falls surrounds me…I'm up to my thighs in the pool, now my hips. As the cold water rises to my belly and then my breasts I experience a brisk moment of complete invigoration. My breath comes in gasps, not from fear but from total release. Without hesitation I sink beneath the water…

…and with upturned hands resting gently on my knees in my yoga pose I open my fingers letting fear stream out. It floats away in concentric rings, widening, expanding, losing vibration, losing force.

The barrier is gone. Power flows fluidly throughout my whole body.

This feels good…I'm awake and so alive.

Blaze looks very much the way it sounds, like many long-stranded whip-thin tongues of fire ranging across every color in the spectrum. Flames lick through my limbs.

Pulsing orbs congregate up and down my center. The strongest glows directly in the middle of my chest. I count three below and three above my heart, spaced at uneven intervals from my crown to the base of my spine.

Your chakras are beautiful, Emily.

My chakras. I nudge them. They flicker in response. I twist them so they flow in a dovetail pattern weaving in and out of each other, spreading back and forth up and down my arms and legs. I make the strands spiral around the orbs one after the other. I change their color by braiding different ribbons together and combining strands to make them thicker. I don't have a clue what it means but it's electric. And all I have to do to make it happen is Intend it.

I envision my tank top and shorts settling on my body in place of the killer eveningwear. Instantly I'm back in the clothes I put on this morning.

The tiniest sound, like the soft cry of a child, alerts me that I'm not alone in the grove anymore.

Quince stands at the tree line with Xander hovering near her shoulder. "Emily," she murmurs. "You're radiant."

I smile, pleased and shy.

Quince cradles a box in her arms. It's about a foot square and made of thick wavy-warped glass crisscrossed by runes. It looks heavy. Something small twinkles inside but the glass itself is so distorted by trapped bubbles, I can't tell what it is.

Anticipation thumps a loud heavy rhythm in my ears.

The third box.

Quince sits on the ground across from me in my yoga pose, placing the crystal box on the ground between us. It's exactly the way I remember it from Aidan's dream except for one thing...the lock is missing.

"Minutes ago it started...*singing*," Quince says, reverent. "The lock. It was steel. It... burnt to ash." She lifts the lid. "She wouldn't speak a word until I promised to bring her here."

THIRTY TWO

My whole body chants her name. "Ava."

"Hello, Sister." She unfolds herself gracefully, standing in her crystal prison.

Chills bloom everywhere because seeing her speak these two words, I know: Ava The White Faerie is my True Voice.

But something is different from the night I saw Ava transform from a silver butterfly and drop like a stone to the counter in Mom's bathroom...

"Ava? Where are your wings? Who locked you in the box?"

She stands. "May I shelter in your hand?"

Sparkles dance over her skin as she steps from the box onto my outstretched palm. I have to shield my eyes. The light emanating from Ava's body makes it hurt to look at her directly. Even peeking through my fingers I'm dazzled. She shines too bright.

"Come closer and I'll tell you all about my wings and the box."

I lean closer but have to shut my eyes tight.

She giggles. "Close your Mind's Eye, Silly!"

My Mind's Eye! I forgot it was still open. Focusing inward I See the pinprick of light pulsing in my chest. Exhaling, I return it to the medallion.

"Can you look at me now?" Ava teases.

She still gleams, but it doesn't fry my retinas. The interface of our fabulously thick ribbon of Connection had been too much for my Keen vision. It's unlike any other bond I have with anyone else, much thicker even than my attachments to Jacob, Aidan, and Claire. It's a broad luminous rope fastening an ocean liner to its anchor.

Ava gathers locks of hair from either side of my face, pulling herself closer still. Releasing and smoothing one fistful, she strokes my cheek with her tiny poised hand. "Sister, I know that you're strong. Now you See that you must hope and be brave, for both of us."

"I took your wings, didn't I?"

"When you absorbed your mother's wings, you pulled too hard. You took mine, too."

"I'm so sorry…"

"Hush. I'm not." There's not an ounce of regret in her body.

"Thank you, Ava," I whisper. "Thank you for helping me, for listening when I was scared. For encouraging me."

"You're welcome, Sister."

"Did I lock you up in the box, too?"

"Not you. The Gray Man."

"I'll find him, Ava. I'll make Margaret and Hannah tell me where they put him. I swear he'll never hurt you again…"

"Shhhh. Sister. You don't understand. His methods are violent and unsavory, yes, but he was only trying to protect us."

"Protect us?"

"He's always been your strongest knight. You set him to guard the borders between our Realms when the psychiatrist told you it was bad to pretend and you believed him. It can be dangerous to meet your voices, Emily. It's not normally allowed. But we had to break the rules. We need each other right now."

"How does locking you up in a box protect you? Protect you from whom?"

"We don't just share a physical and emotional Connection any longer, Sister. You and I share actual emotions. When you took my wings my boundaries disappeared. I have no protection from your sensory input any longer."

The Gray Man was protecting Ava from me.

"Ava, I had no idea…"

"Sister, I'm amazed how quickly you've learned to See through your Eyes. Are you able to draw power from the weapons as well?"

"Drake helped me channel through them for a couple seconds yesterday, but it was scary as hell."

Ava's expression turns grave. "You must try again, Emily. You must try now. Alone."

"Is this necessary, Ava?" Quince asks. "The maidens will work with her this evening to solidify the process in her mind, but Drake will be there to guide her with the weapons tomorrow. He'll help her draw enough power, hold the flow, and modulate her weaving to break the Seal. Perhaps it would be best if she rests this afternoon."

"Drake will hold your flow?" Ava asks.

"Yes, and scorch out my Blaze. If I submit to him he'll be able to deplete my wings so they'll shrivel up and I can go home and live a normal life."

Ava pales. "We're running out of time."

The force of the wingless faerie's dread stipples the skin around my mouth. "I can't use that much power by myself. I'm not ready."

"I know you're frightened," she says. "I am, too. But you can do this. You don't need Drake. You have everything you need inside yourself at this very moment to do what you need to. Do you trust me, Emily?"

"With my whole heart." It's true.

"Will you try?"

Ava's faith surges into me. "Yes." I stand, ready to summon the weapons when Ava instructs. Quince stands, too.

"Your Blaze flows freely. Can you See it?"

"Yes," I whisper, looking with my Inner Eye.

"Now, embrace your gift of Keen." Ava instructs.

I breathe in the glowing ember from the medallion at my throat, joining it with my conscious mind, enfolding myself in light.

Myriad sensations course through me from every direction. I hold both my Mind's Eye and my Inner Eye open but separate, positioning one above the other as if I'm looking through bifocals. I can either focus through my Inner Eye on top or my Mind's Eye on the bottom.

"Well done, Sister," Ava says from the hollow of my cupped hands. "Now, concentrate on the brand of your maiden name around your arm and summon the gauntlet."

I watch the brand flare; morphing into the gauntlet the instant I Intend it to. It settles around my forearm like it did when I was in the diner with Drake, studs gleaming in a thousand faultless facets.

Ava grins up at me. "You're shiny. This is so cool."

"Yeah? Well, you're too shiny to look at."

Like I did in the yoga pose, I create a protected calm at my center. I'm still aware of all the sensory input I'm receiving, but I can process it without reacting emotionally. My anxiety can't influence me here.

"Are you ready, Sister?" Ava asks.

"I'm ready. Maybe you'll be safer in your box, though? I don't want to accidentally hurt you again."

Ava grins. "Yes, the box. But please Quince, will you hold me near?"

When she's safely positioned in her crystal enclosure Ava nods at me. "Remember, go slowly: one weapon at a time. You can do this."

As soon as I Intend the shield it appears, strapped securely to my left arm. The dagger materializes next, sheathed low and loose around my hips.

I don't understand how anyone would ever have reason or desire to reach for more power than already surges through me from my wings, the gauntlet, and the medallion. It threatens to eclipse my senses and swallow me whole. But Ava says it's important. For her I'll try.

I concentrate on my left forearm. The spikes on the shield bristle in the shape of the rune Algiz: Protection. Each razor-sharp tooth is a conduit waiting to channel elemental power. With a gentle tug at the base of a single spike, I activate them all. Energy rushes through the shield abrading my skin.

From deep within the calm I feel my muscles spasm.

"Sister, breathe. You can control the flow of power from the shield, do you See?"

With my Mind's Eye I See countless microscopic openings leading from the shield in through my pores. Weaving together miniscule strands of Blaze, I insulate the channels, narrowing them slightly. The energy slows from a rush to a steady stream. I'm in control. Barely.

"Excellent," Ava praises. "Stay open. Let the power flow free through your channels. When you're ready, activate the dagger."

"I don't like being this open. Maybe this is enough for now?"

"Believe me, I understand," Ava's empathy softens the edges of this impossible task. She's feeling everything I do. "When you're open you have access to vast amounts of power, but you're also exposed. Being closed offers safety and protection, true, but you can't access your power when you're closed. It's a choice."

"I don't even want power!"

"That is, perhaps, why you're blessed with so much."

"What am I supposed to do with it?"

"Nothing for now. We'll practice activating the weapons, modulating your flow, and releasing the power until you're comfortable. We can work on setting boundaries and situating filters. You're a natural, Emily. You'll master this process quickly. You don't need Drake."

"Wouldn't it be easier to let him guide me? He creeps me out, but at least he knows what he's doing. I do *not*."

"I'll explain soon. I need you to trust me. Listen to the sound of my voice. With your right hand, draw the dagger from its sheath," Ava instructs.

My fingers wrap around the smooth hilt at my hip. Effortlessly I pull it from its sheath. The blade sparks with iridescent light.

This time I'm prepared, holding woven strands of Blaze ready when power begins to flood from the hilt into my palm. I narrow the opening, modulating the influx to an almost tolerable level.

I'm vibrating.

The streaming power sings in me. Ethereal music dances through my frame. Blaze is high-pitched—wild boysenberries at the roof of my mouth mingled with gardenia. Keen's scale is the umber of fresh turned soil, an oboe's sinuous ebony. The music moves in perfect counterpoint, melodies intertwining, phrases shifting and eliding, textures blending, evaporating, being reborn. The harmony is mellow honey on my tongue-tip. With new ease I draw power from all three weapons.

A midsummer's evening from my childhood materializes, wavering all around me in the air. I'm a girl of ten, nestled up with my kitten, Butterscotch, on our creaky old porch swing in Utah. Over the tall fence in a neighboring yard a lawnmower's tired engine sputters out, revealing the chirp of a cricket's chorus celebrating the gathering dusk.

The afternoon was too warm for my liking but now a breeze carries the fragrance of fresh cut grass across the baby-fine hairs on my shoulders. It's heaven lying here with Butterscotch purring in the crook of my arm.

Melting ice tinkles as it shifts in a glass of lemonade I placed on the cement ages ago. My fingers play absently with the kitten's pointed ears, burying themselves in the deep fur of her neck. Butterscotch is the softest thing in the world.

I want to stay just like this forever, but the last smudges of light dissolve behind the horizon. Soon Mom will call me in to bed, tsking over the new freckles on my sun-pink cheeks. It isn't fair I have to go to sleep by eight-thirty in the summer. Maybe, just maybe, if I'm very quiet she'll think I'm already tucked up in bed. Maybe I can stay out all night with the stars.

The sky is an enormous watercolor canvas, stained dark at the top and edges, bleeding the indigos, violets, crimsons, and cadmium oranges of a finger-paint handprint where the earth and heavens touch.

Mom's reassuring presence radiates just beyond the walls of the house. She's healthy and happy and Dad is nowhere. This is where I want to stay. But a sharp pang knifes through my ten-year-old chest. Sunset's vibrancy is already washing away.

Wait, please don't go! Pierced by loss and longing, my consciousness separates from my young self, moving back to my seventeen year-old body. *Not yet! Please!*

But the image grows dim, distant, receding.

No. This is *my* memory. I'm in control. I'm not ready to leave yet.

More power. I need to stop from returning to the present. With a little more power I can go back and savor the memory longer.

I yank out the strands of Blaze I'd used to decrease the flow of power through the dagger and shield.

A tsunami of energy crashes over me. I jump as if shocked by an electric cattle prod. Weaving the extra power into strands of Intention, I use them to propel myself back to the midsummer sunset.

It's working. I race toward that reality. My ten year-old self still lays on the porch swing sheltered by a darkening sky. Cut diamond stars punch through the sapphire night.

I'm going too fast. I try to slow down, but speed up instead.

"Emily, stop!" Ava's scream is a world away.

"I don't know how to stop!" Fear pricks my calm as I shoot past the midsummer night. I draw more power, seeking to shelter under layers of Magic. I'm careening out of control.

PLAY DEAD.

I go limp, dropping my grip on all three weapons. The shield and dagger vanish. The gauntlet transforms back into the brands on my arm. My calm shatters in a million frantic bits.

I halt.

Doubled over I grab my knees, sucking huge gulps of air. Slowly the dark spots behind my eyes fade.

The shimmering silver backless gown is back.

"Sister, you're not safe! He'll find you. Return at once!" Ava's words are thin and tinny, like I'm listening through broken ear-buds.

Who will find me? Where is this place?

I cast about for clues and discover I know exactly where I am.

On the sidewalk only feet from where I stand, Peter the Toad and his sign guard the massive Monterey cypress. Behind the dying tree a decrepit parking garage decomposes into rubble. A polluted gray sky suffocates the landscape, exactly as in Aidan's dream.

THIRTY THREE

"**Y**ou have to roll it up, Claire, otherwise it won't fit."

"Aidan? Claire?" I whip around, awash with relief at the sound of their voices. But there's no one here. I'm completely alone except for Toad.

But I can still hear Aidan bossing Claire. I can hear her nonchalant reply.

I cast around for the source of their voices. They're swelling from a crack in the sidewalk.

Dropping down on all fours in the stupid gown, I peer through the crack. I'm above them, watching from the corner of the guest room ceiling I share with Claire at the Vineyard.

"Yes it will," Claire rams her raincoat into her pink flower suitcase with both feet.

Aidan sits on the edge of the bed, worrying at a loose thread on his polo until his shirtfront puckers.

"Why are you so grumpy?" Claire asks.

"Half our family is missing, Claire."

"It's not like they're lost, though, Silly. They just aren't here. Gabe took Jacob to help him with the vans, and Emily is still at her training thingy. They're coming back, you know."

"I don't like it. Everyone else came back from the council ages ago, and Gabe was acting weird. A bunch of elves and maidens are getting ready to go scout out the Doorway and set up a defense against a crimbal ambush. The rest are cleaning guns and restringing bows. I asked if I could help, but they won't let me anywhere near any kind of weapon after Emily's freak-out yesterday. I finished packing in two seconds, so now I'm stuck babysitting you. Maybe that's why I'm grumpy, Claire."

"Oh please, you love babysitting me. Here, pack Emma's stuff for her, that'll make you feel better. Be sure to roll up her underwear so it will fit!" Claire chortles at her own joke.

Aidan flops back on the bed. Hands behind his head he stares up at the ceiling.

"Aidan!" I yell through the crack. He's practically looking right at me.

Nothing. They can't hear or see me.

"Do you think Jacob would really leave us to go with the Fae?" Claire asks.

"No." Aidan's answer is automatic. Then he hesitates. "I mean...I don't know. I think he was just being stubborn. I don't think he'd really go. I hope he wouldn't."

"Hannah says the First Realm is SO amazing," Claire sighs. "I'd go, but only if we all went as a family. What's going to happen to us after the Fae leave, anyway?"

"I dunno. I guess we'll go home with Dad."

"What about Mom?"

"I assume she'll go with us when she's out of the hospital."

"It's going to be so weird."

"What is?"

"Well, I've never met him. I don't know much about him. I ask questions, but no one ever wants to talk about him, like it's breaking a rule or something. Now he's coming home to be our dad and Mom's going to be our mom like she was before she got sick. I've never lived with two parents before."

"You're lucky." Aidan speaks under his breath. I have to lean into the crack to hear him.

"What? Why?"

"He got mad. A lot."

"That can't be the only thing you remember." Claire prods.

"I was barely five when he left."

"Yeah, but everyone remembers stuff from when they're five."

"Spiders."

"You remember spiders?"

"Whenever I think about him it's like I'm covered in spiders."

"Oh, you mean like tingly and tickly because you're nervous and excited to see him."

Aidan rolls onto his side away from Claire. I can see his face but she can't. "Sure. Because I'm nervous and excited."

That's not what he means.

I dig my fingers into the dirt on the sidewalk. I need to know what Aidan means.

"I like his voice," Claire chats on. "It's so happy and loud. He calls me his girlfriend when we talk on the phone. He says everything is going to be just like it was before he left."

Aidan sits up. "Let's go see if Emily's back yet."

The yard is a hive of maiden activity. Aidan and Claire head toward Lady Kaye under the big oak tree by the rope swing. Before they're halfway there the sidewalk beneath me heaves violently. Aidan stumbles and I dig my fingers deeper into the crack to steady myself. Claire continues light-footed.

"Claire, did you feel that?" Aidan asks.

"Feel what?"

I survey the whole yard. No one else seems to have noticed it, either. How is it possible only he and I felt it? It was a huge quake.

"Nothing," Aidan replies.

"Aidan!" I yell, "Aidan! It's *not* nothing." We couldn't have both imagined such a big jolt. Something is *wrong*. Something is wrong is both our worlds.

"Are you okay, Aidan?" Claire asks.

He stares at the ground, turning a queasy gray.

My stomach churns acid at the dread mounting on his face. All at once he grabs Claire's hand and sprints for the forest.

Claire drags her heels. Aidan only gets a few steps before she wriggles free from his grip. "Aidan, what the heck?"

Aidan sinks to his knees, burying his head in his hands, tortured sobs wrack his body. I ache to gather him in my arms and fix whatever it is that's hurting him.

Over the canopy of needled redwood branches a thin pillar of black lightning splinters the cloudless sky. It lasts only an instant, vanishing with a thunderous crack.

Before the after image fades three-dozen elves storm into the yard, weapons drawn.

"Aidan!" I don't mean to scream out loud, but now I can't stop. "Aidan! Claire! What happened? What's going on? Aidan!"

"They can't hear you. You'll only wear out your voice."

I jump to my feet, startled. Toad's hideous slimy mouth hangs open. Inside stands a beautiful woman with her back to me. She's combing her long raven-black hair in slow even strokes. Her brush is inlaid with mother of pearl.

"Princess Nissa?"

"Hello Emily." She pivots to face me. "The light from your wings awoke me. I used to have wings like those, you know."

The sallow gray sky casts dark shadows under her eyes and brackish fog clings to her, dulling her complexion and hair, making her seem old and tired.

"Where are we?"

"The Third Realm is a shadow realm," she answers cryptically, scanning the skyscape nervously from inside Toad. "It's a copy of the First or Second, I forget which. There are countless copies, of course, each more perilous than the last. The air poisons my lungs. Quick, Emily, come inside. Come and see what I've made."

Inside Toad? Am I dreaming?

Descending into the belly of a giant Toad is a lot like descending into an underground cellar—colder and more echoey than I would have imagined.

My bare feet pad noiselessly down the concrete stairs. Naked fluorescent tubes flicker behind metal cages in the ceiling, interspersed between exposed copper pipes. A plunk of water drips on repeat in some unlit corner. Dank antiseptic and iodine almost mask the stale scent of windowless air.

"You're the first visitor I've had in ages," Nissa says. "I'm so happy you're here!"

Everything shifts at the exuberance in her voice. The concrete steps disappear and my toes sink into deep-piled plush carpeting. A burnished handrail appears, reflecting the soft glow of candlelight from sconces set in the walls.

The gloom clinging to the princess dissipates, revealing lustrous skin and glossy hair. Rich tapestries hang from an archway at the landing. Nervousness squeezes my insides, I have no idea what to expect as Nissa parts the lavish drapery. Bracing myself, I follow her through to the other side…

…into an enchanted nursery.

There must be walls and a ceiling, but they're completely hidden behind curling vines and flowering foliage. Blossoms and succulents cover every surface. The twitter of birdsong floats from various hanging perches and brightly winged butterflies decorate the sky as a babbling brook crisscrosses the clover-covered ground leading to a mossy terrace.

The sweetest carved-wooden cradle sits at the center of the raised platform. Nissa bends over to caress the sleeping baby's rose-petal cheek.

A quake shakes the chamber. Fine dust falls from the now visible cinderblock walls. The birds and butterflies disappear. Superficial fluorescence replaces the natural light, illuminating the laminate floor and a metal-rimmed bedrail in harsh shadow.

Nissa coos a lullaby at her daughter, oblivious to the room's mercurial transformation. What's going on? Distressed, I spin around searching for a way out…

…and watch the heavy tapestries reappear, hanging from the curved branch of an oak tree. The cinderblock and linoleum have vanished. Could I have imagined them?

Questions clamor to my tongue, but Nissa gazes uninterrupted at her baby. I, too, am mesmerized by the way the infant's perfect black lashes rest against her porcelain skin.

It would be awkward to interrupt their intimacy with questions. I explore the room instead, my fingers running over the living vegetation on the wall. I bend to pet a fat fluffy rabbit hopping past.

The organic shapes of a birch rocking chair and side table look like they've grown right up through the floor. The rocker takes my weight, adjusting around me for a custom fit.

Next to me a photo album lies open on the slender white-limbed side table, beckoning. I pick it up to find that my favorite pictures of my brothers and sister fill its pages.

I fall in love with them all over again.

There has never been a shape more flawless than Jacob's golden newborn head. Aidan's wrinkled prune-purple skin and bead-button eyes make him look like a little old man in comparison, while Claire is almost a caricature. When she learned to crawl I was amazed every time she managed to lift her head off the ground, her cheeks were that big.

Page after page reveals their quirks and personalities, simple treasured highlights I cherish probably more than they do, as if I hand-picked and compiled these snapshots myself:

Jacob in a white undershirt clutches a red hen to his two-year old chest.

Blonde Aidan takes his first steps on a windswept beach in Carmel, surf crashing behind him.

Claire's chubby dimpled hand in Jacob's skinny fist as she jumps in a pile of crackling autumn leafs.

Nissa takes her place behind an old-fashioned treadle sewing machine, humming while she sews, the needle's happy staccato gives rhythm to her wordless song.

Another jolt rattles the ground. Linoleum instantly replaces the clover under my feet, hospital antiseptic stings my nose.

Nissa's sewing machine morphs into a shabby armchair. The princess's hollow eyes stare at me with her withered hands clasped in her lap. A thin tube connects her to the plastic IV bag hanging from the metal pole at her side. I jump from the rocking chair and rush to her.

Before I've taken half a dozen steps everything morphs back to the way it was … sunlight sparkles off the playful stream, the crushed clover I'm standing on perfumes the air with eternal spring. Nissa busily hums away at her sewing.

I hold up the photo album in my hand. "Why do you have these pictures of my brothers and sister, Princess?"

"Come see what I made for them!" She leaps to her feet, pulling me over to an ornately carved wardrobe.

The weapons are inside.

Nissa picks up the dagger, turning the blade to reflect the light before placing it in my hand. "Have you ever walked so quickly into a room that once you get there you can't remember why you went? That's my brave, brilliant Jacob. This dagger represents him. It's meant to remind you to pace yourself. Most of the time a warrior keeps her dagger sheathed. It isn't wise to always be on offense with your weapon in your hand looking for a challenge. Wearing this dagger sheathed symbolizes preparation and patience." She buckles the filigree sheath around my hips. I slip the dagger inside.

Next, she takes the black leather-bound shield down from its hook inside the door and fastens it around my left forearm. Algiz, the emblem of Protection, bristles in spikes at the center.

"This shield represents Aidan, my blue-eyed knight. Aidan's like you, so sensitive. His imagination is bigger than the world. Sometimes he doesn't know how to turn it off, and it hurts him." The way she talks about Aidan pierces me, as if she doesn't understand that I know him better than I know my own heart. "This shield will act as a filter when too many things press down on you at once."

Finally, she takes the studded gauntlet down from where it rests on a shelf and slides it onto my right hand. "Claire can be silly," she says, "but she is also fierce and beautiful like this gauntlet. If anyone were to discount her as being pretty and nothing else they would only have themselves to blame. They'd be in for a big surprise, wouldn't they? Claire is strong and confident. This gauntlet is a good reminder of those things. Now, Emily, listen carefully, this is important. While each of the weapons work independently, when used together they are virtually undefeatable."

Pride steals my breath. The night the crimbal attacked I was scared spitless. Jacob, Aidan, and Claire united to fight off the monsters so I had time to take Mom's Blaze.

"Look at you, Emily."

I shiver with strange excitement. The weapons fit as if they were made for me. My dress shimmers in the dappled sunlight of Toad's enchanted belly-garden.

When Nissa spoke to me in Aidan's dream she said the weapons would give me Purpose.

"You're a maiden warrior ready for battle."

A rumbling starts all around us. At a ping behind me I pivot to see the mobile suspended above the carved cradle start to rotate in a slow spin. Delicate dragonflies with stained glass wings wobble around the large crystal spider at its center. Another ping and I notice a hairline fissure stretching across the rose orb of the spider's middle.

Nissa races for the wailing baby, gathering her up in her arms. "There, there my sweet little princess. I've got you now. You're my beautiful Emma, aren't you? My brave girl. I won't let anything hurt you."

The pitch and roll of the ground doesn't stop. Another ping. The mobile shatters. Plaster falls from the ceiling. Birds squawk alarm.

"What did you call her?"

"Emma," Nissa answers. "She's my first. My darling Emily Ava Alvey." She bounces the startled infant on her shoulder, singing her name.

"My name is Emily Ava Alvey." I'm trembling.

Nissa dances toward me. The sway of her hips comforts the fussy baby, but the glare she directs at me is pointed like a knife. "Keep your voice down, young lady. If you upset my daughter I'll send you to your room."

"You can't send me to my room." I look down at the dagger, the shield, and the gauntlet to find they are nothing more than the letter opener, wooden shield, and beaded cuff from our box of make-believe. "None of this is real. This is all just a stupid bedtime story I made up…"

"You're confused, Emily, about which parts of your story are real and which parts you embellished. I know I let you down in so many ways, but the weapons are real. I poured all my love into them. When you wear them your bond with Claire, Aidan, and Jacob is your strength."

My anger mounts with every word I hear. "Stop it. Stop it! Stop pretending that abandoning us is okay because you 'poured all your love' into some toys."

"You don't understand!" Nissandra cries, her eyes desperate. "I've been working on your armor, too. Here, hold her." She deposits the squirming baby in my arms and hurries to the sewing machine. "Look!" She holds up a handful of dirty linen.

The earth heaves.

This time I'm expecting it. I drop the breathless baby in the cradle and march to Nissa's side, grasping the cloth in her grip. "This isn't armor. It's nothing but scraps you've stitched together!"

The enchanted nursery disappears completely as the tremors grow stronger. Nissa is gone.

Mom sits in a utilitarian hospital bed in her room at the detox center. A monitor above her head begins a plaintive warning beep, but no one comes to check.

I'm furious, livid. I yank off the toy sheath and dagger, unstrap the shield and rip the gauntlet from my wrist, throwing them to the linoleum floor. I shove the fistful of rags in her face. "We needed you and you *abandoned us*!" I grab her shoulders and lean in. "You *disgust* me. You're a weak pathetic woman pretending to be a good mother to a fake baby!" I point to the second-hand basinet in the corner where a doll lies in a twisted heap. "I will *never* forgive you for what you've done." I spit the words, deliberate and quiet, through gritted teeth.

A low pitiful keening rends my ears. It's the broken sound of a wounded animal, the tortured sound of the abused, the unending grief-sound of self-hate.

This pain bleeding from Mom's throat… I did this. I cut her this way.

"Oh my God I'm sorry I'm so sorry please forgive me I'm so sorry!" I gather her fragile skin-and-bones body into my arms and rock her back and forth like a newborn. My fingers smooth her coarse-thin hair while huge sobs torment her frame. The words of a lullaby she used to sing me bubble up from a deep forgotten place.

"Oh once I had a little swan

She was so very frail

She'd sit upon an oyster shell

And hatch me out a snail,

The snail it turned into a bird

The bird to butterfly

And he who tells a bigger tale

Will have to tell a lie.

Sing terry-oh day. Sing autumn to May.

Her body calms. I stop singing, thinking she's fallen asleep. But from her silence comes a trance-like voice: "My father taught me that being brave meant being quiet. He said it wasn't good to always be whining and complaining. He said I had one purpose: to be a wife and mother, and that if my husband wasn't happy it was my fault. Your father was never happy. I believed that if I hid my bruises and buried my pain and tried harder no one would get hurt but me. But it wasn't all pretend, Emily. I don't know if I can make you understand what it was like, being your mother when you were young. You and Jacob and Aidan and Claire were my whole world and I adored every minute with you. But as you got older you became much stronger than me. I was broken, and I told myself you didn't need me anymore." She starts to shake again, her tears wetting the front of my ridiculous silver gown. "I know I hurt you. I know you can never forgive me. I can never forgive myself."

How can I blame her for burying and hiding the awful things she didn't think she could change? I did the same thing. But now I know: secrets have power. They grow and fester until they leak out as toxic waste.

"I do forgive you, Mom."

Saying it is like salve on wounds I've carried for as long as I can remember. Not just because I can't stand seeing other people in pain. This is for me. I'm ready to heal.

THIRTY FOUR

"**E**MILY! *Where are you?*"

Startled by the sound of Aidan's shout I look down. In the corner of the room where the dull linoleum tiles meet the wall is a mouse-hole gap. Through it I see Aidan where I saw him last, on his knees in the dirt beneath the oak tree by the old rope swing. Claire stands at his side. They look small and lost amid the chaos erupting around them.

Kaillen strides toward them flanked by two elves I don't recognize. He pulls Aidan to his feet. "Are you hurt?"

"She's gone." Red rims Aidan's eyes "There was an earthquake. I tripped and that weird black lightning shot up from the ground…I could feel something—opening—in the grove. Then she was just…gone."

Oh NO. Aidan thinks I left him.

"Aidan!" I yell, dropping to the floor and pounding on the wall. "Claire!"

"I told you, Emily. They can't hear you." Mom's voice is empty.

Panic grips me. I have to let Aidan know I would never leave him on purpose, that I'm coming back. "There has to be a way to make him hear me!"

"There isn't. I've tried so many times. There isn't a way."

"I've never seen a black lightning strike before now," Kaillen says, "but I know what it means. Someone has Traveled."

"Traveled?" Claire asks. "Like on a plane?"

"No. Traveling is a fabled art, as old as legend," Kaillen explains, "something the Ancients were said to have done. Elves still learn the concept of bending space and time to move between places when we're adolescents, but only as theory. No one living has actually ever done it. Honestly, I didn't even believe it could be done. It would require colossal amounts of Magic. None of us has the strength necessary to Travel, not even if we were in the First Realm with our full power. None, of course, except your sister with the weapons."

"Why do you sound mad at Emma?" Claire asks. "What has she done that's so bad?"

"She's infected me." Kaillen mutters. A blush stains his face, betraying his anger. My stomach seizes in a tight thrill. "Your sister is incredibly smart and strong, Claire, but she's put herself in danger. Attempting Travel is completely irresponsible."

"Surely it's beyond her capability," the stocky elf on Kaillen's right says.

"Emily is one of the most capable people I have ever met," Kaillen responds.

Is this detox-center/mouse-hole/crack-inside-a-giant-Toad thingy broken, or did Kaillen just compliment me? My pulse spikes.

"Even if she has managed to learn the lost art, why would she Travel? Where would she go?" the elf on Kaillen's left asks.

"I have no idea," Kaillen says, "but the strain on her physical body will render her useless. It will take days for her to recover enough to open the Doorway."

"Is that all you care about?" Aidan asks.

"No," Mom whispers from her hospital bed.

"No." Kaillen answers.

"When will she be back?" Aidan asks.

"We'll be leaving within minutes to investigate where your sister went and when she'll return. We'll need water. Aidan, will you take the canteens and fill them up in the house? We need to be ready to go as soon as the General gives the order."

"Yes." Aidan stands a little straighter.

"You two, keep with Claire and Aidan," he commands the two elves. "Lady Claire, your job is to go with these men and make certain they hurry back. Can you do that for me?"

"Where are the canteens?" She takes charge immediately.

Kaillen joins the General and Lady Kaye under the birch tree.

"Ava regained consciousness and refused to say anything until Quince agreed to take her to find Lady Alvey." Kaye is saying.

"Were they attacked? Why did Emily Travel?" the General asks.

"From what I can ascertain from Twist, it was accidental," Kaye answers. "Ava was teaching Emily to channel through the weapons, and…"

"Ava was teaching her to channel?" Kaillen interrupts, clearly confused.

Ian ignores him, speaking urgently. "Has Lady Emily returned?"

"No. But her Path is not entirely shut."

Ian mutters something under his breath that sounds like "foolish girl," but his tone is worried, not angry. "Marcus, Jack!" he barks. "Order your warriors to form rank. Lady Kaye, please gather your maidens."

The Fae assemble, men and women standing together.

"General, are we under attack?" yells an elf at the back of the group.

"Has the Doorway been opened?" a maiden calls out.

"Fae, we are not under attack," Ian's voice booms across the yard. "The Doorway has not been opened. Lady Alvey has mistakenly opened a Path, inadvertently Traveling. We don't know where she's gone. It's likely she will return shortly."

Behind me, Mom stares at the hole in the wall, transfixed. She shakes her head, muttering under her breath.

"Marcus, Lizzy," the General barks, "your squadrons will accompany me to the grove to ensure no unwanted visitors enter this Realm through Lady Alvey's Pathway. We must bring her back and close the Opening. The rest of you will remain here and await our word. We will communicate via dragonfly," he indicates Twist who hovers near his shoulder.

"Mom, did you hear that? They're coming to get me!" I scramble back to the metal-railed bed and hug her to me.

"Emily. Please stay a little longer. We could make such beautiful things together."

"We can't stay, Mom. We have to take the weapons you made to Jacob,

Aidan, and Claire, remember?"

"You're leaving me."

"Of course not! You're coming with me."

"I can't leave." The skin of her neck and chest above the threadbare hospital gown is mottled and splotched. "Don't you think I've tried? There's a man, Emily. Covered in Gray. His clothes, his rifle, even his body is Gray. He's out there… watching… waiting. If I try to leave he'll hunt me. He won't let me escape alive."

She has a Gray Man, too. And I know she's right: she isn't strong enough to fight him.

"I'll come back for you, I promise. I'll come back and I won't stop calling until you answer."

I barely feel the pressure of her grip when she squeezes my hand. She studies the faded paisley pattern covering her too-thin knees. "I'm tired Emily. Will you help me with my pillow?"

I lay her back, gently adjusting the pillow under her head. Pulling the covers up to her chin and tucking them in around her shoulders, I place a kiss at her hairline.

"You can't give up, Mom. Not now that I've found you here. Tell me you'll listen for me," I beg.

But she's already fallen asleep.

Ascending the concrete steps of Toad's echoey astringent throat, I emerge into the noxious gray skyscape of the Third Realm.

The scene from the Second Realm plays on through the sidewalk. I clamber over Toad's fleshy bottom lip and hurry to peer into the crack.

The Fae have marched to the grove. Claire and Aidan push their way up to the front of the tightly pressed ranks of elves and maidens who've formed a semi-circle around Quince. Xander weaves in and out of the crowd. "Where is she, Lady Quince? Where's Emma?" Claire yells.

"Claire!" I shout at the top of my lungs. But it's useless. She can't hear me.

Toad blinks his black lily-pad eye at me sympathetically before closing his giant mouth and settling into statue-like hibernation.

Quince bends to gather Ava from the crystal box and places her on the fallen tree trunk. Claire gasps. The General drops to his knees. "Ava," he whispers. "You're alive."

"Hello General," she says fondly.

"We found you unconscious at the Alvey's house. You were so still," The General says. "We couldn't heal you. We thought you'd been lost."

"I was not lost, only hidden."

"Hidden? Where? By whom? How have you lost your wings?"

"You must be patient." Her smile is loving but her eyes are full of pain. "I will explain as best I can."

"Wait," Claire says. "You were at our house?"

"Yes, Bug. I volunteered to watch over Emily when she began to go through puberty much the same as Quince volunteered to watch over your mother Nissa when she left the Vineyard to marry your father David…"

"What?" Claire shrieks.

"Whoa." Aidan presses his hands to his temples like he's trying to keep his brain from leaping out of his skull. "How did I not figure this out before? Claire, think. What is Princess Nissa's full name?"

"OMG. Nissandra! Mom's name is Sandra!" Her mouth is a round O of surprise. I swear she doesn't blink for at least a minute. "Aidan, Mom is a FAERIE PRINCESS!" She shakes his arm. "I'm *really* freaking out about this!"

"Why hasn't anyone ever told us this before?" Aidan demands. "Why are there so many secrets?"

"She was forbidden to leave," Ian says. "She broke the rules."

"We couldn't forgive her betrayal," Quince says. "It's difficult to speak of."

"Then why did you watch over her?" Aidan asks.

"You'll understand when you're older," Ian says. "We've lost our Connections, not the memory of them. She is our Princess."

I've wriggled my head and shoulders into the crack. Roots scratch my face and claw at my hair. Can I crawl straight through? If I push in deep enough will I fall out the other side?

"We'd never witnessed a Halfling Changing," Ava says. "We didn't even know if Emily *would* Change. Nissa could give her a Flame but she was ill, and none of the elves in this Realm are strong enough to give a Spark. We assumed she would remain mortal. But as soon as Emily reached her physical adolescence we could sense her powers awakening even from as far away the Vineyard. I volunteered to watch after her. I was to remain concealed unless there was an emergency."

I'm stuck in the crack, claustrophobic. I can't move forward any further. I inch back, panting. Ava's words are barely louder than my wild heartbeat.

"Three weeks ago, when Gabe saw the brands she'd cut into her arm, Emily panicked. She saw a Spark floating in front of her in the air. Not knowing what it was or what it would do she sucked it inside. It set her Changing in motion. She couldn't contain her secrets any longer. Your father was coming home, your mother was sick. Emily had been self-medicating. She was drowning in fear and despair. I had no choice but to reveal myself to her."

I'm back in the bathroom that dark night holding Mom's lifeless body in my arms watching the silver butterfly flutter down from the corner of the ceiling and drop to the countertop like a stone. "Thank God for you, Ava," I whisper into the crack, "You saved my life."

"I joined with her when she took Nissa's wings, hoping to guide her through the process. But she was too strong. Emily took all of Nissa's Blaze and my wings as well."

A dismayed murmur rises from the crowd.

"No, don't pity me. I knew the risks," Ava says. "I chose to join with her. We make each other stronger."

"No wonder Lady Emily has so much power for a Halfling," Marcus remarks. "She has your Blaze, Nissa's Blaze, her own wings, and Keen as well."

"But where did her Spark come from?" Ian asks. "As you said yourself Ava, none of us is strong enough to give one."

"It came from the crimbal's Master."

"Daughter. We know the High King is the crimbal's Master. He's trying to prevent our return home. Why would he send her a Spark?"

"The High King isn't the crimbal's Master. Emily isn't a Halfling. The crimbal's Master is Emily's father: Drake."

THIRTY FIVE

va's words hang in the air, unnatural twisted birds of prey. I cover my ears with my hands and press my forehead to the ground. No no no no no no no no.

"Impossible," Quince gasps. "David is Emily's father."

"Drake and David are the same man," Ava answers. "His plans have been long in the making."

"But why?" Disbelief and anger fight for position on Ian's face. "How do you know this, Ava?"

"After decades of exhausting every means of breaking the Seal, Drake realized he needed a Halfling Ovate born in this realm to open the Doorway. So he set out to create one."

Shock writhes up my throat, making me gag.

"Drake decided to risk venturing away from the Doorway to carry out his murderous plot. His travels into the Second Realm took a heavy toll on him. Not only was his power diminished when he journeyed away from the Doorway, his immortality was as well. The first time he ventured out he was gone only weeks before returning, exhausted and spent. But he'd planted several seeds and was hopeful at least one of them would come to bear fruit."

"Wait." Claire blurts. "You're saying my dad has two names, Drake and David. You're saying he got ladies pregnant so he could make an Ovate to open the Doorway?"

"That's exactly what he did, Bug. But it was more monstrous than that." Ava's pause stops the breath in my lungs. "None of the women he impregnated survived labor and delivery."

I'm drained. Bloodless. Depleted. I don't want to hear any more. Somehow I know it's going to get worse. I crumple against the unyielding sidewalk, knees to chest ear close to the crack. Tears spill from my eyes. I know with heavy conviction I can never go back to my old life again. There's no place deep enough in my body to bury these revelations.

Ava continues. "For more than a decade Drake waited, regaining his strength, watching with his far-reaching Mind's Eye, sending out Sparks, knowing that if one of his orphaned sons showed potential for power he would receive a vision. He waited in vain. After almost two decades he ventured out again. The second time he stayed away from the Doorway longer, spawning more Halfling Ovate possibilities. He was a shadow of himself when he returned to his sanctuary in the Third Realm to recover his power. He was certain he would have success. He was wrong. Three times he journeyed from the Door, each time reaping nothing. Though his bastard sons each held potential, Drake discerned none would be strong enough to break the Seal. Dismissing his creations as useless to him, he abandoned them to wander lost and alone."

A strange growing lightness wells in my chest, pushing up through the rubble of demolishing horror, contradicting my tears of revulsion and sorrow for Drake's lost children and their murdered mothers because I know beyond doubt: I am nothing like my father.

"His plan had failed," Ava says. "After decades he conceded. A Halfling simply wasn't strong enough. So he turned his sights to the Vineyard, to Nissa. Drake was always infatuated with our Princess. In the years since our banishment she matured, becoming even more lovely and desirable to him than she was as a child in the Seventh Kingdom. Nissa could give him an Ovate son. As a maiden, she would have the strength to survive childbirth. Drake could use her until she gave him what he needed. So he crafted an impenetrable mortal disguise as David Alvey and came to Vineyard to court her, and it worked. She fell head over heels in love with him and we disowned her for leaving."

A low snarl crouches in Kaillen's throat. "He always lusted after her. I could see it in the way he looked at her. It made me sick. I'll rip him to shreds."

"How did Nissa not see through his disguise?" Quince asks, unbelieving.

"Did we, Quince?" Ava chides. "None of us saw through his disguise. Nissa became another victim in a long line of battered women. For years she was innocent and exploitable. Her pride wouldn't let her return to the Vineyard and admit her marriage had failed. She hoped that giving him children would make things better. She suffered Drake's domineering abuse in silence…until she discovered what he was doing to their first born daughter."

No.

I'm on my knees again, clawing at the crack. "Shut up, Ava! Please, NO!"

My nails tear and bleed but I keep digging. I want to disappear. I want to grab Aidan and Claire and RUN. I want this vision to stop. I need Ava to stop talking.

"What was he doing to Emily?" Aidan's eyes are hollow.

"Drake has never believed females are good for anything but bearing and raising children. Because his firstborn with Nissa was a girl, he never considered she'd be strong enough to help him break the Seal. But she did have Magic. Living away from the Doorway drained Drake's power. He had to return to his sanctuary frequently to fill his reserves in order to maintain his disguise. When he detected Emily's power, he realized he had another option."

Is this what burning at the stake feels like? The engulfing heat, the searing pain, the oxygen vaporizing in my mouth? Agonizing screams rage through my arms and legs as I kick and flail, helpless to escape her words.

"He began to take her power through a violent and depraved process. Bewildered and heartsick, Nissa watched her precious daughter wither before her eyes, not knowing what was happening or how to help."

I can't look at their undone faces anymore. I shove my fingers in my ears to halt the words crashing around in me. But it doesn't help. I can still hear.

"Nissa began to keep constant vigil. The third time Drake molested Emily, Nissandra discovered them. She defended her daughter with her life. But she was no match for Drake. While they battled, Drake used the Magic he'd seized from Emily to trap Nissa's mind in the Third Realm. Then, completely depleted, he fled to the Doorway. He's been waiting and watching ever since, regaining his health."

"How do you know these things, Ava?" Quince questions, stunned.

"When Emily took my wings, my consciousness joined with Nissandra's. While my body was in the crystal box, my mind was in the Third Realm with our Princess. She told me this tale."

A collective howl rends the grove. Kaillen stalks behind Ava, muttering dangerous threats. The Fae have knocked their arrows and drawn their guns. Claire shelters in Quince's arms.

Even as my body fights to deny the things I've heard, in my heart I know they're true. I think I've always known. I just wasn't strong enough to accept the ugliness that was part of me. I had to hear it from a distance or it would have destroyed me.

"That's where Emily is now, isn't it? The Third Realm." Aidan stands separate and tall. Iron sets his jaw.

"Yes."

"Where is the Third Realm, Ava?" The General demands.

"It exists between many Realms. It's a shadow realm, a maze of the Mind caught out of Time. Drake poisoned the atmosphere there with doubt, fear, and despair. Every emotion, every decision made there creates a new version of Reality that closely mimics the real world, but paranoia, guilt, and shame run rampant, attacking hope and positivity. It's impossible to separate truth from lies there. The consciousness is trapped in a downward spiral, unable to escape it's own fantasy."

"Why would Emma Travel there?" Claire asks.

"I believe the medallion Drake gave her opened a Path when she channeled with the weapons."

"I swear to everyone who can hear my voice," Kaillen growls, "I will hunt Drake down and kill him."

"We need to continue with our plan," Marcus says. "Let Drake think we're ignorant of who he is or what he's done. When we return home and our powers are restored we can bring him to justice!"

"Drake doesn't believe more than a few of us will survive the ambush he has prepared," Ava says. "He'll siphon as much power as he can hold from Emily's wings, the weapons, and from those of us who do survive. Then he'll march on the throne."

"We've considered an ambush," Marcus scoffs, "but he's one man with a handful of crimbal. He's no match for us."

"It isn't just a handful of crimbal, Marcus." Ava's voice echoes weirdly across the grove. "Drake has been gathering his bastard children. He feeds them lies: that the elves are their fathers, that they were created for sport. He promises them revenge for their murdered mothers and power in the First Realm, playing on the abandonment he himself inflicted, harvesting years of bitterness and loneliness to raise an army bent on justice."

For several seconds there is complete silence.

Finally, Marcus speaks again. "Even so, what are a dozen Halflings? We have Lady Alvey. She controls the weapons, not Drake."

"We *had* Lady Alvey, remember?" Aidan says.

"Aidan's right," Ava says. "Remember, Traveling drained her power. The longer she remains in the Third Realm the more likely Drake is to discover her.

"We can't let that happen," The General says. "Emily's Pathway is still open. One of us will use it to retrieve her."

"That would be unwise. You know the toll Traveling takes on the physical body. With no Magic to protect us the journey would certainly be fatal for any of us."

"What about her?" Claire points at Xander. "Hannah says insects have strong Magic!"

"She's right," Quince exclaims. "Xander can do it, if she is willing. She can follow Emily's Path and lead her back to this Realm!"

At the mention of her name Xander zips to the front of the throng, twirling in the air.

"Xander, can you follow Emily and lead her back to us?" Ava asks.

The dragonfly bobs up and down.

My pulse races. Thank God for little sisters who listen.

"Tell her I love her." Claire's voice is a clamor of fresh hope.

"Me too," Aidan adds. "And tell her to hurry back. Please."

"Tell her Jacob loves her, too," Claire says, "even though he isn't here right now."

Ava's head snaps up, the space around her dims. "Where is Jacob, Bug? What do you mean he isn't here?"

My pulse rockets even faster at the dread in Ava's voice.

"He went with Gabe to put gas in the vans…"

"Alone? How long ago did they leave?"

Claire looks at Aidan and then the General, shrugging. "I don't know. An hour maybe?"

Dismay darkens Ava's face. Her head moves from side to side in a slow arc back and forth.

"What is it, Ava? What frightens you?" Quince asks.

"Drake has recruited Gabe to his cause. When he felt Emily's powers growing stronger he sent Gabe to keep an eye on her. That is why Gabe was at the pool, why he went to her home on the night she began to Change."

Spiders of fear and nausea crawl up the back of my neck. Does that mean…?

"Hold on," Aidan sounds like he's about to gag. "Gabe is one of those Halflings? Does that means he's my half brother? He kissed Emily. I saw them on the path the first morning after we got here."

Kaillen chokes.

I'm going to pass out in my prom dress on the sidewalk. This can't be happening.

"He's not related to you Aidan. Gabe's mother died giving birth to his Halfling sister, leaving him an orphan. His sister took her own life several years ago."

Every new revelation stirs acid in my churning stomach.

"But Gabe likes Emma," Claire insists. "I mean, he *likes* her likes her. And Jacob wouldn't help anyone attack us!

"That's not what she's saying, Claire." Aidan is eerily calm. "You're worried Gabe kidnapped Jacob, aren't you? That Drake will use him to make Emily open the Doorway and turn over the weapons. Am I right?"

"Your Insight is sharp, Aidan," Ava remarks.

"Can that dragonfly understand English?" Aidan points at Xander who perches on the tip of Claire's index finger.

Quince nods. "Yes, she can understand you."

"Xander," he says. "I need you to go find my sister. Please. Tell her not to trust Drake, and tell her Jacob is missing. She needs to come back right now.

Do you understand?"

Xander's antennae wave as if blown by a breeze.

Aidan falls back, landing on his butt in the dirt. "Holy crap!" His eyes are wide with shock. "She just threw a giant wave of color at me! How did she do that?" Ian and Quince exchange startled glances, but Aidan doesn't wait for a reply. "Why isn't she going yet?" he asks, getting to his feet. "You need to go now!"

"Twist isn't here," Quince says. "We left her at camp to communicate with the rest of our group. We need another dragonfly who can exchange messages with Xander."

Lizzy steps forward. A sleek-bodied black dragonfly rests on her shoulder. "Gliss has offered to send and receive with Xander."

"Thank you, Gliss," Ava says. She speaks to Xander next. "Fly swift and safe. Return as quick as you can."

Xander's wings vibrate. Lifting off from Claire's finger, she speeds up into the air, then loops down, flying straight at Claire and vanishing inches from the tip of Claire's freckled nose.

THIRTY
SIX

Unoiled *hinges swing wide behind* me. Without thinking I scramble to my feet and dash toward Toad, desperate to hide.

"Hello, Dear One."

Too late.

"Hello, Drake."

"How unexpected. I was not planning to see you before tomorrow. Welcome to the Third Realm."

I turn to meet him. My father. His eyes are guarded, but he smiles warmly as he steps away from the long wooden box he climbed out of.

"Emily, you gleam so brightly. I see you wear the medallion I crafted for you. Do you find it helpful as a focus?"

My hand rests on the crystal in the hollow of my throat. It's icy cold.

Without glancing down I know it shines with distorted blue light, the same nervous shade that fills my wings.

I return his smile tremulously. "It's incredible. Thank you."

"It serves the additional purpose of keeping me apprised of your whereabouts. I must admit, you departed your Realm so abruptly I briefly lost track of you. Where were you going so quickly just now?"

"To Toad." I confess.

Drake's eyes narrow. "Toad?" he asks softly. Much too softly. "What Toad."

Alarm bells ring in my head. "I…I thought I saw a little toad hopping along the sidewalk."

Drake's fists clench and unclench at his side. A vein bulges in his forehead. "That little bitch," he mutters. The elemental power surrounding him surges, vacillating as violently as his mood. He is not in control. His carefully constructed command of the situation slipped when I mentioned Toad.

Drake stalks back in silence to the box he emerged from, pacing around the portal in an ever-widening circle.

No. He's not pacing. He's searching. Searching for Toad.

He can't See Toad.

I back up onto the asphalt as his frantic search brings him closer to me, away from Toad and the tree.

"Don't play stupid with me," he hisses. "Where is it?"

"I don't know, it hopped away. Drake, please, you're frightening me!" A mad hope takes root in my chest. If I can convince him I don't know what's going on he might let me go.

He stops in his tracks, doubt on his face. But then he shakes his head.

"You're lying. The Princess is obsessed with toads." He steps closer. His unwarmed breath sends chills across my bare neck. "She's hidden nearby. Where is she? Tell me now or you will regret it."

Fear stiffens my limbs. I don't doubt he'll hurt me if my answers don't please him.

"What did that filthy whore tell you?" Drake's voice is soft again, a discordant caress along the curve of my shoulder. His mouth is inches from my ear. "Did the little bitch tell you about my failed creations? About the weak useless women who died carrying my bastards? Did your mother tell you why you and your siblings were made?"

I stumble back another step.

I can tell Drake believes the horror on my face is real. His jaw tightens as a question forms in his eyes.

From the corner of my eye I see something small darting toward me across the slate gray sky-scape. Xander.

"What the hell..." Drake sees her too.

I had no idea dragonflies could move so fast. Even before Xander is close enough to communicate I open my mind wide, pushing pictures of Drake and his rage, his confession.

"An insect?" He laughs, his voice a wicked sneer. "Did Nissandra really think she could thwart me with a girl and an insect?"

He holds his hand up in the air, palm to Xander. His aura shifts. A miniscule weaving of elemental power shoots across the lot, spreading as it moves away from him.

The flow expands, speeding at Xander. A second later she drops from the air, her tiny body crumples against the gritty pavement.

No. Not Xander.

My wings buzz with panic. My friend is injured, possibly dead. I'm heartsick. I'm stuck. Even if I could calm down enough to summon the weapons, their combined power can't help me get back to the grove. I don't know how I Traveled the first time.

"Tell me, Dear One. Was that dragonfly special to you?" His voice is lyrical and deep again, full of fabricated compassion and concern. It turns my stomach sour.

He takes another step closer. "Was it your friend? Was it faithful? Of course not. It was an insect. It didn't have power like you, did it, Dear One? It's entirely replaceable."

He circles to stand directly in front of me. I hold my back ramrod straight, refusing to meet his eyes. He pinches my chin between his thumb and finger, making me look at him. "Not like you, Dear One," he purrs. "No. You aren't replaceable, are you?"

I slap his hand away, step back and scrub at my chin, trying to erase the filth of his touch.

"You're adorable," he chuckles. "You make me proud. Now stop this charade and tell me where Nissandra is."

I will never tell him where she is. I will die first. But I choke down the rebellion kicking inside. I have to convince him I'm clueless, it's my only chance of escaping. "I came here by accident, Drake. Have I done something wrong?"

"I could almost believe you, Dear One." He walks in a slow circle around me, his tapered index finger tracing the outline of my upper-left wing as he passes.

Bile coats my tongue. It takes all my control to keep from clawing the wing out of my back.

"I hope you'll forgive me for my little outburst earlier, Emily." His tone is casual now. "I know you can empathize with me. A century away from home is finally taking its toll. But that will all be remedied soon."

"Tomorrow," I agree. "Everyone's getting ready."

"Yes. I've heard about your preparations. Does it bother you at all how selfish the Fae have become in their eagerness to return home? What a lot of pressure to put on such a young girl. Have you considered the Fae's offer to accompany us to the First Realm, or do you still wish my help in burning out the power in these magnificent wings?"

"I've realized how much Jacob, Aidan, Claire and I can learn from you," I say in my best subservient voice. "We want to come with you. If you show me how to get back to them now, we'll gather our things and meet you tomorrow at the Doorway. "

"I'm afraid that won't be possible, Dear One. As bravely opaque as you appear, I've said far too much. I can't have you recounting our conversation to Lady Quince and the General. No. Aidan and Claire can travel to the Doorway with the elves and maidens tomorrow. Jacob is there now. I asked your friend Gabe to bring him. Consider him an incentive for your cooperation."

"Please Drake. Please let him go. I was always going to open the Doorway for you, you don't need to hold Jacob hostage."

"He came quite willingly, from what I understand. Perhaps your overprotective control began to chafe him somewhat?"

Movement by the Tree catches my eye. Drake is behind me. Has he seen it too? Without turning my head, I shift my gaze.

It's Toad. He's opened one filmy eye to stare at me inscrutably.

LOOK.

The voiceless command tumbles like white water rapids in my mind.

LOOK. SEE.

"Look where? See what?" I call back in my head.

No answer.

"You said to look and See! What am I supposed to be looking for?"

Again, no response.

"Mom?"

Nothing.

"Ava? Hannah? Aunt Margaret"

Silence.

"Toad? Please tell me what to do! If you care at all what happens to me and the people I love, please tell me what to do!"

This time the voice is an echoed whisper rebounding through the slot canyons of my inner ear...

THE THIRD EYE.

"You mustn't blame yourself, Dear One," Drake taunts. "Teenage boys can be so inconvenient."

My resolve crumbles. This is ridiculous. No one has ever said anything about a Third Eye. How many sets of eyes can one person have, anyway? My green eyes, my Mind's Eye, my Inner Eye...

Wait. That's...three.

So what? It's three! I still don't know what the hell it is or how to use it!

There is three of everything: Three weapons. Three siblings. Three Realms. Three voices. Now three eyes, too? *"You're going to have to give me a little more help or there's no point. I don't know what to do."*

All at once I remember Lady Nancy Quince sitting next to me on a bench in the garden. She said I was supposed to make peace with the little girl and the critical woman—Hannah and Margaret—I was supposed to ask what they needed and trust myself so I could find my True Voice. But I did that! That's how I opened the third box. Ava is my True Voice … we listen to the other parts of me and make decisions based on all the information.

What if I'm supposed to do the same thing with my eyes? What if I'm supposed to combine all my Sight to make one Eye…a Third Eye that can see more than any of them can separately?

It's worth a try.

Still looking at Toad I align my Inner Eye so it lies directly over top of my physical sight. Next, I bring my Mind's Eye to the center of my attention, layering it over top of the other two. Not like in the grove when I'd placed one Eye *above* the other. That had been like looking through bifocals. This is like three panes of different colored glass stacked up: red + blue + clear = purple…

…for the first time, I See through all three lenses at once.

Vertigo threatens to bring me to my knees. Jagged needled slivers of texture, light and sound crush against me. I'm blind.

RELAX, says Toad.

I follow my breath in and out, letting my lashes flutter down, softening my gaze. I count back from ten. When I look up, everything has changed.

Toad fills his bloated air sac in approval.

A sudden chill breeze ruffles the surface of my wings as I survey my surroundings with the Third Eye. The sunless skyscape has visibly darkened, revealing a ghostly moon and faint diamond stars just above the horizon. Brittle leaves scuttle past my bare feet on the frozen ground.

"Everything will be fine, Dear One. As long as you cooperate with me fully." Drake's voice is too close.

Something flaps above Toad toward the top branches of the ancient tree.

The sky is wrong, pulled too tight, unraveling at the seams.

Seams? Skies don't have seams.

This sky does, and it doesn't separate just along the edges. My Third Eye reveals holes riddling the air—a 3-D holographic map of the cosmos superimposed over this reality. Every diamond star, every pinprick planet is another rip—tears in the fabric of space.

The Connections emanating from my core are thicker and stronger now that my three Eyes are combined into one. Nausea curdles my gut. The dark heavy coil that had frightened me in the grove slithers darkly to Drake along the ground.

But the ribbons of light are more vibrant as well. I identify the chords leading to Jacob, Aidan, and Claire first, and then Ava, Ian, Quince, and Kaillen. I weave them together, envisioning a fist. With light streaming out between my fingers in every direction I pull their ribbons in closer to my heart.

I inhale relief. They're safe. Worry and waiting thrum through their links. Ava concentrates her whole tiny self on sending love and faith through our bond. I'd give anything to communicate with them, to tell them I love them, to tell them how much they mean to me.

Wait. On the night the crimbal attacked I'd been able to communicate with Jacob telepathically. Could it work again even though we're in different Realms?

"*Jacob.*" I tug on just his link.

His answer is immediate. "*Emily! Where are you? Can you hear me? Something isn't right. I thought we were going to put gas in the vans, but Gabe brought me somewhere else. There are men here. At least three dozen. And they're armed. Can you hear me? Where are you? Emily?*"

"*Jacob, I'm here. Are you hurt? Armed with what?*"

"*No, I'm not hurt. Armed with guns. Lots and lots of guns. Big ones. And they're dressed like a S.W.A.T team, all in black. I've never seen any of these guys before.*"

"*Jacob. I need you to listen to me. It's going to be okay. Do you know where you are?*"

"*In an abandoned parking garage. I saw signs for Highway 1 and Half Moon Bay. I think we got off at an exit for Mt. Hermon. These guys are all just standing around oiling their guns and staring at a wall with graffiti all over it, waiting. Except for Gabe. He's acting like a lunatic. Is this part of the plan? What's going on?*"

I steady my breath, trying to convince myself that Gabe wouldn't let anyone hurt Jacob, that he's only holding him hostage because he thinks he knows what's best for me. Gabe is confused, not evil. He's been deceived and manipulated by Drake like the rest of us.

"*Jacob. Stay calm, I'll be back in a minute.*"

"*Wait! Where are you going? Emily?*"

"*Jacob, you know how much I love you, right?*"

Silence. I can almost feel him shrugging his shoulders. But then his ribbon shines brighter...

"*Yes.*"

"Good. I'll be back."

The musk of Drake's immortal breath grazes my cheek. "If you follow my directions, Dear One, you have no need to worry."

"I'll do anything you ask, anything. Just promise they'll be safe."

"Anything I ask? How nice. I've heard you speak those words before. I like you eager to please."

I shield myself from his vile words, concentrating instead on using telepathy to talk to Aidan and Claire and the Fae in the grove. I tug one link after another: Ava, Quince, Ian, Kaillen. But they can't hear me. Aidan's probably having a panic attack by now. I need to let him know I'm all right.

Except, I'm not all right. I'm far from all right.

My blood turns cold as movement on the frozen pavement catches my attention. I shudder. A swarm of green incandescent cicadas scrabble up and over my feet, flowing toward Toad. They work their way dauntlessly up Toad's slime-covered body, over his desiccated belly.

Toad yawns wide. His thick pink tongue lolls out of his horrible lips—a grotesque red carpet entrance for the locusts' arrival.

The cicadas aren't the only creatures on pilgrimage toward Toad. Bright-colored butterflies wing past side-by-side with dull gray moths. An orchestra of crickets creep forward, their instruments strangely silent. A cluster of wood-brown spiders follows them while an army of red and black ants parade between my feet, all on sudden migration to Toad.

Where are they all coming from, and how has Drake not noticed? He stands behind me, bruising my elbow in his unforgiving grip, waiting for my reply to the question still ringing loud in my ears.

"Where are my weapons, Dear One?"

The ants carry poor Xander's body on their backs. Is she alive? I open my mind again, pushing images of Drake, of Gabe and Jacob, and the army of Halflings. Of Toad and me. Of the pictures in mom's photo album and the smile they put on my face. It has to work.

"Where are they? I want to see them!" The icy blast of his words on my exposed neck breeds goosebumps across my skin.

The breeze that ruffled my wings a moment ago has risen to a steady gust, blowing in from the countless tiny tears in the fabric of the atmosphere. It plasters the skirt of my sparkling gown flat against the backs of my legs, whipping Drake's words around my head.

"I don't have them!" My shout rips from my mouth in the now howling gale.

Drake's hand clamps down on my arm until I'm sure it will break. He circles so we are face to face. His hair hangs perfectly still in the torrent, his eyes are hollows of madness. "Get them. NOW."

THIRTY SEVEN

Dread paralyzes me. I can't let him near the weapons. It isn't just about the Doorway. Drake wants power: my wings, the weapons, and control of the entire First Realm. If I don't give up my gifts willingly he'll take them by force. And then he'll take Jacob's. Aidan's. Claire's.

There has to be something I can do. Someone needs to tell me what to do. I need Ava.

But Ava isn't here.

I See now that the bugs are arriving through the same holes in the sky as the wind. Is Drake making these things happen, trying to frighten me into giving him the weapons?

No. He seems completely unaware of the brewing storm as well as the pilgrimage of insects.

In moments the sky shifts from septic gray to inky indigo. The temperature plummets. The veil of this Third Realm is being riven, like the delicate weave of an heirloom shawl pulled too tight.

Through one gash I glimpse the gnarled oak tree and rope swing. Through another I see the pitted graffiti-covered concrete walls where Jacob, Gabe, and the Halflings prowl. Another reveals a young me with Butterscotch on the porch swing at sunset.

The rip by my shoulder opens on the community pool three weeks ago when I first met Gabe. Through a hole near the ground I see myself at seven, shivering naked on the shower floor.

Aunt Meg rolls pie dough in the kitchen through a gap on my left. On my right I walk arm-in-arm with Kaillen into the throne room of a marble palace, a circlet of blossoms around my head. In a narrow slit I spy myself lying with my head on Gabe's shoulder in a field of wildflowers.

And in a tiny little rift exactly in front of my nose I watch a ready-for-bed five year-old Emily curled up with Jacob in Dad's lap as he shows us the runes on a magic wooden box.

"I'm growing impatient, Daughter. SUMMON THE WEAPONS."

Wait. What if…? I look back down at the crack in the sidewalk. It wasn't just a vision; it's a window between Realms, too, like all the others.

Through the breach Aidan crouches on the ground, poking at the dirt with a stick—there's a line of grasshoppers each waiting in queue for its turn at the front, the first in line squats down, all six legs bent like collapsible tent poles—then launches itself into the air…

… and disappears.

Whoa.

Kaillen kneels next to Aidan. "Your big sister is strong, smart, and very determined. She's coming back."

"Um, Kaillen?" Aidan points at a single-file line of pill bugs marching up and over a small rock before inching straight up into the air at a ninety-degree angle like they're walking up a wall. They disappear about four feet up.

"How are they doing that?" Kaillen speaks from the corner of his mouth without moving his lips as if he doesn't want to disturb the pill bugs.

"I don't know, but check out the hoppers…"

They're interrupted by a commotion near the fallen tree. Kaillen hauls Aidan to his feet.

The sleek-bodied dragonfly, Gliss, zips around the crowd, wobbling in the air. Lizzy closes her eyes, her hands flying to her head as if she's hurt. "Something's wrong!" she gasps. "Xander is wounded—and the sky—the sky is torn!"

"It's torn here, too." Aidan says.

Speak up Aidan! I want to shout, but instead I hold stock-still. Drake is only inches behind me.

"DO YOU DARE DEFY ME, DAUGHTER? WHERE ARE THE WEAPONS?" Waves of maniacal fury radiate from his body.

"I'm trying!" I whimper.

"Ian, Quince!" Kaillen's voice carries clearly through the grove and through the crack in the sidewalk. "Aidan has discovered tears in the fabric of the sky in this Realm as well. The insects are leaving through them."

Gliss takes a nosedive, recovering just before crashing into the dirt. She pulls up, hovering inches from Aidan's head…

…oh WOW…

…Fireworks coruscate behind my eyelids and suddenly…

…I don't need to watch through the crack in the sidewalk anymore. I'm connected with Aidan through the dragonflies.

I am one with Xander. The sulfur of a struck match burns my nostrils. My tongue recoils from the taste of smoldering tar. Just beneath my skin the torpid purples, browns, and yellows of an unhealed bruise stagnate my blood.

Xander is dying.

Tears well in my eyes. She's fading fast.

On the surface of her pain I experience Aidan watching, waiting. I push my memory of us on the path sharing a bucket of raspberries, of the sweet grass field where he told me his dream. Of him strapped in his highchair as a toddler while I played airplane with his mashed peas, making the most absurd noises I could think of just to hear his giggles. I send him my determination, my self-believe: *Aidan. I have a plan.*

The connection severs. Xander is dead.

Aidan heard me. They know Xander can't guide me back, but they also know I have a plan. Anticipation and faith surge through Ava's ribbon. Courage comes from Aidan and Claire and just about every other elf and maiden assembled in the grove. I savor their support, letting it buoy me up.

"Don't make me ask again, Emily. SUMMON THE WEAPONS."

I cower under Drake's ruinous stare, stalling. "I'm sorry," I stammer. "I don't know why it isn't working." I just need a little more time.

With every ounce of concentration I can muster I join my consciousness with the Third Eye. Shrinking down, I hover just outside the wall of lights at my center. With the smallest trickle of Intention I set the mass of lights spinning like a top, focusing my vision until it's razor sharp, searching for two specific spheres—one Spark and one Flame. It takes only an instant now that I know what I'm looking for.

I pluck two glowing stars from the swirling galaxy and quickly float outward, back to the edges of my body.

Directing all my attention on my link with Jacob, I will the gifts to him. They speed along our bond for a moment before winking out of sight.

His ribbon vibrates.

"What was that? Emily? What did you just do?"

I almost smile at the surprise in his voice.

"I guess you got your Spark and Flame?"

"Yeah. I feel really strange."

"It's a little unsettling."

"You think?"

"I'm sorry you don't have time to ease into this, but you're ready, Jacob."

"What's happening? Why are you doing this?"

"Don't freak out, okay?"

"No, not okay! Emily?"

"Jacob. We aren't safe. Drake isn't who anyone thought he was. He had Gabe take you to the Doorway to make sure I do what he wants."

"I'm a hostage?"

"Yes."

"Where are you?"

"*With Drake in the Third Realm. I'm his prisoner. But don't worry. I have a plan.*"

"No. No plans, Emily! Just do what he says so he'll let you go."

"It's not that simple. Drake is our Father. He'll hurt you to make me open the Doorway and then give him the weapons…"

"Just open it and give them to him!"

"It won't be enough. He wants my power. And yours, and Aidan's, and Claire's. He won't stop until he gets it. He wants to rule the First Realm and enslave the Fae. It won't ever be enough. He won't ever let us go."

Jacob groans. "*This is all my fault. I've been such an ass. I'm so sorry…* "

"*Shhhh. Listen. It isn't and you aren't. I have to stop Drake, alone. I can't hide behind the weapons. I'm sending them somewhere safe*".

"*Emily, if you're going to fight him you need the weapons!*"

"*Don't worry. I have something else.*"

"*No Emily! This is CRAZY…* "

"*Trust me, Jacob. Trust yourself. I do. If I don't face Drake I'll never be free.*"

I drop all the ribbons and steady myself.

Drake stands directly between me and Toad, enraged. I look past his shoulder.

Toad's mouth gapes wide, thick strings of saliva flapping behind him in the wind.

It's frigid cold now. My bare shoulders shiver against the onslaught of descending endless night. But Blaze thrums in my wings, pouring white-hot power into my bloodstream. The medallion around my neck pulses with elemental energy, begging to be used.

The brand around my upper arm flares bright like a beacon before transforming into the gauntlet and fitting itself snugly around my wrist, spikes extending between my fingers.

I'm ready.

For a moment, I rest in the warmth of my calm. Heat and raw energy radiate from my center, pushing the frozen wind away from my skin for just a little longer, the maelstrom a distant rush. The skirt of my shimmering gown relaxes, falling gracefully around my legs. I blink slowly, relishing this peace before the real storm is unleashed. I look up at the tortured sky. Fear and dark Night poise to strike.

But I See something else too—Ian and Quince, awe on their faces, looking down at me from a tear in the branches of the Tree as if I'm some amazing mythical creature. They seem confused and maybe a little lost, but when I meet Quince's eyes we share a look: Hope.

I lift my chin, gathering that hope and placing it in my heart.

I'm afraid. If this doesn't work, I don't know that I'll ever find my way back. But I have to try. For them. For me.

I summon the shield and dagger.

"I see you've managed to find your senses and my weapons, Daughter. That is good."

Elemental energy pours in through all three weapons.

"You may stop, Dear One. That's enough. Give me the weapons and we'll go meet Gabe and Jacob at the Doorway. I'm sure they're both anxious to see you. We have work to do."

I don't stop. Energy rushes through my pores. I draw power from my wings, pulling pulling pulling until they start to wither, until I'm laid almost bare.

Like an artisan working at a loom I weave strands of Blaze and Intend the weapons away from me.

"*Remember, Jacob, don't freak out.*"

Drake's screamed profanities lance through my calm as all three weapons wink out of existence.

The last thing I hear before I lose contact with Jacob is his stunned curse, "*What the fu … ?*"

"DAUGHTER…" Drake's shout trembles with fury. And panic.

"Did it make you feel more like a man to dominate a little girl, Dad?"

My question is quiet, but he staggers back, a welt rising across his cheekbone.

"You were my hero, my guardian, my first crush."

Cruel lacerations spread up his arms, opening his neck. The front of his shirt sticks wetly to his chest. He looks down. A pained, disbelieving grunt is forced from his lungs.

"I was confused and scared," I step toward him. "You said you loved me. I couldn't understand the things that I was feeling, what was happening to my body. But I wanted to be a good girl. I wanted to please you."

He doubles over, gasping for air.

"Emily…" he groans. His aura wavers, folding in on itself as he sinks to his knees.

"You said I was special. You said I was different from anyone else. You said it was because I was so soft, so young, so smart. You said I made you feel better than anyone else, that you couldn't help yourself, that it was my fault."

"Stop Emily, please! Help me," he moans.

"It wasn't my fault."

"No, no, it was mine! I'm so sorry. I was sick. I hurt you. I'm going to make it right, I promise. I've changed. Please Emily, stop. You're hurting me." Blood slides from his ears. Bubbles form at the corners of his mouth.

"Dad?" No. What have I done? I didn't mean to…

I rush to his side.

His aura ripples with menace. He grabs my wrist and straightens, towering over me. The blood vanishes, gashes stitching themselves together.

"Oh, Emily." His lips twist in a mocking sneer. "You've been through so much, haven't you? Are you still taking the medicine the psychiatrist prescribed? I think it's time we got you in for counseling. You're having those delusions again, aren't you? I thought you'd have outgrown your ludicrous fantasies by now."

My Third Eye snaps shut. Blaze and Keen snuff out. With no buffer to protect me, the maelstrom envelops me from every direction, threatening to shred my soul.

"I can take the weapons from any of my children, Emily. I believe Jacob has them now, is that right?"

"I'm not letting you anywhere near him," I scream.

His laugh booms louder than the howling wind. "I'm their father. Jacob chose to go with Gabe, remember? I hear that you've been stealing pills and telling stories. Do you really think anyone will believe your word over mine?"

"It doesn't matter. I believe me. And I'll keep talking until someone listens."

"Who will you tell? You're stuck here."

"Look around you, Dad. This place is being torn apart. It's unraveling as we speak. All I have to do is open one Path to return to the Second Realm."

His aura ripples with doubt as he casts his eyes around.

All of the sudden what Ava said clicks: Drake's Blaze binds the Doorway. He doesn't have a Third Eye because his Inner Eye is useless. That's why he can't See Toad or the tears.

But he knows I'm telling the truth.

"There are literally *infinite* possibilities, Emily. Do you really trust yourself to choose the right one? Let's be honest, you were never very good at making decisions on your own."

"There isn't only one right choice. I choose all of them, every memory, every emotion, every experience, every mistake, every dream, every fantasy. They're all part of me, even the ones that are unpleasant or uncomfortable, and no one can take them away from me."

I reach up, placing chilled fingers into the holes twinkling like diamond stars along the unraveling seams of the sky. I gather the silky edges in my hands, pulling them down around me as I would a cloak, wrapping myself in the very fabric Drake used to conceal his hiding place.

Now *he* is vulnerable and exposed.

Drake's howl of impotent rage encircles me. He lashes out in fury. A bolt of pure hatred shoots from his hands.

I feel the impact before it arrives. I have just enough time to pull my wings in close and cover my head in Night before my world goes black.

THIRTY EIGHT

"**E**mily, can you hear me?"

"Open your eyes, Sweetheart, or squeeze my hand if you can hear my voice."

"She had a pill bottle in her hand. How many did she take? Do we know how many there were? How many are left?"

"As far as I can tell she didn't take any, there's still seven or eight in the bottle."

"Then what could have happened?"

The voices of the people I love are distant, the pressure of their fingers, too. I want to shout to Aidan and Claire and Jacob. I want them to know I didn't leave them on purpose.

But my mouth is glued shut, my jaw set in plaster.

It will loosen. Too soon.

It's weird how much it hurts, knowing that it wasn't real.

I know it will take a long time to sort through reality and fantasy, but right now it's enough to have this moment of awareness: I created my own version of Oz and populated it with the people most important to me. Even my egos became characters in my fairytale.

What if this awareness doesn't last?

I lie here just beneath the surface of consciousness, grieving the loss of my innocence. There are no enchanted weapons. The weapons were my brothers and sister. Nancy and Lady Quince aren't two different people. Mom isn't a fairytale princess. Kaillen probably still thinks I'm an immature brat, while the guy who actually likes me might have even more issues than I do.

A heavy weight sits on my chest. I want to sink further down from the surface. There is no White Faerie who revealed all my secrets. I'm still going to have to tell everyone that we can't go home with Dad because he molested me when I was seven. That I'm pretty sure he abused Aidan, too. That I'm terrified he'll hurt Claire.

But the despair and confusion locked up inside me are gone. I'm not conflicted anymore. I'm learning who I am, and Mom is right. My strengths do define me and will help me tell my story.

A peaceful glow dissolves the pressure on my chest. Irresistible warmth enfolds me in her arms. I let go, knowing I will wake with the strength to confront my demons, no matter how long it takes or where the journey leads me. As I drift off the loving voices hover around me, keeping me safe.

EPILOGUE

"How much do you think she'll remember?" the man asks in his gruff voice.

"I don't know. She's been through so much," the woman replies. "How can we keep doing this to her?"

"She is strong. Stronger than any of us realized. When she pulled down the sky of the Third Realm she didn't just break the Seal, she obliterated the entire Doorway. Drake has disappeared, but so have Gabe and the Halflings. They took Jacob with them."

THE END

DEAR
READER,

Like all fiction, this tale is a combination of imagination and experience. In weaving the two together to write RIVEN, I did hijack the names and personalities of my children and a few close friends, with their permission. And yes, Emma's voice is very similar to my own voice, (how could it not be?) though she is vastly more patient and far (FAR) less obnoxious than I am in real life. Also, my maiden name is actually Alvey and it really does mean Elf Warrior, (how cool is that??).

Emily's story, while fictional, is sadly one that is all too familiar. Statistics show that you, or someone you know, has been affected by some form of childhood abuse. Many victims cope with abuse by escaping through fantasy, which is why I chose to include fantastical elements in this novel about true things.

I have had the distinct honor of being an Outcry Witness for half a dozen people. Six adult men and women shared their story of abuse with me, for the first time ever, decades after it took place. I did not seek out these confidences, but keeping them is a trust I hold sacred. Their stories inspired me to research and write my debut novel.

The message of RIVEN is empowerment and the integration of all our many parts through self-acceptance, self-mercy, self-love, and self-trust. Instead of hiding and burying parts of ourselves that have been wounded, we can come to celebrate every single inch of our beauty and Magic. This is when we transform from Survivors to Thrivers.

If you, or someone you know is struggling as a victim or adult survivor of childhood abuse, I urge you to seek help. Childhelp National Child Abuse Hotline 1-800-422-4453 is open 24 hours a day 7 days a week. Adult survivors can find resources at www.ascasupport.org.

Thank you so much for spending time with Emma and her siblings in *Riven*. Our lives are adventures... part psychological thriller, part romance, part comedy, part mystery, part tragedy... and if you're at all like me, you might be convinced you have magical wings lying just beneath the surface waiting to unfurl. I'm endlessly excited to share more with you in *Secret Keeper* and *Primed*.

Xo,
Jane

ABOUT
JANE ALVEY HARRIS

 I have a Humanities degree from Brigham Young University with emphases in Art History, Italian Language, and Studio Art. I'm CRAZY about the visual and performing arts! I enjoy playing classical piano, painting & sketching, singing & acting, and especially writing poetry & prose.

But my real passion is PEOPLE. I love to watch and study what makes us tick as human beings. I'm definitely a dreamer, and my favorite thing to do is weave together sublime settings and stories for characters to live and learn in... myself included.

I currently live in an enchanted fairy-princess castle in Dallas, Texas, with my three often-adorable children and their three seldom-adorable cats.

KI a¹

CPSIA information can be obtained
at www.ICGtesting.com
Printed in the USA
LVOW10s2248280617
539681LV00014BA/1125/P